Fox Is Framed

Also by Lachlan Smith

Bear Is Broken
Lion Plays Rough

Fox Is Framed

A Leo Maxwell Mystery

LACHLAN SMITH

The Mysterious Press
an imprint of Grove/Atlantic, Inc.
New York

Published simultaneously in Canada
Printed in the United States of America

FIRST EDITION

ISBN 978-0-8021-2350-3
eISBN 978-0-8021-9182-3

The Mysterious Press
an imprint of Grove/Atlantic, Inc.
154 West 14th Street
New York, NY 10011

Distributed by Publishers Group West

www.groveatlantic.com

15 16 17 18   10 9 8 7 6 5 4 3 2 1

To My Parents

Fox Is Framed

Chapter 1

The night before I drive out to San Quentin, I have the dream again.

It's the same dream that used to wake me every night when I was young. Now, in my thirties, it's begun to afflict me once more.

In it, I'm a child again coming home alone from school to our second-floor apartment in Potrero Hill. In the shabby hall, our once-familiar door looms over me, either because I'm small or because of what's behind it. I know what the child's going to find when he opens that door, but I'm powerless to turn his steps.

What he saw, I see. My mother's body lies on the floorboards, naked under her robe. The shattered bones of her skull pierce her ruined skin, so that her face looks inside out. And this part is added: standing over her, his hair wet as if from the shower, my father holds a paper sack of what I assume must be clothing in one hand.

Lawrence steps past me and goes out. There's nothing to speak, no lines either of us may utter. No touch passes between us. Sometimes he isn't there, and my dreaming self understands that he's already fled. Sometimes he's still wearing the bloody clothes. Then I know that the crime is fresh.

~ ~ ~

Two-plus decades inside had marked Lawrence as indelibly as a cellie with a Bic pen and a paperclip. He had a look I'd noticed in other longtime prisoners, a ghost of youth lingering beneath the ravaged surface of old age. His arms, sticking out from the rolled sleeves of his CDC denim, were sinew and bones, I saw as the officer led him into the attorney consult room at San Quentin.

"Don't tell me you didn't bring pictures of the baby."

My brother, Teddy, and his wife had just had their baby, and Tamara and the baby were still in the hospital, or Teddy would have been here with me today. Only after Teddy'd been shot five years ago did I learn he and our father had maintained a close relationship, and that Teddy had been working to reverse my father's conviction. These revelations left me dumbfounded. I'd spent my young adulthood blaming my father for the hole at the center of my life and for the lousy job Teddy had done in filling it, and I'd found it tough giving up the habit.

"There's even bigger news. It's about your case." My voice was perfectly even, delivering the most stunning news he'd ever received in his life. Except, perhaps, the news that my mother, Caroline, had been murdered and he was the only suspect. "The judge granted your habeas petition yesterday."

He sagged, his hands trembling on his scrawny thighs. "Jesus."

I had a copy of the order and slid it across the table. He touched it gingerly. I'd helped Teddy with the brief, but it'd basically been complete when he dropped it on my desk. I suspected that Lawrence, who had been an attorney before his incarceration and, more recently, one of California's most sought-after jailhouse lawyers, had had a hand in it. (As a backdrop for his own claims of innocence, he'd succeeded in obtaining freedom for a number of other men.) The legal issues weren't complicated; what was crucial was the legwork Teddy and his investigator had completed five years ago.

"So why am I still here?"

"It's either here or in County. That's where they put pretrial detainees. Wouldn't you rather be in low security in a place where you've spent the last twenty-one years, instead of San Bruno jail with a bunch of psychopaths?"

For an instant his eyes seemed to film. "They can't retry me."

"The physical evidence from the crime scene has been lost. There aren't any witnesses left. I would think it would be nearly impossible to get a conviction. That said, the state can do whatever it wants until the judge tells them otherwise."

"And you think there's a chance they might try to put me through hell all over again."

"They may try to leverage you into a plea. I figured you wouldn't want that."

He stammered. "I want my law license back. I want my livelihood. I want what they took from me twenty-one years ago. They should compensate me, not try me again."

"I agree. That's what I'll tell the DA when I talk to her."

He wouldn't look me in the eye. I could tell he wanted Teddy. With each year of his life that passed behind bars, the thought of this moment must have seemed more and more like a dream.

When his outrage had finally passed, he took a deep, shuddering breath, and looked up. "I've kept something from you. You deserved to know. I guess I was afraid of what you might think."

"What is it?"

In his face I glimpsed the effect my lack of faith must have had on him, like the remnant of illness. "What were you expecting, a confession? Don't worry. It's just that I got engaged to a woman ten years ago. That's the big secret."

I was astonished. Of course I knew that women—certain women—formed connections with men behind bars, and sometimes even married them. "Who is she?"

"Her name is Dot. Short for Dorothy. She lives in San Rafael. Don't look at me that way."

"I'm just surprised. That's all."

He was getting angry. "You're thinking what the hell is wrong with this person, that she would chain herself to me? The truth is there's nothing wrong with her. Or me."

"Why are you telling me all this now?"

His anger seemed to boil away. "Because I've sheltered her from certain things. The possibility of me getting out of here, for one thing. See, the deal was we'd get married if and when I made parole. I've led her to believe that there wasn't a chance, that the visitors' room is the only kind of life we could ever have together. She took me on those terms. Now it seems the game may be changing. I don't want her to feel . . ."

"Feel what?"

"Obligated." His Adam's apple lurched. "Or tricked. I'd ask Teddy to do this, but she and Teddy haven't ever gotten along. You know how your brother used to be. He looked down on her. Dot's not the kind of woman who'll stand for that."

"What do you mean you'd ask Teddy to do this? Do what?"

"Someone has to tell her what's happening. I want you to let her know that she doesn't have to go through with it, that if she doesn't want me now that I'm out of prison, if me being in here is part of the deal for her, then I won't force the issue. I'll make it easy for her, if that's what she needs. She doesn't have to marry me."

"Dad." The word was strange on my lips, and I realized I'd never called him that in my adult life. His shame and fear were nakedly displayed in his face, kindling a long-dormant spark of loyalty in me. "I'd like to meet her, but I'm not going to say anything about your engagement, and I'm not going to give her this news. You'll have to tell her yourself. What's she going to think if she hears it for the first time from me?"

He agreed and wrote down her name, Dorothy Cooper, and her phone number, along with an address and apartment number. At last, to our mutual relief, I left him with a copy of the judge's order with its heading, Petition Granted, the legal deliverance he'd always dreamed of but in which he'd never quite dared to believe.

Chapter 2

Tamara and Teddy had a bungalow in Berkeley with persimmons and lemons in the backyard, guarded by a fat Labrador who slept twenty-two hours a day. They'd met in the same brain-injury rehab group, Teddy suffering from the bullet that had almost killed him as a consequence of his digging into our father's case, Tamara from a virus that made it hard for her brain to form short-term memories. Like him, she'd learned to cope with her impairments, which in her case meant living her life from one scribbled reminder to the next. They'd both been told they might never live on their own, might never be able to earn an income. A promising artist before her illness, she'd resumed painting and illustrating after their marriage, and a few months ago her first children's book had been released.

She was strikingly beautiful, African American, only twenty-six to Teddy's forty-five. Talking with her, you'd never know anything was wrong with her. She was bright, friendly, and engaging. Still, those of us who knew her had learned to wait and draw back when we saw the flash of confusion and panic cross her face, a look that meant the slate of her mind had just been wiped clean.

Teddy's ex-wife, Jeanie, was visiting when I arrived, two days after Tamara and the baby had come home from the hospital. In the kitchen they were giving Carly a bath, Jeanie stooping over the sink, her blond-brown hair falling around her freckled face while Tamara supported Carly's head, smiling and making cooing noises as she tenderly washed her. Teddy was unshaven, his bearlike bulk draped in a white guayabera. He'd begun to affect a straw sombrero with enough brim to hide the craterlike dimple in his brow, the scar left by the bullet that should have killed him. His pants sagged and the cuffs trailed over the heels of his thin-soled shoes.

Carly's face was a pinched, pinkish purple. She began to scream as Jeanie diapered her, wrapped her in a towel, then handed her to Teddy. "Here you go, Papa," she said with a funny look, as if she hadn't quite gotten used to the idea of her former husband fathering a child.

In her father's arms the baby quieted. "Look at you," I said, watching from the living room, having just walked in. "The family man."

Tamara was jotting a note in her baby log, a special notebook where they recorded the daily details of life with Carly. It covered feedings, diapers, naps, baths, and was not just for their own reference but also for when Tamara's former mother-in-law, Debra Walker, Jeanie, or I checked in. She took the gift I'd brought and pecked my cheek. "Hey there, Uncle Leo. What's this, a set of bike tools?"

"I wish. Is she almost ready for her first day out with the boys?"

"I don't *think* so."

Teddy winked at me. "The racetrack?"

"Two-dollar beers . . ." I said.

"Which of you guys is the bad influence again?" Tamara asked.

"That would be Leo," Teddy said. "He doesn't know the first thing about babies."

"Well, you're the expert now," I conceded.

"We're all learning together." This from Jeanie.

Holding his child, gazing down at her, my brother looked strikingly whole.

"I'm not sure I've ever seen you this happy before," Jeanie said, noticing what I had. Tamara shot her a quick glance.

Teddy looked up, blinking, shy. "Was I unhappy?"

"It never occurred to me. You were just . . . *different*."

Teddy handed Carly to Tamara, catching her eye. A silent message passed between them, Teddy assuring her that Jeanie was no threat, that his regrets were ancient history. I touched his arm and tilted my head toward his desk in the living room, adorned with Post-its, and mouthed the word "talk."

"Jeanie doesn't mind listening to a little shop talk, do you, hon?" Teddy said. "She's just dying for a chance to congratulate me on the big win."

Jeanie shrugged. I poured myself a glass of lemonade, and the three of us walked outside while Tamara went to the rocker to feed Carly. The threat posed by Jeanie was now gone from her attention, either because Teddy's look had comforted her or because she'd had another of her cognitive breaks. It was a fine day in the first week of March, sunny and warm, the hills green from the winter rains. The magnolia by the fence was in bloom. Jeanie and I sat around the glass-topped patio table while Teddy sprawled on the chaise.

"You pulled it off!" Jeanie said. "You really did. Especially considering what you've been through, you ought to be so pleased." It was Jeanie who'd once told me that my father was a master manipulator, ensnaring Teddy in a web of lies. None of us believed that anymore. Even I'd come to feel that he'd been wronged. Of course, coming to believe that I'd been wrong about him didn't mean that I knew how to feel about him possibly getting out of prison. My guilt over the way I'd rejected him made it all the harder for me to come to terms with this change.

"It's been a long road," Teddy agreed. It was hard to read his expression. In the old days, he'd have worn a look of catlike satisfaction, like he'd pulled something over on the world, but the new Teddy just looked tired, like he was aware that even this great success couldn't make up for all he'd lost. I hoped he didn't see it that way.

"I had a call from Angela Crowder this morning," I told them.

In response to my brother's blank look, Jeanie, annoyed, said, "You tried about two dozen felony cases against her. You thought she was arrogant and underprepared. She was on the Santorez case. She was the one who reported you to the bar afterward, tried to get you in trouble for suborning witnesses."

"Still doesn't ring a bell. Some things, I don't mind forgetting."

Jeanie had little patience with his impairments. She expected him to have the same quickness and sting he'd always had.

"They're going to retry Lawrence?" Jeanie asked. "Is that what her call means?"

"They're investigating, she says. She was trying to feel me out, seeing if I thought he'd accept a plea."

"And?"

"No way, I told her. Dismiss the charges."

"The city's trying to avoid a lawsuit," Jeanie said.

"What do you know about cold case prosecutions?"

"More than I used to. Usually they've got DNA. When they do, it's damned if you do, though, damned if you don't. The DNA matches, so it must be true. Juries don't want to understand the science, the way the statistics can be manipulated to make it sound more conclusive than it is, especially in large populations. Unless you get someone with a good science background on your jury, it's usually lights out for the state."

I'd worked for Jeanie for three years after Teddy was shot. She'd recently left private practice and gone back to her job in the Contra Costa public defender's office. By then, I'd already hung out my shingle. I missed our conversations, afternoons spent in each other's office, one of us propped on the edge of a desk or leaning against the wall, bouncing ideas, time that to outsiders might seem wasted.

I'd meant to speak with Teddy about Dot, but with Jeanie there I held my tongue. I knew what her opinion would be of a woman who could fall in love with a man who, like Lawrence Maxwell, was in prison for life.

Teddy let out a snore. "This is a big step," Jeanie said, watching him.

"It's a big step for anyone," I told her, instinctively defending him, though her tone seemed to echo my own fears as Teddy and Tamara sailed into the unknown.

"Two years ago they could hardly take care of themselves. And now they have an infant. Have you talked to him about getting some help with it all?"

"What do you mean, like social services? Big Brother watching for an excuse to take Carly away?"

"Private help, then. Or, Little Brother."

I winced at her implicit rebuke that I wasn't doing enough to support my brother since he'd moved out from my condo when he and Tamara bought the house together. "Debra has been helping. And I'm here often. Nothing's stopping you from coming by, right?"

"Tam doesn't want me here," Jeanie said. "The last thing any woman wants is her husband's ex-wife looking over her shoulder. Sooner or later she'd tell me to back off, and I wouldn't blame her. I'd like to avoid that conflict."

I didn't argue with her. I'd seen the look on Tamara's face and knew Jeanie was right. "It's a different world for both of them compared with two years ago," I said. "I worry about them, but Tam's going to be fine. Maybe she even has a certain advantage. She has the luxury of not getting frustrated because she already put Carly to sleep five times."

"Well, Teddy, then."

"He knows how to ask for help when he needs it. Not like before."

I hadn't meant this comment to sting Jeanie, but I saw that it did. He'd never wanted kids when they were married. He'd never believed in days off or downtime, other than the rare occasions when he decided to get high or drunk. And he never recognized such weaknesses in others, including Jeanie, who'd been both his spouse and his law partner for over a decade.

"Teddy deserves this," she said. "All of it. And they're much better than they were. But I still think we need to get them some help. A professional, a person who's being paid to be here, not just us checking in whenever we have the time." She sighed, then changed the subject. "I just hope he's right about your father."

"Keith Locke was the real killer." Just as my brother had been preparing the habeas corpus petition summarizing the discoveries he'd made in his own personal investigation into my father's case, he'd been shot in the head by the son of the man who'd been my mother's lover. Having discovered the existence of the affair, Keith, then a teenager, had gone to confront my mother. Probably he hadn't known what he wanted from that encounter until he saw her. In a blind fury of rage and shame and lust, he'd raped her and beaten her to death, leaving her for me to find. My father had been convicted of the crime, and I'd accepted his guilt.

Teddy, however, had not. But instead of trying to convince me of my father's innocence he'd hid his loyalty to him, in the mistaken belief that he was somehow sheltering me from knowledge that would torment a more loyal son than I was. A few years ago, feeling that Teddy was getting too close to the truth, Keith Locke once again had turned to violence.

"I still can't make up my mind. All I've seen is the evidence Teddy submitted, and the judge's order. It doesn't say that your dad's innocent, only that evidence was withheld showing she'd been with another man. What the order doesn't point out is how that withheld evidence possibly could strengthen the prosecution's case. If your mother *had* been with another man, and your father caught her at it . . ." She glanced at my face, then looked away. "All I'm saying is that if there's a deal on the table, he might want to take it," she finished.

I looked away, suddenly annoyed with her for her unsolicited advice, and with myself for feeling that she might be right.

Chapter 3

A few days later, figuring that by now my father must have told her the big news, I called Dot. "My name is Leo Maxwell," I said. "My father gave me your number."

"Oh," she said and laughed with a richness that gave way to caution. "This *is* a surprise. Is something wrong? Has Lawrence . . ."

"No, nothing's wrong." From her surprise, I knew my father hadn't told her about the judge's order. Was he unable to work up the courage to share the best news he'd ever received in his life? "Dad just wanted us to meet. He asked me to call."

A pause. "Look, you'd better tell me what's going on."

"I'll explain everything when we meet in person," I promised.

She told me to meet her at a Starbucks near her apartment in San Rafael. "I'll be the fat one wearing leather."

A hog was parked prominently near the Starbucks entrance, one of the deluxe model Softails, the sun gleaming off its polished chrome. I went in, and my eyes immediately found her. As promised, she was a large woman in leather chaps and coat, with the flourish of a flowered silk scarf. She was about five ten, two hundred pounds, between fifty-five and sixty, with gray hair pulled back. Her tiny mug of espresso stood untouched. As I walked in her eyes took my measure.

We shook hands. She wore no wedding band or any other visible jewelry. "I'm not what you expected," she said, her gaze easily holding mine. "You thought you were coming to meet some emotional invalid. That's what your brother thought. That's what he was hoping for. When he saw his error, he tried to run me off. You're looking at the bitch who wore Teddy Maxwell down."

"You're right," I admitted. "You're not what I expected at all."

"But then again, you hardly know your father, so how could you know what to expect in the woman he's engaged to?"

"Right again."

"I know plenty about you. Normally that would put me at the advantage, but you wouldn't be here if you didn't know something I didn't. Lawrence is proud. You didn't want him in your life, and he's going to be damned if he's going to beg you to be involved in his. He wants you to make the first move. It's asinine. You going to let another twenty years go by? To hell with pride."

"He doesn't have much choice about it. Neither do I, for that matter. You see, there's been an unexpected development. His sentence has been vacated. There's a possibility that he may be getting out."

She just stared, her face gone rigid with shock. Then without a word she rose and walked past me out of the coffee shop.

I heard the hog fire up, and, deciding to follow her, made it to my truck just in time to see the motorcycle growl past out of the lot. I followed and managed to keep Dot in sight as she turned onto Sir Francis Drake Boulevard, heading west toward Fairfax, where she turned onto the Bolinas road over the mountains to the sea.

I stayed behind her. That scenic road up the flanks of Mount Tamalpais was a favorite of mine, and I'd ridden it several times in both directions on my road bike. At the top of the climb, she pulled off at the Pine Mountain trailhead and killed her engine.

I parked beside her. She took off her helmet, freed her hair, and glanced over at me with displeasure but not surprise. "He couldn't even tell me himself," she said as I got out of my truck. "He has to send the son who despises him."

"I don't despise him."

"I'm supposed to go to *him*, not the other way around. I'm to make the first move. Court him the way he courted me. Well, what did he think it meant when I told him I'd marry him?"

"I suppose he thought you never believed he'd get out, so you'd never have to go through with it."

She was still straddling the bike, staring out over the hills, mottled brown and green. The wind was fresh on our faces. "*Have to.* He's always been tormented by the fear that I chose him only because I want a man someone keeps in a cage, like a pet that you take out when you're ready to play with it." She glanced at me. "The truth is him being locked up is the second biggest tragedy of my life."

"How'd you meet?" I asked, with delicacy.

"He helped my son make parole. Scotty was dead of an overdose six months later. I started visiting Lawrence after Scotty's death, try-ing to get to the bottom of what that place did to my boy. Believe me, I'd never have stepped foot in that prison if I'd known where it would lead. But I didn't seem to have any choice. I wanted to marry him, but he wouldn't agree. He said we should wait until he got out. I thought he was the one who didn't want *me*."

"Don't take this the wrong way, but it doesn't sound like you're happy that he might be getting out."

She gave me a sharp look. "It's the best news anyone could have brought me. But I'm worried that he's going to push me away, reject me before I can reject *him*. Precisely because happiness is within our reach, and because he doesn't think he deserves it."

"I think you ought to talk to him."

"He wanted you to give me the news because he wants to make it easy for me to back out and prove his deepest fears."

She must have seen the truth in my eyes. "Shit." She looked away. "I can't tell you how much that stings. He's going to make this so insulting, so painful for us both. But I'm not going to give him what he wants. You tell him that I won't let him ruin the best thing that ever happened to me. To us. If he wants to break our engagement, he can tell me himself."

She put her helmet back on, kicked the bike to life, swung it back around in a half circle, and drove away toward Bolinas and Point Reyes.

~ ~ ~

On Tuesday I again drove out to San Quentin, this time bringing Teddy with me. He'd been reluctant to leave home, but Debra was there, and I'd convinced him that his wife and child would be fine. "Dad wants to thank you in person," I said. "And he'd like to see the pictures of Carly."

During the drive Teddy was tense, stressed out with fears about what could happen at home in his absence. I'd told him about my visit with Dot, but his only reaction had been a grunt. "How could you not have told me that Dad was engaged?" I asked, though I suppose the answer ought to have been obvious. Where our father was concerned, Teddy'd always had a talent for keeping secrets.

"Dad didn't want me to tell you," he said. "He thought you'd think less of him, or something. And, he and I never saw eye to eye about Dot. I never understood this so-called engagement of theirs. It seemed to me that she was using him to fulfill some need of hers, that him being inside was part of the attraction."

"I guess now we'll see. If he gives her the chance. After all these years, she deserves a chance, don't you think?"

Teddy just shrugged, obviously uncomfortable. To change the subject, I described in more detail my conversation with Angela Crowder.

"So they've dumped this one on me," she said to me on the phone. "For the last week I've been trying to figure out what to do with it. There's no one around here who has any connection to the case. I'm not that old, for Christ's sake. So I'm not sitting here thinking I have to cover my ass or anyone else's. That's not the kind of prosecutor I am. You know that, Leo. You know I always give it to you straight."

"Do I know that?" I asked her.

"So here's the deal," she said. "It's only good until the hearing next week. If we have to go before the judge, it comes off the table. Second-degree murder, time served, the usual conditions. He walks out of that courtroom a free man, and we all put the past behind us."

"The past isn't even the past," I told her. "Not for him, and not for me. Not until the state dismisses these charges."

We'd see her at the hearing, I said.

"So what do you think, should he take the deal?" Teddy asked when I finished recapping my conversation.

"Jeanie has a point. The withheld evidence could actually bolster the prosecution's case, give him a motive he didn't have before. But no, the thought of him pleading guilty puts a bad taste in my mouth. Obviously we've got to tell him about the offer, but it seems to me that they ought to dismiss the charges."

"I agree," Teddy said, looking uncomfortable with the reversal of our roles, me automatically taking the lead and he looking to me for confirmation of what he was thinking. "But if he's got a chance to walk away from it, time served . . . Part of me thinks he's dumb not to grab the deal."

"That's *his* decision," I said. "We don't get to make it for him."

My tone was sharper than I'd intended, and my words had the effect of shutting down further debate. I wanted our father to fight, and at the moment I wasn't interested in probing my motives. As with my last visit, we had to wait over half an hour at the guard shack in the wind and cold out there on the bay before they'd let us in. During our wait, we didn't speak any more of the deal that was on the table, a deal that Teddy clearly wanted my father to take.

One of the officers had decided to be a hard-ass. He wanted us to see Lawrence in the regular visitors' room, where conversations were recorded and there could be no expectation of privacy. After making us wait around just because he could, he finally let us go through to the attorney-client conference area.

"Hey there, Papa," Lawrence said when the guard finally brought him in.

Teddy rose, and our father clasped hands with him, the closest he could get to a hug with the olive-jacketed guards watching through the glass. "I knew you could do it." Lawrence's voice was tight, higher than normal. His excitement was palpable, in contrast with the impatience he'd shown toward me the other day. "Teddy, they can't stop talking about you in here. People coming up to me I've never met, saying, 'That boy of yours, he never gave up on you.' You're a hero to every poor son of a bitch in this place. You had every reason to give up and you never did."

"We had a little holdup there," Teddy said, his hand still in our father's.

"You got shot in the fucking head. You call that a holdup?" Lawrence shook his head disbelievingly. "You know I'm the whole reason he was so hot to get his law license back, just to show those fuckers that Teddy Maxwell always wins."

Lawrence took his time with the photos Teddy'd brought. Finally he slipped the stack back into the envelope. "She's beautiful," he said. "You ought to be goddamned proud."

"You keep them," Teddy said.

"Don't need to. I'm getting out of here soon, aren't I?" He slid the envelope back. "You get real tired of living your life secondhand. Or thirdhand, as it is." He turned to me, drumming his fingers excitedly on the table. "So where are we at with the case?"

"Angela Crowder is the DA. She made an offer. You plead to second-degree murder and the state will agree to recommend a sentence of time served, meaning you walk out of the courtroom a free man. You'd be on parole, so they could always violate you. I told her you wouldn't take it. The offer's good until the hearing, though."

"They're bluffing," Lawrence said.

"I wouldn't be so sure. What she said is that they're investigating. It sounds to me like they're thinking about retrying you. It's been pointed out to me that the evidence withheld from the defense wasn't necessarily inconsistent with guilt. I think a lot of judges would have denied Teddy's petition on that basis."

I tried to explain it as succinctly as I could. "All the evidence shows is that Caroline was with another man before her death. It doesn't show that this other man killed her. In fact, some people might think that it supplies the missing link of motive. You come home in the middle of the day, find her in bed with another man, and in a jealous rage beat her to death."

"We got lucky, is what you're saying. Unbelievable."

"There's also the possibility of an appeal by the state. The court of appeals might look at this one and shrug. Harmless error is what they call it when they think you might be guilty anyway. If the judge denies bail, you might find yourself stuck in here longer than you think. It's a dirty bargain, making you plead guilty to a crime you didn't commit, but you've got to remember that this mess could drag on for years."

"I'm not pleading guilty to anything. They don't even have probable cause."

"Then we've got to be ready to bring a bail motion at your hearing. Teddy can handle it. Or I can, if you want."

Teddy stirred in his chair, glanced at me. We hadn't talked about this part. He was still technically the lead attorney on my father's case, but he hadn't made a court appearance since before the shooting, and a first-degree murder case wasn't exactly the place to start.

My father spoke carefully. "Teddy hasn't been in front of a judge in over five years."

I didn't say anything. But the expression on my face was enough.

"Oh, shit, kid. Now you're going to make me cry. I feel rotten about it. I really do. But it's my life here. Teddy did his job, now it's time for you to come in and do what you do."

"You're the alpha dog, now," Teddy said. "No point beating round the bush."

"It's not a good thing or a bad thing," Lawrence continued. "It's just a fact."

I nodded. "Okay, I'll do the hearing. There's no conflict with that, but you'll need to find another attorney for the long haul if they don't drop the case. There isn't a better public defender's office in the country than San Francisco's."

My father nodded. It was settled, then. "What are my chances of making bail?" he wanted to know. "It's not one of the legal issues I've kept up on. It's not really a factor in my client group."

"Decent," I said. "Let me ask you this. If you do get out, what are your plans?"

"No such thing as plans in here. Once you start making any, you're finished for life inside." He sat back and sighed heavily. "I wouldn't impose on you, if that's what you're asking."

"I talked to Dot."

He seemed suddenly to become still. "And?"

"You told me you were going to give her the news, but she had to hear it from me. You can imagine how that made her feel."

"I couldn't do it," he said woefully. "Every day, I meant to call her, believe me."

He seemed truly ashamed, but also helpless and paralyzed by the new possibilities life had opened before him.

I looked at him with pity and frustration. "What's wrong with you? She's clearly devoted to you, and for someone as independent as she seems, that's saying a lot. What's she do?"

"Trauma nurse. She doesn't like to talk about her work."

"So you're going to act like you don't believe she'll honor your engagement if and when you get out? What's that say about your respect for her?"

"Sounds like you're making judgments you've got no business making."

"You made it my business when you sent me to tell her what you should have told her yourself. She should have been the *first* person you told."

"So what did she say?"

"What do you mean, what did she say? You think she's going to talk to me about you and her? She got on her bike and drove off. I followed her. When I finally caught up to her, she was furious."

"She isn't ready for this any more than I am."

"No, I don't suppose she is. But at least she's willing to face it."

"It's just . . ." His jaw worked up and down a few times. "I'll talk to her," he finally said. "I'll make it right."

"Good, because I can't do *that* for you."

"But if for some reason she's not ready . . ."

"Teddy can't put you up. Not with Tamara and the baby."

"Leo—" Teddy began, then closed his mouth, realizing I was right.

I had an extra room at my place, which he possibly knew. But I didn't want him living with me. It would be too near, too fast. It was one thing getting to know my father again after years of believing the worst about him. It was quite another to share a bathroom. I'd gotten used to living alone again after Teddy moved out.

He went on, his voice roughening. "There's guys out there who would still be in here if not for what I did for them. Put up bail, too, if you're telling me you don't want to do that."

"I'm not saying we don't *want* to do anything." I flushed, suddenly wishing I were almost anywhere else, wishing I hadn't gotten into this. It demeaned all of us. I knew my brother would front the bail money in a second if asked, but Teddy had a family to worry about, and he couldn't be financially liable for Lawrence's bond.

He went on. "I know you pretty well, Leo, even though you and I haven't said two words to each other in twenty years. You worried I'm going to run?"

He was behaving just as Dot had described him, taking the offensive rather than risking rejection. "That's not what I'm telling you. Not at all."

"I've got people who'll post any bond that judge will set. I don't need a handout."

"There's this guy who owns one of the residence hotels in the city," I said. "Who owed Teddy a favor, gave him a room for years rent-free. The Seward. If you're on bail or parole with conditions, the judge may not approve it."

"See, he *does* care," Lawrence said to Teddy. There was no mistaking the sarcasm.

"Take it easy on him, Pop," Teddy said. "He wants the best."

"For the record, I don't think you should stay at the Seward, or anywhere else. I think you should go home to Dot, if she'll have you. You're engaged. What that means in this day and age is that you can live together. You don't have to wait to be invited. You can just ask her if it's okay. She shouldn't have to beg."

The meanness suddenly drained from Lawrence's face, and his head went down for a second. When he spoke, it was in a tone I hardly recognized. "*Home.* I don't even know what the word's supposed to mean."

I didn't, either. "Probably, it means what you make of it."

"See, now, that's exactly what I'm afraid of." Hearing him say this, it occurred to me that perhaps his imprisonment was as necessary to his idea of togetherness as it had been to Dot's, at least according to Teddy's view of her. He went on. "I keep forgetting, you're the one who found her body." He looked up again. "I want you to know that I don't blame you for the way you felt about me, for thinking I did it. You were just a kid."

"For Christ's sake, that's not what this is about."

He was shaking his head. "Teddy and I, we kept you in the dark all these years. Somehow I thought you'd come to me on your own one day. But now I realize it wasn't fair of me to put that responsibility on you. I should never have assumed you'd reject me out of hand if I were the one to make the approach."

I would have, though, and he knew it. Rejecting him is exactly what would have happened if he'd made such an effort. His protests of innocence weren't a viewpoint I wanted to hear.

"And you shouldn't assume the same about the woman who's agreed to marry you. It's not like she didn't know your past. You *both* knew what you were getting into."

"Caveat emptor. Except the terms have changed."

I suddenly found that I was out of patience with him. "Look, I'll see you before the hearing," I told Lawrence. "Teddy, take your time."

Outside, I walked out the front gates and down the narrow road to a little cove with a shell beach barely wider than a man. In the distance across the calm water, San Francisco prickled with tiny spires, like trouble itself on the horizon.

Chapter 4

"Be seated," Judge Liu said, taking the bench.

The courtroom was half filled with spectators, most from the press. Lawrence sat shackled between Teddy and me, still wearing his CDC blues. The bailiff had refused to take off the hardware. Dot sat in the front row behind him. Angela Crowder stated her name for the record. I did the same, then added, "Your Honor, my client is in restraints. At this moment he's presumed innocent. Can we have these shackles removed?"

The judge, a big man, was imposing in his dark robe behind the bench. He gave me a look without an inch of yield in it. "The deputies and I have an understanding. I don't tell them how to do their job and they don't tell me mine. In ten minutes this issue may be moot. Can we all be a little bit patient with the conditions here?"

"Your Honor, my client has been patient for the last twenty-one years. I'm sure he can be patient for ten minutes more."

"I'm certain he can." Judge Liu eyed my father appraisingly, then turned to the DA. "Now, Ms. Crowder, it's my understanding that the state has not filed a motion to stay my ruling pending appeal."

"That's correct, Your Honor. We respect this court's judgment and have no plans to appeal the order granting habeas relief."

Angela Crowder was in her forties, plump and barely over five feet tall, with a mass of tightly curled dark hair. Her freckled face belonged in a Dutch painting. She had a dime-sized mole on her chin that any competent dermatologist might have removed. Eye contact was her weapon of choice. When things didn't go according to plan, she grew vicious and ran the risk of stinging herself.

"You have no realistic chance of success, is what you mean."

In the back of the courtroom I heard a cough that had obviously begun as a laugh. Liu's eyes sought the offender, not with displeasure. He went on. "Mr. Maxwell has a right to a speedy trial if the state intends to recharge him. If the state doesn't intend to charge him with this crime, then he has the right to walk out of this courtroom today a free man. What are the state's intentions? Ms. Crowder, are you prepared to refile the first-degree murder charges?"

"Your Honor, the police department and the district attorney's office are investigating. As we're all aware, this is a very old case and most of the people who were originally involved are now gone. We're having to start from scratch. The state, nevertheless, believes it can present evidence of Lawrence Maxwell's guilt. As his attorney, Mr. Maxwell, has observed, his father has been patient for twenty-one years. The state is sensitive to the fact that any delay at this point must be difficult to stomach. Nonetheless, extremely serious charges remain pending. In two weeks, I promise the court, we can have a definite answer."

Seeing in the judge's face that he was going to give her what she requested, I stood. "Your Honor, if I may be heard. I would ask that if the court is inclined to grant the state's request, which my client opposes, that Your Honor set this case not for a status conference but for a probable cause hearing." A probable cause hearing, otherwise known as a preliminary hearing or preliminary examination, was a required stage in all felony cases.

"Do you have any authority for your entitlement to a probable cause hearing?"

"Penal Code Section 995. The conviction has been vacated, so we're starting over. Essentially, it's the same as if Mr. Maxwell had been arrested for the first time last week on suspicion of this murder. If the state wants to retry him, it should present its evidence now."

"I agree," Liu said, surprising me. "Ms. Crowder, any reason why the state should not have to show probable cause?"

She rolled her eyes. "We've already shown it. Twenty-one years ago."

"Precisely. You've just told me that most of the people involved twenty-one years ago are now gone. That includes investigators, many of whom would need to be questioned about the physical evidence that I found was wrongfully withheld from the defense. If those people aren't available, then the defense won't be able to question them. Mr. Maxwell will probably argue that as one reason why this case should be dismissed."

I spoke up. "The defendant expects to file a motion to exclude the use of any transcripts of testimony from the previous trial."

The man we stood before now gave Crowder his best fuck-you smile. "Any thoughts, Ms. Crowder?"

"I don't have an argument prepared right now, Your Honor. We can brief the issue . . ."

"I'm sure that both sides will enlighten me when you file your briefs a week from today. Simultaneous briefing, please. I'll grant the state's motion for a continuance and set this case for a probable cause hearing in two weeks. After that hearing, if necessary, I'll also hear the defendant's motion to dismiss this case. Anything else?"

I stood. "The defendant requests bail."

"We can take that up after the hearing," Crowder said.

The judge studied her. "No," he said. "I think we'll take it up now. What bail is the defense requesting?"

"Ten thousand dollars." A shot at the moon.

He didn't blink. "That's lower than the usual amount for a first-degree murder charge. A lot lower. Give me your reasons."

I summarized my father's clean prison record and the lack of any evidence that he posed a danger to anyone. With no money, credit cards, driver's license, or passport, he posed no flight risk. "As for my client's ties to the community, I'll have to switch roles and speak not as Mr. Maxwell's attorney, but as his son. For twenty-one years my father, my brother, and I have never stopped seeking his exoneration." My feelings about my father were no one's business but my own. The truth, at least for me, was otherwise. But that was a private truth, one I had no desire to reveal in this public forum, with journalists scribbling or typing every word I said.

"There's no reason," I continued, "he should have to post such a high bail while the state dithers and delays the inevitable decision to dismiss these charges. We ask that the court recognize the special circumstances of this case and set bail at ten thousand dollars."

I sat down and felt a hand squeeze my arm—my father's. I glanced at him, and the nod he gave me conveyed urgent approval. He seemed to recognize that his freedom was at hand, closer than he'd ever dared dream, and his eyes brightened in hope. I hardly heard Crowder's response.

Judge Liu made his ruling. "The defendant's motion to reduce bail is well taken. I find that the special circumstances in this case— including the defendant's many years of incarceration, excellent behavioral record, and the likelihood that the state will not be able to meet its burden of proceeding—warrant a substantial reduction; however, not to the level requested by the defense. Bail is set at fifty thousand dollars cash bond."

~ ~ ~

As soon as Liu had left the bench, Dot came through the swinging gate, took my father's face in both her hands, and kissed him on the mouth. Cameras flashed, capturing the moment. My father's face was flushed. His hands shook with excitement.

More reporters were waiting as we came out of the courtroom, making me remember that today was the first time Teddy had appeared at the Hall of Justice since he'd been shot. He'd once owned this place. Back then, people would have turned to look at him as he strode down the halls to a court appearance, the cops staring with open contempt, the defendants acknowledging his magic reputation as a fixer. The hearing today could have been his coming-out party, his return to the practice of law—except I hadn't given him the chance to say a word.

Dot had her bike, and planned to meet us at Teddy's. She'd brought an extra helmet for my father, but Lawrence balked. "Not unless you're going to let me drive," he said.

"And kill us both?" She masked her disappointment with feigned disgust.

As we drove across the Bay Bridge, sitting three across in my pickup, Dot passed us, and my father peered out the window for a glimpse of the skyline between the decks. When we were halfway across, he said, "I guess they fixed it after it fell down." It took me a moment to realize that he was talking about the upper deck's collapse during the quake of '89.

I said, "Things must look different." I was wary of drawing him out, afraid to know too much about what he was feeling. He would be like a skinless man, all his protective instincts turned inside out, a condition likely to put him wrong in any normal interaction. As he stared out at the landscape unscrolling outside the window, I was sensitive to how I must figure in the tumult of emotions he was experiencing.

"Funny," he said. "I was just thinking how everything looks the same. Same old world. And same old Lawrence Maxwell." What he meant by that I didn't ask.

I'd called as soon as we left the courtroom, and the others were waiting at Teddy's house: Jeanie, Tamara, Carly. The welcome home party that wasn't. Because where was home for a man who'd spent the last twenty-one years in San Quentin? Dot was waiting outside, and the others were all out back. As we joined them, Tamara, who'd been sketching, rose, laying her pad aside.

"I hear you're a wonderful artist," Lawrence said, taking her hand. "You're just as lovely as Teddy described you. Or rather, lovelier."

I introduced everyone to Dot, whom my father seemed to ignore. She wouldn't look me in the eyes, but hung back, seeming to take in the scene. Tamara deflected Lawrence's compliment by introducing him to Jeanie, who seemed uncomfortable and out of place, and kept staring at Dot as if she were some exotic species. But since Teddy had asked Jeanie to come, she was here.

"Let me show you the baby," Teddy said, moving between Lawrence and Tamara. "This is Carly."

"Don't wake her—" Tamara started, but he was already lifting the sleeping child from the bassinet, remembering to support the head. Her black hair was finely kinked, the skin just a shade darker than Teddy's, every human detail perfect in miniature. Then, without warning, Teddy handed the baby to her grandfather, who to my surprise took her as if being handed an infant were the most natural thing. He held Carly, jiggling her gently to keep her from crying.

"Isn't that nice," he said, peering at the tiny, oblivious face. "Isn't that something. I was always good with babies," he said, looking up with flushed happiness at the rest of us.

Dot said, "This is certainly a side of you I've never seen."

After a pause Jeanie said, "I suppose you never forget."

"I raised two of them. I changed the diapers, fed them in the middle of the night, rocked them to sleep. Happiest days of my life. Every second is precious. Every single one."

Dot watched him with her jaw tense, vulnerability behind the customary hardness of her eyes. I tried to guess what she was thinking. All of us except Teddy had wanted nothing to do with Lawrence for twenty-one years. For nearly ten of those years, she'd been there for him, but now, it seemed, she was being asked to take a backseat. Of course, she wouldn't be interested in such an understanding from me.

Or maybe she was thinking of her son, who'd died after Lawrence helped him win his freedom.

"Back to Mama," Lawrence now said, breaking the tension of the moment as Carly yawned and awakened. He handed the baby to Tamara.

Jeanie had brought a tray of cold meats, antipasti, fresh fruit, and grilled vegetables. "There's stuff here I haven't seen in two decades," my father told us. "Kalamata olives . . . We used to go to this little place in North Beach—"

He stopped, looking apologetically at Dot, and I realized that by *we* he meant he and Caroline, my mother. Dot nodded and touched his wrist, as if giving him permission to speak of that still-unfinished business. I both wanted and didn't want him to go on. There was a nearness in the way he spoke of her, as if she were a living presence to him still, accessible in a way she never would be to me. At the same time, hearing him speak like that filled me with foreboding.

As I'd tried to make clear to Crowder, the past wasn't finished for any of us, not with the case hanging over our heads. I believed in my father's innocence, but not as Teddy believed in it. I was a skeptic converted to uncertain faith. My eyes found Dot's.

We filled our plates and found seats. Jeanie wanted to know about the hearing, so Teddy and I filled her in. When I came to the part about Judge Liu granting my request for a probable cause hearing and scheduling it for two weeks out, I downplayed the news. She opened her mouth, but I gave her a warning look. The last thing I wanted was to talk legal strategy here, today, in front of the man engendering it.

"Liu's a good judge," Jeanie said. "No surprise he granted bail. He *gets* it." She looked from Teddy to me and back again, but she didn't ask the question that seemed to be on her lips, the question of where Dot had come from.

My father reloaded his plate with the good roast beef, deliciously pink, the plump red organic strawberries, the grilled asparagus, the olives. It was distracting, watching him eat. Our conversation kept stalling around the force of his hunger, the way he bit into the strawberry and sucked the fruit away from the greens, took a thin slice of roast beef between thumb and forefinger and folded it whole into his mouth, a bite so big that he had to swallow four times, still chewing, eyes watering, to get it down. Watching him with obvious pleasure, Dot lifted a napkin to his lips and wiped his mouth, then leaned forward and in sight of all, kissed him again.

When he'd finished, he leaned back in the sun and said, "Now I think I'd like to spend a little more time getting to know my granddaughter."

~ ~ ~

The rest of our welcome home party went equally well. My father was charming, reminding me of Teddy in his prime. He'd talked in a steady stream to Tamara and Jeanie, making them laugh, putting them at ease. He'd paid the small gestures of affection that he owed to Dot, and she'd spent a few moments in conversation with Jeanie and even held the baby, though it appeared that she and Teddy still weren't speaking. I couldn't help seeing them both from the point of view of Jeanie, who watched my father with barely hidden skepticism, no doubt searching for telltale signs of the master manipulator presenting himself as he wished to be seen. He held the baby for nearly an hour more, charming Carly, too.

As the afternoon sun declined, we gathered in the front yard to see them off, like a wedding party watching newlyweds embark. Lawrence, having been persuaded to accept Dot as a driver, fit the helmet she'd brought him onto his head and swung his leg over the saddle. As Dot kicked the bike to life he wrapped his arms around her and held on tight. Dot pumped her fist, sounded the horn, and bore him away.

Chapter 5

I hadn't been quite straight with Lawrence when I praised the public defender's office before his release. In fact, I'd known it was unlikely that an attorney from there would be appointed. A man named Keith Locke was in prison after having pleaded guilty to attempting to murder my brother. Locke had been defended by the San Francisco public defender's office. That was enough of a conflict of interest to keep the PD from also representing my father, so it was no surprise to me when later that week they filed a notice of conflict. This resulted in so-called conflict counsel being appointed for Lawrence. What it meant was that a private attorney from the court's panel would be paid on an hourly basis to juggle Lawrence's case along with those clients who'd chosen her to be their lawyer.

Wednesday morning, Teddy and I caught the BART into the city for our first meeting with the new lawyer. Her name was Nina Schuyler, and her office was on Sixth Street south of Market, not far from Teddy's old building. Lawrence and Dot arrived soon after we did, Dot parking her bike on the sidewalk. A bored-seeming security guard looked the four of us over, took a peek inside the file box I'd lugged with me on the train, then summoned the elevator to take us up.

I hadn't seen my father since he rode off with Dot after our welcome home party last week. He seemed harried. Dot was short with him. Maybe they were just nervous. They'd never been allowed to touch, and now they were living together. Neither would look me in the eye.

Four of the five chairs in the third-floor waiting room were occupied. The lone woman, white, wore short short cutoffs and a fringed vest. She sat beside a sprawling man dressed completely in red. There was an empty chair, and on the other side an Asian kid scratching at a bandage. Beside him sat a middle-aged Latino. The office had potted trees and framed prints by Kandinsky, cubist Picasso, and Chagall. The carpeting was aged but clean, and the large windows admitted plenty of light.

A quick online search had revealed that Nina Schuyler had graduated from law school in 1996, three years before me. She'd worked for the San Francisco public defender's office for six years, then opened her own practice. She'd tried a few high-profile murder cases and made something of a name for herself. She was just thirty-three, two years older than I was, having graduated from Stanford and begun her studies at Berkeley at the age of twenty-one.

We didn't have to wait long before the inner door opened and Nina came out, tall but slight, long limbed but not willowy. She had a piano player's delicate-fingered hands, and dark hair swept back from a no-bullshit face. She wore suit pants and a sleeveless blouse, and she studied her BlackBerry as she walked.

"Marcella, who are all these people? I told you I'm booked solid today."

Her receptionist just shrugged, not taking her eyes from the phone screen. "They say they want to see you. I tell them you're booked, but they think if they wait, then maybe . . ."

"Excuse me for a moment," Nina said to my father. Putting a hand on my arm, she stepped around me. "I'm not taking new clients now," she announced to the room. "Even if I were, I wouldn't have time today. And even if I had time, you'd need appointments. Marcella can give you the names of attorneys I refer cases to. Otherwise, I'm afraid you're only wasting your time."

The man in red started to rise, but she turned without seeing him, the room instantly becoming invisible to her, her body language communicating refusal so clearly and forcefully that the pimp sat back down.

Nina held the door as we filed into an inner hallway, me lugging the file box. As the door closed I heard her would-be clients begin talking all at once.

"You're having to beat them off," I said. She was an attractive woman and I wanted her to notice me.

"I swear to God, if it weren't for the trouble of having to hire someone to replace her, Marcella would be out on the street." Nina showed us past a small, cluttered office and a tiny kitchen to a small conference room. On the table were a vase of lilies, a water pitcher, a coffee carafe, and three fresh legal pads and pens. "Nina Schuyler," she said. "Call me Nina. Please, set down your things."

I put the box on the floor and we took our seats. "I've followed your case with interest. And was thrilled to get the draw. I've read the court's order, and I've read the briefs. Yours was well done," she said to Teddy, who simply nodded. Despite all her years practicing in the city, she made no direct acknowledgment of his reputation. Lawrence introduced Dot, and Nina graciously took her hand.

I gave her one of my cards. "Leo Maxwell."

She placed the card on the pad in front of her. "Here are my ground rules. Right now, it's a bit crowded in this room for my taste. I'm happy to keep the two of you informed, but you shouldn't expect to be included in decisions. You'll sit in the gallery, not at the counsel table. You won't be second chairing this trial. This is a vessel with one captain, and that captain is me."

"Okay," I said. She appeared not to notice the look my father was giving her. "You want Teddy and me to take a walk?"

She considered the question. "No. You can stay. You all can, for now." She turned a few pages of the file in front of her, which as yet was thin. "We're set for a probable cause hearing next Friday," she said, reading from her notes. "According to the court's order, motions to dismiss will be heard at that time. Briefing is due"—she consulted the file again—"in two days."

"Leo can handle that," my father said. "I don't want us asking for a delay."

I offered her an apologetic look, only to be shut out by the intensity of her focus. "It would be a mistake to give the state more time," she said, carefully returning Lawrence's stare. "You know how they're using this time."

He held her gaze grudgingly, then looked away. "I have a pretty good idea."

Nina leaned slightly back in her chair, now including me, Teddy, and Dot in her attention. "They're interviewing your old cell mates, everyone you might have spoken to during all those twenty-one years you spent in prison. Most men who do time, like you, make enemies inside. I'd be very surprised if you were any different."

Teddy leaned forward. "You're saying they're trying to drum up a snitch."

"Isn't that where you'd direct your efforts if you were in their position? In a case like this one, DNA or other physical evidence couldn't possibly be conclusive, given your marriage to the victim. And after so many years, it's unlikely that any new eyewitness would come forward. No, I think their only path to a conviction is through your own words, something you let slip to someone who now believes he might have something to gain. Or just as likely, something you didn't say. What other new evidence could the district attorney hope to find after all this time?"

I watched Dot out of the corner of my eye, wondering what she made of my father's alleged crime. If Dot had never bargained on him being released, she certainly hadn't signed on for this.

My father had gone pale. I saw his fear and knew Nina was right: an informant was the state's easiest route to conviction. I'd thought they might revisit whatever evidence they had, test it for DNA, but a match would be meaningless. My mother had been killed in the home she shared with Lawrence, and his DNA would naturally be all over any sample collected from the scene. A snitch, on the other hand, didn't need science, and such testimony would be free of the taint of the prosecutorial misconduct that had served as the grounds for the judge's order reversing my father's conviction. No doubt San Quentin was full of men willing to give false testimony for a ticket out of prison.

Nina went on. "From news reports covering the bail hearing it's clear that the judge is disposed to dismiss the case. So we have to move quickly, before the state has time to locate or manufacture the evidence that will convince him otherwise. That's why I'm not planning to ask for a postponement, even though I don't expect to be fully prepared for the preliminary hearing."

My father's eyes were shut. When he opened them his expression was unreadable. But, to me, he looked as if he knew already that the police would find the informant they were looking for. "Okay."

Dot put her hand on his arm, gripping it above the elbow, but he didn't react.

"So do you believe I'm on your side?" Nina asked.

"I'll believe anything if it'll keep me out of prison."

"As for your suggestion that Leo draft the brief that's due in two days, I think it's a smart one, given that I've just come on board."

"I already made a start," I told her. "An outline."

"Then you should be able to send me a draft tomorrow."

I was annoyed by her assumption that I might have nothing else to do, but merely said, "Fine. I'll have it for you tomorrow afternoon."

"Very good." She gave me a quick smile, which had the warming effect it was intended to have on me. "Now why don't you show me what you have in that box."

Before I could open the box, Dot rose, as if afraid what the contents might reveal. "Sorry," she said. "But your lawyer doesn't want me here, and the truth is I don't want to stay. This is the unfinished business. There are things here that I don't want to see."

"You'll be at the trial," Nina said. "That's what's important."

"Of course," Dot said and went out, with a quick smile at Lawrence. Nina looked worried. I could see that it took all Lawrence's self-control to let Dot go. When the sound of her bike had faded from the street, half of his attention seemed to have fled with it.

Over the course of the next ninety minutes Teddy and I walked Nina through the old case file, with Lawrence offering details as needed. Then Teddy outlined his theory of Keith Locke's guilt and our father's innocence. If Nina was skeptical she kept it to herself for now.

We made a few decisions, none earth-shattering. First came a no-brainer, that Lawrence wouldn't testify at the probable cause hearing. Because the standard for finding probable cause was so low, the defense rarely put on any evidence. Typically the only effect was to give the prosecution a preview of the defense's case. Second and more significant was that Lawrence and I would begin making a list of prisoners who might hold grudges, men who might be tempted to give false testimony to put him back where they were.

"If they find a witness, they'll try to keep his identity secret as long as possible," Nina said. "I'll need to be prepared to make an argument and cite cases saying why we need to know who the informant is."

"I have a pretty good investigator I use on most of my cases," I said. "I'll put him to work."

Leaning back in her chair, she stretched her arms, surveying the table crammed with transcripts, notes, and photographs. "Make sure you get me a good list of anyone who might testify against him. A complete list," she emphasized. She was addressing me, not my father. "That's the main thing."

I gave a nod. It hadn't escaped me that she'd avoided asking Lawrence whether he'd confessed to anyone inside. If he'd confessed, and told her so, ethically she wouldn't be able to put him on the witness stand later to deny the confession. Her comment made clear—in terms that only another lawyer would understand—that it would be my role to get vital information from my father and pass it on to her in sanitized form, allowing her to learn what she needed to know, and nothing more. This arrangement would free her to ethically and imaginatively defend his case. It was clear she was taking all the precautions a good defense lawyer would take with a client whom she believed to be guilty.

Without further ceremony she rose. "Now if you don't mind, I'm going to try to put all this in some kind of order, and start on the research I'll need for Friday. We'll speak again tomorrow after I've reviewed your motion."

~ ~ ~

"About that list," I said to Lawrence when the three of us were on the train back to Oakland. He'd decided to spend the afternoon at the office with us, and then I would give him a ride to San

Rafael. "Don't leave anyone off. I don't need to know why the names are on there."

He was staring into the blackness of the Transbay Tube outside the window. Looking at me, he said, "She thinks I confessed."

For a moment I wasn't sure whom he meant, Dot or Nina. If that's what Nina thought, she must have considered me some kind of deluded half-wit, I reflected, working to free the man who'd killed my mother. I remembered Dot's sudden departure. Suddenly, the familiar doubt surged through me, and I had to push it down. "She's a good lawyer. It doesn't matter what she believes." Hesitating, I then said, "Look, I hope that you and Dot are able to enjoy this time."

He glanced across the aisle. "I don't want to *enjoy* myself. I can bring in business, you know. I'm not a lawyer anymore, but if I have someone handling the cases, I can work them."

"Prisoner lawsuits? I'm not that desperate. But stick around."

"Appeal work, for a start. Guy gets convicted, sentenced, people inside refer him to me. We write the appeal, make a few gestures of appreciation—it wouldn't take much—and pretty soon you've got a steady stream of paying clients."

It sounded pretty implausible to me. "I'm a trial lawyer, not an appellate lawyer. I make the messes, I don't clean them up."

"Maybe, but this contingency work of yours—these civil cases—the defense lawyers have to be afraid of you or they won't pay. You and I both know they're not going to be afraid of Teddy anymore." Lawrence spoke intently, peering into my face, his eyes avoiding his older son's. Teddy registered the slight only in a faint tightening of his shoulders, a readiness for a movement that never came. It angered me that Lawrence could be so blunt in front of him.

"He isn't going to be trying cases anytime soon," Lawrence went on. "But he can write an appeal."

"Dad's going to be bringing in fresh cases, as well as appeal work," Teddy said.

I turned to Teddy, my displeasure with my father turning to understanding as I realized I'd been railroaded, or rather that Teddy had, with Lawrence extracting a promise from Teddy without either of them consulting me. "Fresh cases. What do you mean?"

"You ever heard of a guy named Bo Wilder?" Lawrence asked. "He ended up in Quentin right about the time of that blowup I had with Ricky Santorez. If it weren't for Bo, I'd have been dead after that stunt I pulled. He needs a lawyer his guys on the outside can call in a pinch."

"What did you promise him?" I spoke to Teddy, ignoring my father.

"Dad'll take twenty percent of every fee he generates."

Teddy was bringing little money in, and therefore shouldn't have had much say in our financial decisions, and shouldn't have been agreeing to share his small income with anyone. But, clearly, money wasn't what this was about for Teddy. Now he looked at me as if I were somehow to blame, even though it was he who'd been colluding with Lawrence. "I'm happy to write appeals even if you aren't. I'll work whatever comes in."

"You're going to be sharing every fee you earn. Is that what you want?"

"Yeah, that's what I want, Leo," Teddy said with a flash of anger, his face set in a variant of the stubborn squint he once wore in moments of decision, a look that used to suggest a mind six or seven moves ahead of everyone else. He was right, though, I realized. Our father deserved to be able to work, and the cost to us was less than the benefit to him in dignity.

The issue, for me, was that Lawrence had gone behind my back, intuiting and exploiting a conflict between Teddy and me to get what he wanted. Not to mention that he evidently wanted me to become the go-to lawyer for someone who sounded like a major criminal player, just as my brother had been for Santorez. As the train emerged into the sunlight of West Oakland, Lawrence closed his eyes and turned his face to the window like an old dog savoring the warmth while it lasted.

Chapter 6

My father within a few days had acquired a motorcycle, leather jacket, and chaps to go with the helmet, a getup he wore with evident self-pleasure. Though he was no doubt too proud to say so, he didn't need to explain to me that Dot had bought him these things. He took advantage of his newfound freedom to spend weekday mornings at the office.

He parked himself in front of the computer in the reception room. I gave him small tasks—had him fill out subpoenas and answer the phone. But he seemed never to stay interested in any assigned work for long. I asked him to catalog documents in my civil case, but his attention flagged. Often I'd come in and find him at the window. Thinking of what, I could only imagine. The past, the present, Caroline or Dot. When I next noticed the box of documents, it was shoved against the wall.

"What kind of help are those two getting?" he asked the morning after he first showed up on the motorcycle, the week after our meeting with Nina.

I knew that he was referring to Teddy and Tamara. "Debra is there pretty often. Tam's former mother-in-law. Also Jeanie and me."

"You ever change a diaper in your life?" he asked. When I shook my head, he went on. "You're running a law practice. You don't have time to be checking in on them every day, even if you did know anything about babies."

"Not every day."

"Not even every week. Couldn't those two use more help than they're getting?"

"We've talked about it, but it's expensive, and Tam's resisted. She's tired of being looked after. She wants her own independent life, and who can blame her? So far, at least, the two of them have managed to handle everything life has thrown their way."

"I'm not saying they haven't. But this is a baby. You screw up, you don't get a second chance. If I've learned anything in life, I've learned that it's better not to mess up in the first place than regret it the rest of your days."

He said no more, but I guessed what he was thinking, that he could help them. He was looking for a new sense of purpose in his life after prison, and here it was, staring him in the face.

After the first few days Lawrence didn't come back after lunch. Instead, Teddy would be there, and I realized without needing to be told that our father was with Tamara and Carly. Most evenings, he remained there for an early dinner, then went home to what, for me, remained an unimaginable domesticity with Dot in San Rafael.

On the Saturday before the hearing, Teddy and Tamara invited everyone to dinner. Around the table were Teddy and Tamara, Dot and Lawrence, and Debra Walker. Dinner was takeout from an Indian place nearby: chicken, lamb, and beef in rich sauces.

Tamara, sitting next to Dot, kept glancing at her shyly. Finally she said, "I don't want to intrude, but I can't help wondering how the two of you are holding up. What's it like to have been engaged all these years, and only now to be living together for the first time?"

Dot seemed momentarily taken aback. Then her face softened. "Imagine waking up every morning and not knowing who the hell this is in the bed next to you, or how he got there. Only *you* don't have to imagine *that*."

"It gets easier," Tamara said.

Teddy and our father exchanged a glance, one of Teddy's eyebrows raised.

"It's a temptation to think of myself as the one whose life has been overturned, because it has. But this hasn't been any easier for Lawrence. He may have been used to sharing a cell, but he isn't used to sharing anything else. Neither am I. I keep threatening to have bunks installed. Stainless steel."

"So that's how you think of me, as your cellie," Lawrence said, turning to face her.

"I'm just trying to find a common frame of reference. Wouldn't you prefer that I think of myself as your cell mate rather than as your jailer?"

"Sounds a little kinky," Lawrence said dismissively.

"Well, it doesn't turn *me* on," she told him. "And it's not doing much for you, either, if recent experience is any guide. I'm waiting for the news of your release to reach your brain, but that doesn't seem to have happened. Until it does, we're both still in San Quentin."

Lawrence frowned, pushed food around on his plate. "Reminds me of something about ten years ago," he said, seeming to launch into the story as a means of changing the subject. "This young kid, eighteen years old, from right here in Oakland. He's a churchgoing kid from a decent family, but on the day of his high school graduation, he goes out with the crowd and gets drunk for the first time in his life. He goes to party after party, gets separated from the people he started out with, and ends up in a car with three dudes who promise him a ride. On the way, they pull up to a gas station. The guy in the backseat gets out, goes in. Three gunshots later, the guy comes running out with a pistol in one hand and the cash register drawer in the other. They tear away, but get pulled over two blocks from the scene.

"The kid ends up taking a plea, ten years for felony murder, on the premise that he must have been involved in planning the robbery, even if he hadn't intended the clerk to get shot. Ten years for a terrible mistake. He's engaged to a beautiful girl. 'Marry me before they lock me up,' he says. They've waited, both of them, because their parents wouldn't let them marry until they finish school, and she won't sleep with him until they're married, and he's had eyes for her as long as he can remember. They have their church wedding and their honeymoon night and then he surrenders to the state. She promises him that she'll wait, but they're so young. Neither of them even knows what that means."

My father took Dot's hand, and she squeezed his as if she feared that at any moment someone might come through the door and tear him away.

Debra said, "I think I know the child you're talking about. Or someone just like him."

My father nodded. "One look at this kid, anyone could tell he wasn't prison material. I saw him the first day he was processed in, and he stood out like the bull's-eye on a target. Unlike his three so-called accomplices, he had no record. He wasn't headed to Stanford, but he'd been planning to enroll at Laney College, and he seemed to have his head on straight. Except for that one night."

"So what happened?" Tamara asked.

"Not what you'd think." Lawrence shared a glance with Debra Walker, who nodded again, as if giving him permission to tell it. "What you'd expect, at least what I would have expected if I hadn't seen it with my own eyes, is she visits him a few times, then yanks the eject lever. Remember, these kids are just starting their lives. She's the kind of girl could have any man. You'd expect her visits to grow further and further between. Then one day she tells him she's met someone else and wants to move on with her life. He takes it as best he can, but he knows that without a good woman waiting on the other side, he doesn't have a chance of keeping that ember of hope alive. He surrenders to the darkness, and hope dies."

"There's no darkness where Jesus is," Debra admonished him.

"True." Lawrence gave a little frown. "But I'll tell you from firsthand experience, ma'am, Jesus is cold comfort for a convicted man during a long prison night."

Debra made a disapproving face, but her eyes communicated understanding.

"Anyway, that's not how it went down. For seven years she was there every weekend. I'd see her sometimes, when Teddy came to visit me. In that crowd of poor, angry people, she stood out like a beacon. He didn't have an easy time, but he survived. He changed from a boy into a man, as much as anyone can call himself a man inside that prison. He gave her a child and he watched the child grow. And when he got out, she was waiting for him. Just like she promised."

Dot was still gripping his hand. "But what about his feelings? Did he love her? Or had he just come to depend on her? Or to feel that he owed her?"

"I'm not sure what they thought they owed one another. They were still together, last I heard. He'd found a job, was contributing to the family. Devotion's an interesting word, by the way. You go back to the old French it means sacrifice yourself, take a vow."

Dot released his hand, gave him a pat on the wrist. "It means a lot of things."

From the other room I heard the baby begin to cry. Tamara made as if to rise, a look of exhaustion on her face. "I'll go," I said, glad to escape the tension between my father and Dot.

The baby's room had space only for a crib, a dresser, and a rocking chair. The small window was curtained. In the crib, Carly's arms had come free from her swaddle. I slid my hands between her body and

51

the mattress and picked her up, supporting her head. With the baby on my knees, I tightened the swaddle around her as I'd watched her mother do. Leaning back, I held her against me, her face resting on my shoulder, and began to rock.

It was the first time I'd been alone with Carly, and her seeming trust in me was foreign. I was surprised that she settled back to sleep so easily. It was frightening, in a way. If anything ever happened to Tam and Teddy . . . I pushed the thought away, but I realized that I now lived in a world where, should the unimaginable occur, it would fall to me to be a father to my brother's child. Teddy didn't and wouldn't need to tell me that this was so. There was no one else but me.

I closed my eyes and rocked to the sound of the voices in the other room, Carly's breath hot against my neck.

~ ~ ~

On the Monday morning before the hearing Lawrence rose from his desk every twenty minutes. Several times he went into Teddy's office and closed the door, and I heard him talking on the phone. Finally, just before lunch, he knocked on my door and came in. "I think I might have that name Nina was looking for," he said. "The snitch. His name is Russell Bell."

The name sounded familiar, maybe because I'd once heard it in the news. But if so, the memory was faint. "Who's he?"

"He got out a few years before I did." He dropped into the client's chair across the desk from me. "I wrote the brief that freed him. I figured he owed me everything, but I guess he's the kind of old buddy who'd rather cancel a debt than pay it."

A wilderness of secrets seemed to hover behind this revelation. He'd known this for a while, I guessed, possibly even before Nina brought the idea up in our first meeting. "So you got him out, and now he wants to put you back in? Why on earth . . . ?"

He looked away. "He must see me as a liability, now that he's out. He *did* the crime he was in for. Not like me. Still, he should never have been convicted. The DA fucked him, and his lawyer was asleep at the wheel. Ineffective assistance of counsel, of course. What he must be thinking is that he'd actually told me how it went down, this kidnapping and rape that landed him in prison. A confession, basically. He thought I'd get a kick out of the lurid details, I guess, or maybe he got a kick out of telling me. And he seemed to think there was some kind of privilege that prevented me from repeating what he was saying. Now he's learned different, and he must be afraid I'm going to use his confession against him. Call it a preemptive strike."

He'd mentioned something about having people on the outside who owed him. Russell Bell fit that description. Lately, my father had been on the phone far more than could be accounted for by any of our business, and with Teddy working from home in the mornings, he'd taken the liberty of either making or receiving calls at Teddy's desk.

"So Bell informs on you to prevent you from doing the same to him?" I was incredulous.

"I guess he thought, hey, easier to screw Lawrence than help him, which is what I was asking. Just a hand up until I got back on my feet. That's all I wanted."

I looked at him, trying to figure out what he was telling me.

"Leo, what I'm trying to say is I may have fucked this up."

I was filled with dread at what he might have done, worried that he might have threatened Bell, tried to manipulate him the way he'd played Teddy and me. He'd tried this little game before: after Teddy'd been shot, Lawrence had gone to the police and told them that Ricky Santorez, one of Teddy's former clients and an inmate at San Quentin, had confessed to ordering the hit. But it hadn't been true. Why he'd done this was still a mystery. The uncharitable view was that in the shooting of his oldest son, Lawrence had glimpsed the possibility for personal gain and had sought to exploit it, but even I found that hard to believe.

"You tried to blackmail Russell Bell. Is that what you're saying?"

"Blackmail's an ugly word. I was only asking for a favor."

"What favor would that be?"

"Money."

"You didn't confess to him, did you?"

"Hell, no. He confessed to *me*, like I just said."

"I'll get Car on this." My brother's go-to investigator now often worked for me. I called him and gave him Bell's name. It was Car who mentioned Lucy Rivera, reminding me why Bell's name had sounded familiar. Twelve years ago Bell had been the perp in an infamous abduction and rape of a fourteen-year-old San Francisco girl. I told Car to find out what he could.

~ ~ ~

"Your investigator will just have to catch up with us at the courthouse," Nina said that Friday morning as she filled a file box with everything she'd need for the hearing. She and I were in her office, while my father, Teddy, and Dot waited in the conference room, all of us dressed for court. "Even if he does find Bell and confirms he's the snitch, the questions the judge is going to ask are first, how we knew there was one, and next, how we knew it was *this* guy. And the DA's going to say, of course, the defendant knows the identity of the person he confessed to. This may have not been the best play."

"You told me to find the guy Lawrence might have talked to. I was only doing as asked." I'd taken her request further than she'd anticipated, maybe, but I'd thought that my zeal would earn me recognition for a job well done.

She seemed not to realize she'd changed her view about a hundred and eighty degrees since we'd last discussed the subject. "The problem is I don't think we can accomplish anything today if what your father says is correct. If the DA has an informer, then it's going to trial, and there's nothing we can do to stop it."

"Let's see what Car comes up with," I said.

"*If* he shows up."

"Let's get Bell on the record, then, if he turns out to be the snitch," I said, pushing the issue even though she no longer seemed to be listening, and even though I knew that what I was urging was foolhardy, pushing the point because I couldn't stand being dismissed. "They won't have him prepared today. Surprise will be on our side."

"It's a preliminary hearing this morning, not a trial. We're not calling witnesses."

I tried to get Car on his cell to tell him not to serve Bell with a subpoena, but he didn't pick up. Probably he hadn't found him. At eight fifteen we left for court. We arrived at Judge Liu's courtroom at the same time as Angela Crowder and a very tall, silver-haired, expensively suited SFPD detective. We all had to wait outside the courtroom for the deputy to unlock the door. The detective, whom Crowder introduced as Neil Shanahan, stood aloof, his hands folded, his chin lowered but his eyes on Lawrence. Nina glanced at him only once.

On the hour, Judge Liu took the bench. His gaze held no amusement as he took in the detective sitting next to Crowder at the prosecutor's table, the reporters and other spectators half filling the gallery. He knew as well as the rest of us what Shanahan's presence meant. He'd be here only because Crowder had decided not to dismiss the case, because she intended him to testify and provide evidence that she believed would ultimately support a murder conviction.

"We're here today in the matter of the people versus Lawrence Maxwell. Counsel and others present at counsel table, state your appearances."

Crowder rose. "Your Honor, Angela Crowder for the people. Here with me is Detective Shanahan from the San Francisco Police Department."

"Welcome, Detective Shanahan. And I see we have new counsel for the defendant." Nina introduced herself, and Liu said, "Ms. Schuyler is no stranger to this court. Anything else we need to take up before we begin?" Hearing no response, the judge went on. "Very well, then. The state may call its first witness."

Crowder rose. "The state calls Detective Shanahan."

Crowder stood at the podium while he was sworn. Two weeks ago, arguing against bail, she'd been tentative, almost reluctant. Now she radiated intensity, her stubby hands gripping the edges of the open binder before her. I knew from previous experience that her excitability often tripped her up. At the same time, it gave her a powerful presence in the courtroom, like a flood that overwhelms all obstacles.

Crowder and Shanahan worked through the preliminaries, establishing that he was the lead investigator, that he was trained and qualified, and that he'd reviewed the complete investigative file. The next part of her examination was devoted to establishing that a homicide had in fact been committed on that April morning twenty-one years ago, the day my life shattered. She introduced my mother's death certificate, the coroner's report, and finally, the crime scene photos.

One by one Crowder had the pictures marked, then handed them to the clerk, who passed them to Judge Liu. He studied each intently, as if the waste that is violent death was being revealed to him for the first time. Between photos he glanced at my father with new and keener appraisal. Though his sympathies had seemed to rest with Lawrence during the bail hearing, today his mood, like Crowder's, was somber.

He'd freed Lawrence, and he'd clearly considered the prosecutorial malfeasance that necessitated that freedom as something akin to a personal wrong, a violation of the processes and principles that he administered. However, all that now was behind us. The books were cleared, the slate wiped clean; we were starting over. And Liu, who in two years would be required to run for reelection, could be counted on to treat my father like any defendant accused of a heinous crime.

I'd seen the pictures he was looking at, of course. Since discovering that my brother was working on my father's case, I'd been through the file from front to back numerous times. It wasn't their gruesomeness that affected me. After all, I'd seen crime scene photos of dead bodies before. Rather, it was the details of the scene, the deeply familiar patterns of wallpaper and carpets, objects long forgotten that seemed to leap back to vivid life in my mind's eye.

Watching Liu study the photos, and noticing him glance solemnly at my father, I felt my own doubts return. The DA's version of events was certainly the most probable story from the perspective of anyone on the outside looking in: that he'd caught her with her lover or come home just after the man had left, then beaten her to death in a jealous rage. Such a scenario was wholly consistent with the semen samples taken from my mother's body showing that she'd had sex with another man shortly before her death. This evidence had been concealed from the defense by Gary Coles, the DA who'd prosecuted my father, necessitating his retrial now.

I heard the courtroom door creak open. Turning, I saw Car, my investigator, beckoning me. I slid from the spectators' bench and went out through the double doors into the hall.

"I talked to Russell Bell, served him with a subpoena. If you want him in court, you'll need a body attachment. He isn't coming on my say-so." Car handed me a file folder with the subpoena return inside it. What this meant was if the judge allowed it, we could have Bell arrested by a sheriff's deputy and brought to court.

"So he's the snitch?"

"Apparently. He didn't deny it."

"What've they got hanging over him?"

"Nothing, far as I can tell. He's been clean since the day he got out of prison. He's right here in the city. At city hall, in fact. He works as a driver for Supervisor Eric Gainer." Car delivered this astonishing news without blinking.

"You've got to be kidding me," I said. Eric Gainer had been my high school classmate and the star of our state championship basketball team my junior year. Five years later, he'd also been an eyewitness to the abduction of Lucy Rivera. His role in the drama had involved a heroic attempt to save the girl. He'd managed to yank the driver's door open as the kidnapper sped away. Eric would end up dragged along for half a block before he was shaken loose, yet he'd managed to get a look at the kidnapper's face. Lucy was herself unable to identify her abductor, as she'd spent the long hours of her captivity blindfolded while being repeatedly raped.

In many ways, Gainer's heroism and his testimony identifying Russell Bell as the kidnapper had launched his political career. From the beginning, Gainer seemed marked for higher office: the governor's mansion, perhaps. Now, in what appeared to be a stunning reversal, Bell worked for Gainer and had ratted out Lawrence, who'd helped free him.

I wondered why on earth this hadn't made the papers, why we'd heard nothing about it. Nothing Car had said so far contradicted my father's story that Russell Bell had snitched on him before my father could do the same. Yet there had to be more.

Car and I returned to the courtroom to hear Crowder ask, "Detective, how long have you been the lead investigator on this case?"

"Two weeks," Shanahan said.

Sitting at the defense table, Nina glanced back. I held up the folder containing the subpoena return, and she rose to take it. Returning to her chair, she opened it partway to glance at the contents, then gave a frown.

Crowder went on with her examination. "In those two weeks, have you learned of any information that was not contained in the investigative file?"

"I have. I interviewed a new witness earlier this week, who provided important information."

So here it was, exactly as Nina had predicted. The DA was going to solve the problem of relying on stale and tarnished evidence by building its case on words allegedly from Lawrence Maxwell's own mouth.

"Does the name of this witness appear in the original investigative file?"

"No. The individual wasn't a witness at the time of that investigation."

"Explain to me, if you can, how you came to interview this person."

"Sure. Maxwell'd been in prison twenty-one years. It seemed logical to me that at some point he would have talked about why he was there. I obtained a list of individuals with whom he might have communicated, including prison staff and inmates. I contacted as many people as I could whose names appeared on that list, and interviewed them, either in person or over the telephone."

Nina was jotting notes, presumably a reminder to request a copy of the list from the DA.

"And what information, if any, did you learn from these interviews that was relevant to your investigation?"

"Last week I spoke to a former inmate who told me that Lawrence Maxwell had confessed to murdering his wife."

"Did you obtain a statement?"

"Signed and sworn."

"Without revealing any information that might identify that informant, please read his statement into the record."

Nina rose to object to the statement being admitted without Bell's testimony. But Liu overruled the objection and told Shanahan to go ahead. The state wasn't required to bring Bell into court until the trial.

Shanahan proceeded in a monotone, paraphrasing from the document in front of him. "The informant told me that one morning in 1991, he and 'Larry' were in the yard at San Quentin prison, where they both were inmates. Larry remarked to the informant that his younger son was graduating from college, and that he hadn't spoken to the son since Larry's arrest. Then Larry made the comment, 'The boy hates me. I killed his mother.' He went on, 'It was a terrible thing, but it had to be done. I just wish he hadn't been the one to find her. I'll have to live with that for the rest of my days.' "

The younger son referenced in the supposed confession, of course, was me. I heard the murmur of hushed voices, muted exclamation, and a buzzing in my ears. The courtroom seemed to swim. The gist of the confession, even if manufactured, struck me as the sort of remarks my father might make. It pierced me to the core.

Crowder moved on quickly, establishing that Bell was out of prison but entirely omitting any mention of Lawrence's role in getting Bell exonerated. They went on for about ten more minutes, Shanahan testifying that the details of Lawrence's confession matched those of the crime.

At last, Crowder yielded the podium to Nina. "Detective, please identify the informant and give his current address and telephone number," Nina said.

Shanahan looked at Crowder. She promptly announced that the state would not disclose the informant's identity out of concern for his safety.

"Ms. Schuyler?" Judge Liu said.

"We're entitled to this informant's identity. The prosecution can't withhold evidence."

"If the defendant wants to learn this informant's identity, he can follow the procedures in the Evidence Code," Crowder said. "But that's for another day. We're here to establish probable cause."

"I agree," Judge Liu said. "Ms. Schuyler, you can raise this issue again at the proper time, by motion. Your questioning today should be limited to matters that would conclusively establish your client's innocence."

"But we can't possibly prove that this informant is lying without knowing his identity," Nina protested.

"I won't allow a fishing expedition. If you develop something, I'll give you leeway, but right now you've got nothing other than conjecture, and that's not enough for me to disbelieve the informant's statement."

Nina drew an impatient breath and turned to the witness. "Detective Shanahan, do you share the DA's opinion that disclosing the identity of this informant would pose a safety risk?"

"I do. Absolutely. He begged me not to let the defendant know that he was the one who'd given this information. He told me that if Maxwell found out he'd come forward, his life would be in danger. He said that Maxwell had orchestrated several violent reprisals. In one of those attacks, an inmate had ended up stabbed to death."

At the defense table Lawrence loudly muttered, "Jesus." Judge Liu shot him an angry glance. Nina didn't turn, but I saw her shoulders tighten. My own blood boiled at his loss of self-control. She must have been even more furious. On the stand, Shanahan now wore a look of self-satisfaction.

"Did you make any attempt to verify whether what he said was true—whether Mr. Maxwell had been responsible for such attacks?"

"Mr. Maxwell's name never came up in the original investigations of those attacks."

"So this part of the informant's story didn't check out, correct?"

"That was actually the point, that he'd been able to cover himself by acting through intermediaries. So no, I wouldn't say that it didn't check out. I was able to confirm that the inmates in question were, in fact, assaulted. And that one died as a result."

"Are there any facts independent of this informant's statement that allow you to connect Lawrence Maxwell with those incidents behind bars?"

"Not yet." The detective looked straight at Lawrence. "I've only been investigating this informant's information for a day and a half."

"Did this informant tell you any information that was not publicly available regarding the murder of Caroline Maxwell?"

Shanahan thought for a moment, then said, "No, he didn't."

Quickly, Nina said, "What was the informant's conviction?"

"Excuse me," Crowder said, rising. "Objection. She's doing it again. She's just trying to fish for information to uncover the informant's identity."

"It's obviously for impeachment," Nina said. "We know he was convicted of something. We're entitled to know whether it was a crime of dishonesty or moral turpitude." Such crimes, of course, being admissible evidence for the purpose of establishing that the unnamed witness had a character for dishonesty.

Quick thinking. Especially as Nina knew from the note I'd passed her that Bell's conviction had been reversed. But Crowder didn't rise to the bait and contradict her. The judge deliberated a moment, gazing at the clock at the back of the courtroom. "How about this? For the purposes of this hearing, to avoid disclosing information that might identify the informant, I'll assume that he was convicted of a crime involving moral turpitude or false statement."

"That's fine," Crowder said. No doubt she recognized that there was no way Liu would disregard the informant's story based on this hypothetical assumption.

With no choice but to move on, Nina asked whether the detective knew if the individual, while incarcerated, had provided

information in connection with any other pending case. Again
Liu shut her down. "You'll have your day to pursue these areas,
but none of them is relevant today unless you can show that the
informant is a material witness with evidence that might exonerate
your client. Do you have anything else?"

Like all good attorneys, Nina knew when to fight and when to
shut up, how to walk the line between earning a judge's respect
and needlessly awakening his anger. "Nothing further."

"Does the defendant have witnesses?"

"Your Honor, if we could have a minute," Nina said. The judge
nodded, surprise visible on his face.

Nina whispered something to my father and grabbed the folder
containing the subpoena return. Accompanied by Lawrence, she
beckoned me and pushed through the swinging doors into the
hallway outside the courtroom. I followed her. "What am I supposed to do with this?" she asked, swatting me on the arm with the
folder. "You didn't tell me you were planning to drop a subpoena
on him."

"Yes, I did. We talked about it this morning. What was Car going
to do, invite him to lunch?"

She turned to Lawrence. "Russell Bell. You're saying he's the
snitch?"

"Russell is a liar. That's what I'm saying." Lawrence's hand trembled as he fingered the cigarettes in his chest pocket.

"How am I supposed to show that?"

Lawrence didn't make any response, just stood there.

"You want me to put him up there when I don't have any
ammunition? Is that what you want? Me standing up there firing
blanks, showing an empty hand?"

"Yeah," he said with sudden heat. "Put the fucker on the stand."

Nina asked him to go inside and wait at counsel table. Once the
door had closed behind him, she turned to me. "Why would we
want to call him? Who are you trying to impress?"

"You don't have to call him. It's your case." But I reddened at the obvious answer, that I was trying to impress her. I saw in her face that she'd been aware for some time of the attention I paid her. Now, for the first time, that awareness was shading into anger.

"It's supposed to be. But I can't *not* call him now. Look, I don't practice law by ambush. Maybe that's how you do business in Oakland, but not me, not here. We gain nothing by pulling tricks. It makes us look amateurish. It turns the court against us without any tangible benefit to your dad. Who happens to be *my* client."

She turned away, and it was as if she no longer saw me, the same way she'd looked right past the collection of characters in her waiting area the first day we met.

Nina strode through the gates to the podium.

"Your Honor, the defense calls Russell Bell. Mr. Bell has been served with a subpoena but refuses to appear. We request a body attachment."

At the mention of Bell's name Angela Crowder threw herself back in her chair, arms crossed, with a smile of disbelief. Seeing her face, I knew we'd miscalculated—or rather, I had. Shanahan's eyes were on Lawrence.

Crowder stood and said, "May we approach the bench?"

A whispered debate then took place between Nina and Crowder at the sidebar of the judge's bench. Shanahan looked on, arms folded, and Judge Liu officiated, his chair wheeled to the edge of the platform. From where I sat, I couldn't hear a word, but I could tell that Nina was defending the corner I'd put her in as stridently as if she'd chosen that ground.

When they returned Nina was visibly upset. Crowder, on the other hand, was satisfied and triumphant. From the bench, Liu announced his ruling. "Having heard counsel's explanation, I find that the testimony would not be relevant to the issue of probable cause. Since the defense intends to call no other witnesses, I'm ready to hear argument."

Crowder kept her remarks to a minimum, emphasizing that the informant's statement, if believed, was sufficient in itself to sustain a conviction. Nina used her time to reiterate and clarify her objection to the informant's testimony and to Liu's refusal to allow her to call Bell to the stand.

Liu promptly announced his ruling. "I find the state's informant to be credible, and I find that his statement gives rational ground for a strong suspicion that Caroline Maxwell was murdered on June twentieth, nineteen eighty-three, by the defendant with malice aforethought. In accordance with these findings I order Mr. Maxwell to be bound over for jury trial." After consulting the calendar he set a trial date in mid-May, sixty days out. "Anything else?"

Crowder stood and made a motion to increase bail. Liu again heard arguments. In the end, he left Lawrence's bail unchanged, allowing my father to walk out of that courtroom a free man, if a man could be called free when both the past and the future pressed in on him with literal prison bars.

After the hearing Nina left without speaking to anyone other than Lawrence, taking his arm and whispering a few words, my father nodding in response, both of them avoiding my eyes. Lawrence had to use the men's room. Waiting for him in the hallway, neither Teddy nor I said a word.

Chapter 7

On the last Saturday in March, two weeks after the hearing, I took advantage of the unseasonably warm weather and went for a ride. My head needed clearing, and biking was the only sure way I knew to do that. I was still bothered by the mistake I'd made at the preliminary hearing, forcing Nina's hand in a half-conscious effort to impress her. Ever since then, I'd noticed tension between us, as if she were holding herself aloof.

When my legs needed punishment, I typically looked to the horizon. Mount Tam and Mount Diablo, the Bay Area's two highest peaks, both offered steep climbs and amazing views to accompany my skyrocketing heart rate. I decided to tackle Diablo, in the East Bay, both because the air was extraordinarily clear after a few days of rain, promising views for hundreds of miles from the summit if I made it that far, and because I wanted to avoid the necessity of leaving my car in Marin County and having to ride a loop.

I rode the BART to Castro Valley station, and worked my way north and east, gaining altitude most of the way, to Diablo Road. At South Gate Road the climb began. It'd been a while since I'd made a climb as difficult as this one, and I tried to go easy on my legs. Sweat ran down my forehead and poured down my sides. My calves, quads, and ass ached as I pumped, straining to find the familiar rhythm. I had to remind myself to lift my eyes to the ever-expanding vista as the road wound around to the north side of the mountain.

I told myself that instead of trying for the summit I was going to peel off and coast north to Walnut Creek, there to catch the BART back to Oakland, but at the turn I surprised myself and kept going with a surge of power I hadn't known was there. It wasn't, really. The rest of the climb was a slog. The only thing that kept me from stopping was the knowledge that if I did, I wouldn't have the heart to point the wheel up the mountain again.

The last two hundred meters were little more than a footpath, with a grade of over thirteen percent. Near the top I finally had to let myself tip to one foot, shoulder the bike, and walk, but I'd made it and was rewarded with the view I'd hoped to find. To the west, the Sierra Nevada rose in a jagged, snowcapped line. On a day like today, supposedly it was possible to see Half Dome in Yosemite with binoculars. I'd never seen it.

Riding down, my legs were shaky, my quads aching as I coasted. There were a few moderate hills to surmount, and I was out of gas, but at last I was navigating the busy city streets to the BART, where I collapsed gratefully into a seat in one of the nearly deserted end cars where no one would mind my sweat.

Coming into MacArthur, I checked my phone and saw that Nina had left several messages, including two texts telling me to phone her right away. "I've been trying to reach you all afternoon," she said when I did.

"I've been out of service. What's happened?"

"Russell Bell was shot to death today in San Francisco. The police have arrested your father."

For a moment, I couldn't say anything. Then I told her that I needed to get home and shower, and after that I'd be at her office as soon as I could.

~ ~ ~

That evening, everyone except my father, who remained in custody, met in Nina's office. She'd been to the jail to see him and now had just returned. Before Dot showed up, Nina had taken the opportunity to give a lecture, with me and Teddy sitting there like a pair of kids being reprimanded. "All I can say is that it's unfortunate now that we identified Bell in open court as the snitch. If we hadn't tipped our hand, the police would have no clue that your father knew Bell's plans. Now, everything lines up to suggest that your father had him murdered."

"What can I say?" Under different circumstances, it might have been me behind her desk, handling a high-profile case like this one. I knew that I'd made the mistakes I'd made precisely because I *wasn't* in charge. I'd wanted to show Nina I was every bit the lawyer she was, and, in doing so, I'd screwed up. "You're right, but obviously I didn't anticipate this development."

Nina glanced at my face, then Teddy's. "Well, somebody did."

I heard the edge in her voice, and could only partly blame her. She'd just been slapped in the face with the most deflating news a criminal lawyer can receive, that a client with an upcoming trial has been arrested for another serious crime. Dot arrived, and Nina stepped out to let her in the street door. When the two of them returned, Car quickly filled us in on what he'd learned of the murdered man. "Eric Gainer hired Russell Bell to drive for him two years ago, a month or so after his reelection, right after Bell got out of prison. Thanks to your father for that. No one seems to know about their previous connection. Bell was shot in Gainer's car this morning on a dead-end street outside a warehouse down near Mission Bay. No witnesses." Car closed his notebook. "For the record, I was sitting at home with my dick in my hand."

Nina stood at the window, arms clasped to her chest. She wore tight charcoal jeans and a sleeveless pale-green blouse that showed off her slender, toned arms. A pendant and matching silver earrings contrasted with the darkness of her loose-braided hair. She gave an impression of fatigue tempered by discipline. "I think they'll have to release him by Monday," she told us.

Car said, "I'd been following Bell, just like Leo wanted. Dogging his every step. They start questioning witnesses they're bound to find someone who recognizes me. Not from the scene, but still . . ."

Ignoring him, I spoke to Nina. "So we wait. We don't do anything."

"I don't see what other option we have." Her eyes went to Car. He was a compact, muscular man with a shaved head, dressed in jeans and a blazer, tattoos showing at his wrists and neck. He'd worked for Teddy a long time but, with me, was always his own boss.

"He was with me all day," Dot broke in. "I don't see why they're still holding him. I don't see what you all are so worried about."

Nina turned from the window. "It's clear that the police don't believe you."

"Well, that's what I told them, and that's what I'm telling you. We went for a ride down the coast, bought lunch in Half Moon Bay, then came back via the Peninsula."

"Someone must have seen you eat lunch. The waiter, other diners at the restaurant."

"We bought sandwiches, then took them to the beach. When I went in to get the sandwiches, Lawrence stayed outside with the bikes."

No one said anything for a moment, and then Teddy spoke. "Like Nina says, they'll hold him over the weekend. Then on Monday they'll have to cut him free."

Nina's tone was neutral as she went on speaking to Dot, the voice of a defense lawyer closing down her critical instinct. "You'll testify to everything you just told me, that he was with you the whole morning."

Dot returned her stare. "That's right. We weren't anywhere near the city when the shooting went down."

"What about the two of you?" Nina asked, turning to Teddy and me.

"I was on my bike at Mount Diablo. Alone," I said. "I'm sure Teddy was at home."

Teddy nodded to confirm this. "That's the point," Car broke in. "You weren't alone, but I was. I'm not going to be hung out to dry by you or any other defense lawyer." He rose and walked out.

Teddy got up with an apologetic glance at Nina and followed him. Nina nodded, as if Teddy's going after the investigator only confirmed her suspicions. Dot glanced between Nina and me. After a moment of silence, she rose. "You'll call me with any updates," she said. Nina nodded and Dot went out.

"You're misjudging Teddy and my father if you think either of them could have been involved," I said to Nina when we were alone.

"Am I? I look at Teddy and I see a mind working, scheming. Lying in wait."

Ever since Teddy's shooting I'd nurtured the fantasy that my brother's old personality, his skill and guile, had somehow survived intact behind the shell of his diminished self. But the truth was his disposition had changed. All his ruthless instincts had drained away. Her vision of him conniving behind the scenes awakened a certain longing in me, even if it was murder she was accusing him of. I had to wonder if that's what I wanted, if I would trade my brother's new gentleness for his former duplicitous strength.

"None of us had anything to do with this, Nina," I told her. "You must know me well enough now to realize that."

She sat behind her desk, arms folded. "I'm supposed to be the captain of the ship—and I'm not. It's becoming clear to me that someone else has his hand on the tiller. You say it isn't you. Well, I'd like to know whose hand it is."

"If what you say is true, if they've got no evidence, then this whole thing could be over before it starts. I think you're right. There's nothing to do but wait."

She nodded, and it appeared for a moment that the conversation was over. Then, seeming to change her mind, she went on in a rush, holding out a hand to stop me from interrupting. "Listen, people say things about your brother and this investigator of his that concern me. We don't need to get into specifics. I'm sure much of it is overblown. I just want you to know that such rumors make me very uncomfortable with the situation that's developing. I shouldn't need to tell you this, but I'm your father's lawyer, and a damn good one. I don't represent your brother. Or you."

I didn't trust myself to speak. "You're way off base," I said at last.

"I don't care how off base I am as long as we understand each other."

I dropped onto the sofa in her office, tipped my head back and simply looked at her, more pained by this accusation than I ought to have been. She faced me across the room. She'd just let me know that if she could pin anything on me or on my brother, she would. I didn't think Lawrence would permit that, but still, the prospect sobered me. She kept on staring at me, not flinching.

I rose to leave.

Chapter 8

At the Monday morning calendar call Nina didn't have to say a word. The assistant DA working felony arraignments cut Lawrence loose without explanation. Without grounds for revoking his bail, and without any evidence that he was involved in Bell's murder, the law had no power to hold him. That wasn't the end of it, of course. They could still pick him up and charge him at any time. For now, however, I gave him a ride back to Dot's place in San Rafael.

During the ride, I told him what Dot had told us about his alibi. "She's not lying, is she?"

"How do you expect me to respond?" He glanced at me forlornly across the cab. "We didn't have a chance to discuss what she'd tell the police, or if she'd tell them anything. We didn't know they were coming until the moment they knocked on the door."

I knew better than to ask him too much more. He was in an impossible position. Dot was possibly lying to give him an alibi, and if so, she hadn't cleared the lie with him in advance. "Where were you really?"

He just sighed, shook his head. "Nowhere near Bell. About that, she's telling the truth."

I parked my truck and walked inside with him. Dot had been at the hearing, but she'd had her bike and Lawrence hadn't, and she'd gone home ahead of us. While Lawrence went to shower, I sat with her in her kitchen. She looked wan.

"They arrested him here," she told me. "There must have been a dozen police cars. If anyone in this building didn't already know who I'm living with, they know now. I didn't sign on for this, Leo. I was just getting used to having him out. I don't know what I'll do if they put him back in. I don't know what *he'll* do."

Or what he'd already done, her tone seemed to imply. "We're going to do everything in our power to make sure that doesn't happen. But Dot, you've got to trust his lawyer. You shouldn't have talked to the police. All it takes is for them to be able to poke one hole . . ."

"I'm no idiot," she said. "Don't speak to me like I'm some dumb kid. Can't he make a deal, take a plea? I know he has his heart set on winning the case, getting a big payout in a civil suit, but the risk . . . We're not going to be rich, but I can make enough for two."

I knew that money was foremost on my father's mind, but it hadn't occurred to me that he might be rolling the dice in the retrial in the hope that the city would have to pay him a settlement if he won. With a guilty plea, of course, such an outcome would be foreclosed.

My father came out dressed in jeans and a flannel shirt and microwaved a cup of instant ramen. After initially indulging his taste for foods he'd long been denied, it seemed that he'd returned to a diet of items that might have been purchased from the prison commissary. With both of them in the room, no further conversation on this subject was possible. I left him to his breakfast and drove back to Oakland.

I spent the rest of the morning and early afternoon catching up on my e-mail and getting out letters I'd meant to write weeks ago. Then I went online and accessed the billing records for my home and office phones, both of which my father had been using since his release. If the police were looking for a link between my father and Russell Bell's murder, then the phone records were one of the first places they'd search. I needed to know what they were going to find.

I made printouts showing outgoing and incoming calls and began crossing off numbers I recognized and calls I knew I'd taken or made. I pulled up my calendar, and with its help I highlighted the calls that I couldn't have made or received. Between the office and home phones, I identified a dozen calls to two different San Francisco numbers, none of which appeared in the billing records prior to the date of my father's release. The earliest one had been placed from my home phone that first afternoon. It took me half a minute on the Internet to determine that the number was a landline listed as Russell Bell's.

Based on what my father had told me, I knew that they'd been in contact. Still, I felt a rush of anger and had to stand and pace with my hands behind my head for several minutes before I could think. Lawrence had called Bell a total of six times, three from my apartment and three from the office, a call every two or three days right up until the day before the probable cause hearing. Two of the incoming calls were from the same number. One of the other outgoing calls was to city hall.

After anger came a gnawing, cold fear I couldn't make go away. The police were going to get these records, and they were going to use them to spin a motive for my father. There was nothing I could do about that. These calls were now part of the net that was closing around us. Dot was right, I thought. He ought to try to take a plea. I would advise any client of mine in Lawrence's position to do so. But with Lawrence, I couldn't take that step.

Throwing myself back on my only refuge, I worked diligently on my other cases for the next three days. There was always plenty to keep me busy. Then the *Chronicle* put us on the front page.

The reporter had evidently been thoroughly briefed by someone in the DA's office or the police department. The story, which ran to nearly three thousand words, must already have been in the works before Bell's shooting. Headlined BETRAYAL AND REVENGE, it opened with several paragraphs describing my mother's murder, my father's conviction, and his subsequent imprisonment. The article went on to describe my father's activities as a jailhouse lawyer, culminating in what the article ironically labeled his greatest success, the freeing of Russell Bell.

The article told me something I should have remembered on my own: the DA who'd prosecuted that highly publicized case was Gary Coles, the same one who'd prosecuted my father seven years before that. However, instead of emphasizing Coles's repeated misconduct, or the DA's decision not to retry him, the piece placed the blame for Bell's freedom squarely on my father's shoulders. Also, it made no mention of Gainer's inexplicable decision to employ Bell after the state had dropped the charges. Instead of probing for the truth, the writer was interested only in implying a cause-and-effect relationship between Bell's decision to testify against Lawrence and his murder after Lawrence had learned of this plan.

It was a lurid and maddening piece of reporting, and it would quickly be picked up by local TV and radio. In a city as small as San Francisco, the effect would be to convict my father in the court of public opinion before a jury ever even saw him. By the time of his trial, we'd be hard-pressed to find twelve jurors who didn't already know he'd confessed to Bell in prison, and then had him killed to keep him from testifying. The question was whether potential jurors would admit to having watched these news reports and having been swayed by them.

With an idea of learning more on my own, on Thursday evening I decided to drop in on Russell's visitation to see who cared about his death enough to show up. I thought there was a chance Eric Gainer might be there to pay his last respects to someone who, despite his background, had evidently become a valued employee. If he was there, I wanted to talk to him.

The funeral home was an ugly long building a block or so from McLaren Park. In the foyer, a signboard behind glass told me that Russell Bell's visitation was in the Violet Room. There, four rows of folding chairs stood empty. The casket stood flanked by two meager floral arrangements. Standing over the casket, I took out my flip phone and snapped a shot.

Russell Bell's head on the velvet cushions seemed small. His hairline was receded, his jaw narrow and somehow misshapen. I couldn't tell how tall he'd been. He had a look on his face like he knew the answers to all my questions, even the ones I hadn't thought of yet. Behind me someone coughed. I turned and saw a giantlike figure standing near the wall just inside the door, wearing a navy pinstripe suit that sat on him like armor. I recognized Jackson Gainer, the older brother of City Supervisor Eric Gainer and a lawyer at one of the city's white-shoe firms.

I was taken aback to find him there instead of Eric. But, saying my name, I extended my hand.

He didn't seem to remember who I was, which was in line with his reputation for showing utter disregard for those outside of the city's highest sphere of power and influence. He just didn't give a fuck about you if you couldn't do anything for him. In that regard, he couldn't have been more different from his brother.

Jackson and Eric Gainer: everyone knew their story. Two white kids from the neighborhood, their background not so different from mine, a year apart in school and both standout basketball players. Jackson had landed a scholarship to St. Ignatius High and had spent three years as a power forward. Eric, though smaller, had filled the same role for Balboa, the public school he and I attended.

In Jackson's senior year, when Eric and I were juniors, the teams met in the first round of the Division I Boys Basketball California State Championship, played at Kezar Pavilion here in the city. Five minutes into the fourth quarter, Eric had been driving to the basket and Jackson floored him with a flagrant foul.

The whistle blew, and Eric, without so much as a glance at his brother, went to the sideline for a towel to staunch the blood pumping from his nose. He made both free throws and remained in the game. On the strength of those shots, the Balboa Buccaneers, who'd been down by three at the time of the foul, pulled ahead and ended up winning by seven points. No one who'd been in the bleachers would ever forget Eric's performance, the utter disregard he showed when Jackson's palm went into his face.

We shook hands, his huge one swallowing and crushing mine. Seen together these days, Eric, despite his similar size, looked more intellectual than Jackson, owing to his receding hairline and rimless glasses. There were those who said that the older Gainer brother was the moving force behind the younger's career, that he'd installed Eric on the board of supervisors and kept him there by arm-twisting and willpower. On his own, people said, Eric would never have risen so far. But I only had to remember Eric with bloody wads of cotton jammed up his nose, calmly sinking shots over Jackson, to know that he'd done what he wanted with his life.

Just as I started to say something, Jackson Gainer revealed he knew exactly who I was. "Look, Leo, let's cut to the chase. I can't tell you anything. That's why you're here, isn't it, to see what we have on your father? You're not going to get anything out of me. And let me just say now's hardly the time to be playing Perry Mason. The body's still warm. Everyone's in shock. Although, considering Russell's background, maybe we shouldn't be surprised."

"Meaning?"

"Don't play stupid. He was a con. And it sounds like he was asking for what he got. If it wasn't your dad who killed him, then it was someone else he crossed. Someone like Bo Wilder. From what I hear, the DA's office thinks that Bo and your father were pretty tight while your father was inside. And Bo has plenty of muscle on the outside."

This was the name my father had spoken on the train, the guy in San Quentin who'd protected him when Ricky Santorez, my brother's former client, wanted Lawrence dead. The guy he'd wanted me to work for now. "I've never heard that name," I said.

Glancing now at the visitors' book, I saw that only two other mourners had left their names. My blood boiled when the first signature turned out to be Lawrence Maxwell's. The second was Detective Neil Shanahan's. Suddenly in a hurry to leave there, I pressed my card into my companion's hand. "Tell your brother I want to talk to him."

Jackson Gainer started to protest, clearly resenting my tone. But then I said, "Just say it's for old times' sake."

I left, hoping to catch my father. After driving around for ten minutes, I spotted Lawrence just about to descend into the BART station at Sixteenth and Mission. Pulling to the curb, I blew my horn, rolled down the window, and called to him. He turned from the escalator and came over to the curb. "What are you doing? Following me?"

"Save yourself the fare and get in."

He came around and climbed into my ride.

"You and Shanahan have a nice chat?"

"So you were at the funeral home."

"And I saw the guest book, with your name and his."

My tone gave him his cue. "Was it stupid of me to go there? Probably. I won't tell you that I'm not glad the man is dead. Of course I am."

"You didn't say anything to Shanahan, did you?"

"Don't worry. I didn't go running my mouth."

"Shanahan say anything to you?"

"'Dead Henry's wounds bleed afresh.' Thinks he's a smart cop, that one. He told me, 'That's Shakespeare, case you're curious. *Richard III.*' Fuck him."

"He's going to know some things," I said. "He's going to have a warrant for our phone records soon if he doesn't have them already."

After a pause Lawrence said, "So what?"

"All those calls to Bell up to the day of the hearing. He's going to see those."

"Let him. I helped Russell and I thought he'd want to help me. Can't I ask for help from a pal?"

"There's asking and there's asking."

"Want to learn who your real friends are? Go to prison and then get out."

I pulled over into an empty space. There wasn't another car parked on the block. "Look, it's time for you to be straight with me. I can't help you if I don't know what's going on. You told me Russell raped a girl and liked it. That's what you said the other night, that he admitted the crime he was in for."

"I got him off because his lawyer, in his opening statement, stood up in front of the jury and promised an alibi witness he couldn't deliver. The lawyer hadn't interviewed any witnesses and he didn't have them under subpoena. After the reversal, from what I understand, the state didn't retry Russell because they couldn't get certain witnesses to testify the same way again. It's a miracle they prosecuted him in the first place. Any competent lawyer should have been able to turn that case inside out. But the bottom line is Russell raped her. He's guilty."

"And he confessed to you, right? That's why he had to go and invent a confession from you, because in real life he was the one who'd confessed. That's what you said."

"He might as well have confessed. He was dumb enough. He told me plenty." Seeing the disappointment in my face, he went on. "You know everybody in prison is innocent, Leo. None of those guys doesn't dream of one day getting out, and as soon as Russell fell in with me, he realized he had a chance. So he knew better than to confess. But I'm a good judge of character. Innocent men don't get convicted and locked up. It doesn't happen, popular myths aside." His looked away, as if realizing that his cynicism was self-indicting.

"*Might as well have* confessed. So they let you out and he won't help you, won't pay you for your services rendered. In return, you decide to threaten him with this confession he might have made but didn't."

"What I know is that Russell kidnapped and raped that girl, and he didn't have to confess for me to know it. I didn't kill him. What I think is maybe someone did the world a favor, shot the son of a bitch as revenge for what happened all those years ago."

"Jackson mentioned Bo Wilder to me. It sounds like the cops have a theory that Bo was behind the hit. That he did it on your behalf."

"Well, if he did, he didn't tell me about it. And it's not like I've got anything to offer the man."

His quick dismissal of the idea only aroused my suspicion. "The main thing in our favor is that the cops still don't have the shooter or the gun. Still, Bell was murdered in broad daylight. It's hard to believe there weren't witnesses." My tone sounded harsher than I intended.

"Don't get too used to picking out my own clothes is what you're telling me. Or rather, to having Dot pick them out." He stared a thousand yards down the road. "Tell me this. Friendship aside, how much would it have cost him to hire a lawyer, and how many lawyers would have done as good a job as I did? Don't you expect to get paid?"

"It's called a retainer, and I collect it in advance. Why are you so worried about money?"

"Why aren't you? Why is anyone? It's self-respect. If you'd been inside, you'd understand the code. I had a right to name my price when I got out. It was a fair price, but that doesn't matter now. Bell's dead, and I won't pretend I'm not glad for that, when it's just you and me talking."

His eyes went to the rearview.

An unmarked Crown Vic rounded the block and veered to the curb, leaving one parking spot between his bumper and mine.

"He's been with us the whole way," Lawrence went on. "He picked me up as soon as I left the funeral home. Let's sightsee a little. Take him for a ride. You know where I want to go. It's about time I saw the old place again." He glanced again at the mirror.

With Shanahan following, I drove slowly up into Potrero Hill, to the apartment building where it had all begun. A light showed in the second-floor window. It was possible the people who lived here now had no clue what had happened years ago. Probably there were few people left in the neighborhood who did. "It's almost like I could walk right back through the door, go back in time," Lawrence said. "Although I wouldn't want to walk back into *that*."

He glanced at me as if checking whether I was okay with him talking this way about our shared past. I stared up at the building. I'd been down the street plenty of times, of course, but never like this—never with him.

"Even if you didn't kill her, you came pretty damn close a number of times," I said. "I remember one time you were hitting her, and she was screaming at you. Teddy finally called the police, but only because I begged him to." Not for the first time I wondered what had been wrong with my brother that he didn't intervene more forcefully, knock my father down the way the older brother is supposed to do in the movies. In any case, he never had.

"I don't expect you to forget that. There's no excuse for a man to use his fists on a woman. The mother of his children. But I did my time for that, and I'm not the same man I was. No matter how much we may want to, neither one of us can undo the past.

"Go ahead," he went on, seemingly oblivious to the terrible thoughts that filled my head. "Ask me anything."

"I know Russell was lying. I don't need to ask you that again."

He seemed to avoid answering the question I hadn't asked. "I can't imagine how that must have been for you, finding her. For years I felt it was my responsibility, to try to understand. But the mind just breaks down. Plus, I never saw you again after that day. You were a little kid. You didn't have any reason not to believe people who told you I did it. There was a trial. None of it came out right. And just when you needed me the most, I wasn't there. They wouldn't let me see you. For years, it ate me alive. I wanted to reach out, try to make you see I was innocent, but Teddy thought it best to let you alone. I'm not so sure."

"It's my whole life," I told him. "It doesn't turn on a dime. Certainly not on this one."

"I know it, Leo, and I don't blame you for it. If you can learn to trust me . . ."

"No more surprises," I said. "You need to trust *me*. And you need to trust Nina." I realized the question I should have asked, which was where he'd been the morning of Russell Bell's murder, but somehow the moment for asking such questions had passed.

Lawrence nodded. "No more surprises." He rolled down his window, stuck out an arm, and waved the Crown Vic forward. The unmarked car flashed its lights and drew up alongside, and the driver's side window slid down.

Lawrence leaned to the window and shouted, " 'They do me wrong and I will *not* endure it!' "

Chapter 9

On Monday Nina filed a motion under Penal Code Section 995 seeking to have the case dismissed. Her reason was that the state's only witness was dead and thus no longer available to testify against my father. Seemingly in response, Crowder moved to revoke Lawrence's bail. Both motions were heard the following Friday in Judge Liu's court.

Liu heard bail arguments first. At the podium, Crowder said, "Two weeks ago, the state's confidential informant was murdered. For nearly six hours, investigating officers from Oakland, San Francisco, and numerous other jurisdictions tried but were unable to locate the defendant. He was finally taken into custody in San Rafael, where he's been living out of the court's jurisdiction. The state asks the court to revoke bail."

Lawrence sat stone still, not reacting after the lecture Nina'd given him following his outburst last time. She now turned in her chair to stare at Crowder with disbelief.

"You're not contending that he violated any bail condition?" the judge asked.

"His only alibi is a story from his girlfriend that they were out riding motorcycles together a hundred miles from here. This is a defendant out on *bail*. The whereabouts of Mr. Maxwell's sons are also unknown at the time of the crime."

A murmur ran through the courtroom, and I sat bolt upright as if I'd received an electric shock. I could tell by the anger on Judge Liu's face that Crowder had miscalculated. I felt Dot lay a hand on my arm. Her eyes were cold, and she gave me a nod. *Let's get them*, her gaze seemed to say.

"It's not my place to question her story, at least not now. You don't have the murder weapon, or any evidence of his involvement. So far, all you have is motive. Am I right?"

"I'm told that phone records reveal numerous instances of contact between the defendant and the victim beginning the very day the defendant was released by this court."

"That's pretty thin. As I understand it, they were friends in prison. Anything more?"

Crowder glanced at Shanahan, who shook his head. "The state can't reveal any more details. Especially not with the subject of the investigation sitting right here."

"Then I'm going to deny your motion to revoke bail," Judge Liu said. "If you'd charged him, it would be a different story. I will, however, add a no-travel condition. The defendant shall restrict his movements to San Francisco, Alameda, and Marin Counties unless he first gives notice to the prosecution and obtains permission to travel from me."

Crowder sat down. Now it was Nina's turn. She took the podium with quiet anger but said nothing.

"I've read your motion to dismiss," Judge Liu said. "You correctly point out that the state's case is based entirely on Detective Shanahan's testimony. You also note that with Russell Bell dead any statements Bell made to the detective or anyone else can only be introduced as hearsay. The Constitution says that criminal defendants have the right to confront their accusers. This means no hearsay. However, if it's the defendant's fault that the witness is unavailable—for instance because the defendant had him murdered—there's an exception to the no hearsay rule."

"Your Honor is referring to the forfeiture by wrongdoing exception."

"You'll agree with me that if Maxwell arranged for Bell to be murdered, it follows he can't reap the benefit of that act and keep Bell's hearsay statements from coming into evidence."

"The forfeiture doctrine doesn't apply until he's proven guilty of murdering the witness," Nina said. "As you've just noted, my client has an alibi. In addition, there would have to be a specific finding that Bell was murdered for the purpose of keeping him from testifying in this case. Not some other reason. The prosecution hasn't even come close to making that showing."

"Thank you," Liu said. With Crowder back at the podium, Liu probed her with questions regarding our backup argument: that the potential harmful effect of the confession might still require it to be kept out, even if the state met the low bar of producing "evidence sufficient to support a finding" that Lawrence was involved in the hit. As the judge pointed out to Crowder in a question she couldn't satisfactorily answer, he could always instruct them to ignore the confession after they'd heard it, but the jurors were human beings, and unlikely to forget it.

Seeing the battle slipping away from her, Crowder at last said, "Russell Bell's body is hardly cold. The state ought to at least be given the opportunity to develop proof that Maxwell was involved and that his alibi was a sham."

Liu agreed, and scheduled an evidentiary hearing prior to trial. "The bar is going to be higher than just *sufficient to support a finding*, Ms. Crowder, given the devastating effect of Maxwell's alleged confession to Bell, and the likelihood that the jurors would be unable to put it out of their minds even if I instructed them in the strongest terms to do so. To get that confession into evidence without Bell as a witness, you're going to have to prove to me that it's at least more likely than not that Maxwell was behind Bell's murder—and you've got five weeks to do it."

~ ~ ~

"I'm incensed," Nina said after the hearing. The others had gone home. I'd accompanied her to her office to take stock. She went on. "It's one thing to accuse your father, but now they're trying to drag you and Teddy in. The implication of what she said is that you and your brother are suspects in Bell's murder. A family vendetta is what it's starting to look like."

"You think they're going after Teddy and me." I was struck again by how she'd reversed positions. Just last week, she'd all but accused Teddy of being involved.

"It's what they'd like to do." Seeming to become aware that she'd changed viewpoints, she said, "With every case, every client, there's an initial holding back. You want to maintain that distance, that objectivity, as long as you can. But for me, when it comes to certain cases, there's a tipping point. Starting today, I've reached it."

"You seem different. Maybe more relaxed."

"I'm angry. It's a good anger. Invigorating." She looked at me for a moment across the desk, and I felt a spark pass between us before her focus snapped back. "Now what's this about calls from your office to Bell?"

I told her what I'd found in the phone records, information I should have given her before. I had no good explanation for having held back, so I offered no excuse.

The spark was extinguished now. "Anything else I ought to know?"

"I went to the funeral home. Dad was there. So was Jackson Gainer. Like he was standing guard. Shanahan, the detective, also turned up." I thought of my father's admission that he'd tried to get money from Bell. No point in sharing that with her now.

"Jackson Gainer. Standing guard over what? What else?"

"He told me that the DA thinks that a man named Bo Wilder may have been behind Bell's murder. Bo's in San Quentin, but he has people on the outside. He protected my father when there was a price on his head."

She studied me skeptically, processing this new information. "I don't want to lose this case because you end up stumbling on something best kept under wraps."

"Don't worry, I've got plenty of my own cases to work."

"Good. I'm glad to hear it."

Chapter 10

My practice was in the doldrums, and little money was coming in. Ever since Lawrence's release, I'd more or less stopped meeting with new clients. This was foolish, yet his case seemed to loom over everything, eclipsing more lucrative bids for my attention. Teddy's phone, on the other hand, was ringing off the hook.

Despite my doubts, our father seemed to be living up to his end of the bargain he'd made with him. Every week it seemed another incarcerated client or family member called wanting Teddy to write an appeal or a habeas petition, and his tiny office was suddenly cluttered with boxes of transcripts. I had depositions to take in my civil cases, discovery to review, motions to file, but whenever I turned to this real work I had to fight through dread.

The next Saturday, the sky was gray outside my office window, and around two a misting rain began to fall, dashing my plans for a ride. I'd been up late at my desk going through transcripts of my father's first trial, adding to the collection of empty beer cans in my wastebasket. After three hours of desultory effort, I moved to the wing chair in the corner and closed my eyes, a transcript open on my lap.

The phone rang. When I answered it, I heard, "This is Eric Gainer. How are you, Leo?"

Hearing his voice instantly conjured up those old pot-smoking, punk-rock-listening days. Even back then, when he was a teenager, Eric could be irresistible. His attention, when he turned it on anyone, was like a beam of warmth. His voice was familiar to me in recent years only from the news. We hadn't spoken directly to one another since high school.

"It's been a while," I replied. "I don't get over to the city much these days." There was nothing much else to say.

He got to the point. "Jackson said you wanted to talk to me."

"That's right. Strictly off the record. For old times' sake."

"Why don't you come to my place. It's Jackson's, actually. Give me a ring when you're almost here. I'll open the garage and you can park inside." Was it that he didn't want to be seen with me? It made sense, since my father'd been accused of murdering a man who'd worked for him. I tried not to let it bother me, but it did.

I drove into the city to the address I'd written down. The impressive Cow Hollow house was perched three stories above a garage, which opened as I turned onto Gainer's street. I pulled up over the sidewalk and inside. Eric met me at the door. We stood in his kitchen swapping reminiscences, quickly exhausting the safe subjects in our shared past. "You shoot pool?" he presently asked.

He led me upstairs to a den with bookshelves, a fireplace, and a pool table. There was also a corner bar and two narrow windows facing the street below. The books on the shelves appeared to have been read, their spines creased. Along the rails, the only way to complete cross-table shots was to clear the books from a section of shelf, providing another foot of space to draw back the cue.

I'd asked for the meeting, and I knew that if I wanted answers, I needed to take the lead. "I won't beat around the bush. I came here because I wanted to ask you about your relationship with Russell Bell. Do you mind telling me how on earth you came to hire him?"

He nodded, unsurprised by the question. "You and I both know that it doesn't fix anything to lock people up. The most advanced civilization on earth, but we're still medieval in the way we punish crime. Someday, with luck, I'll be in a position to have a real influence on our policies. Imprisonment isn't a solution. It's the heart of our problem. When these people finally get out, no one will trust them. What choice do they have but to go back to a life of crime?"

"You can't mean that hiring Russell was about practicing good public policy."

"Of course not. It wasn't anybody's business but mine. He was on my private payroll, not the city's. Actually, I hired him because it was the only thing I could think to do to make amends for the mess Gary Coles and I made of his life."

So that was it. Liberal guilt. I ought to have known. "Then I'm more impressed. You're the first politician who behaves in a worthy manner and doesn't feel the need to tell the whole world about it."

"Worthy? I don't know. I haven't talked about this with anybody. Not in the sense of what it means to me, privately. What it's meant in my life." He was arranging the balls in the triangle, clacking them back and forth. He looked up. "The thing is, I'd actually like to talk about it with you."

It struck me that I was about to cede control of our conversation. But if he was willing to talk, I was ready to listen.

Eric handed me a cue. "You take the first shot. We won't play for money."

I broke, but nothing fell. Then it was Eric's turn. The intent, familiar way he moved around the table made me realize how much time he must spend here. It was where he did his thinking, I guessed. He'd poured us both Scotch. He made his shots with casual ease, hardly seeming to notice that I was in the game. I wasn't, not really. The game wasn't the point. It was just something to do with his body while we talked.

"I know what people say about me, that my whole career is built out of what happened the day of that kidnapping, my feeble attempt at heroism. Without that experience, I don't even think I'd ever have dreamed about going into politics."

"You were a hero," I said. "I remember that much."

"But I didn't *do* anything," he said, as if still angry at himself after all these years.

"You did everything you could. You chased the van down. You all but pulled the guy out from behind the wheel, with the girl lying there, terrified, a sack over her head. You got all skinned up when he sped away and you finally fell off, and then you were out there nonstop, putting up posters, comforting the family until she was found alive. You were a legitimate hero. Everyone admired you."

"And I took full advantage of it, didn't I." *Thunk* in the corner pocket. "It was just like being a basketball star, everyone looking at me, thinking how great I was. Then Gary Coles came along and I signed my deal with the devil."

I wondered why he was telling me all this but I didn't interrupt. "Christ, he made it easy to lie. I don't think I'd ever felt so good about anything as I did about the lies I told during that trial. He made lying seem like a selfless, heroic act, like the natural culmination of what I'd done out there on the street, chasing the abductor down and trying to grab him. All I had to do was say that I saw his face, that they'd gotten the right guy, and I could go on being a hero. And that's what I did, Leo—and I never looked back. Not until they came to me years later and said he was getting out, that I needed to testify in the retrial. The thought of it made me physically ill."

I looked at him with new understanding, and new caution. "A lot of well-meaning people lied because Gary Coles made them feel it was the right thing. You weren't the only one."

"That's cold comfort for someone who's always held himself to a higher standard. Or tried to. Anyway, the majority of those people weren't actually well-meaning. From what I understand, most of the cops had figured out that Coles would cover their tracks for them. Anything for a conviction. And no one ever caught him."

"My brother did."

"Maybe, but only after he was dead, and only by using Coles's own tactics." He missed his shot and straightened. "Or are you going to tell me you really believe your father's innocent?"

I missed badly. He caught the cue ball as it dropped into the corner pocket.

"I do," I answered him. "I wouldn't have been involved with freeing him if I didn't."

"Principled stand. I hope you believe it. Well, here's to avoiding hypocrisy." He raised his glass and positioned the cue ball where he wanted it. "Russell sent me a letter after I was first elected. He wanted my help reopening the case. He wanted me to admit I'd lied in my testimony, sign a statement to that effect. I left that letter out on my desk for a long time. It was followed a few months later by a second one accusing me of the most cynical motivations: of using the opportunity his case had given me to launch my political career and reap personal gain, all at the expense of his life.

"It struck me as the letter of an innocent man. It affected me more deeply than you could imagine. The consciousness of that lie had been stewing in me, and the letter was like a storm breaking. I'd put all that behind me, I thought, made amends in my own way. But, of course, not to Russell. His life was still ruined. He was still in the joint. I never responded to either letter, but after Russell got out with your father's help, and after I told the DA that I couldn't testify in the retrial, Russell came to see me, and I offered him a job as my driver."

"Just like that," I said. We were standing across the pool table from one another. Neither of us had taken a shot in some time.

"Just like that," Eric repeated, as if bewildered by his own act. "What would you have done? What can anyone do for a man like that?"

I wouldn't have lied and helped Gary Coles frame the man in the first place, I wanted to say. Instead I asked him, "How did you stand it, having him there in the car with you day after day, reminding you of what you'd done? He was in prison for how long, twelve years?"

Eric moved the cue ball, giving himself a better line on the corner pocket. I hadn't scratched, so he shouldn't have touched it, but it was his table. His rules. "The more pertinent question is how did I stand it knowing he was in prison, knowing it was my fault, during all those years when he *wasn't* driving my car?"

"What was he holding over you, Eric?"

He grabbed the cue ball and rolled it fast into the corner pocket, then flung his cue onto the table. "I don't know what you're hinting at. The reason I asked you here is that I just need your father to—back off for a while."

"What do you mean, 'back off'?"

"Your father called the office a number of times. I asked Jackson to handle it, and I told Jackson I didn't want to hear the details. From what I gather, your father thought he could shake down Russell, or shake me down, about something connected with that old case. Maybe he wanted money. Maybe he thought I could have some influence on his behalf in the DA's office, get the charges thrown out, who knows. I told Russell that if he ever had trouble with anyone about the past, if anyone ever tried to use his background as leverage, he should come to me."

"Maybe he wanted to warn you about Russell."

"I hardly needed *warning*. I knew all about Russell."

The edge in his voice made me look up. "What is it? What's going on?"

Gainer just shook his head. "You need to make your father understand that he's not going to get out of this mess by threatening me."

"*Threatening* you? I don't know what you're talking about, Eric."

"You really don't know what he's been doing, do you?" He left the room. I followed him. There was an office nook in the corner of the next room. From a desk drawer he took out a sheet of paper and held it in front of me. I reached for it, but he snatched it back. "Look, but don't touch."

It was a printout of an e-mail sent to his official city e-mail address. The From line was an e-mail address composed of gibberish letters, from an anonymizer website. A picture had been attached to the e-mail, but it wasn't displayed on the printout. Rather, a file name was listed in the attachments field in the header, a series of digits corresponding to a date and time, like the file name a digital camera automatically gives to a picture.

This one had evidently been taken on the eleventh of February at 3:32:29 AM, because the file name was 0211033229.jpg. It was April now. I made an effort to burn those digits into my memory. The message said, *You've been a very bad boy, Eric, and I know all about it. Now will you follow my instructions? Keep ignoring me, and you'll get what Russell got.*

"Now do you see?" Eric asked me. "You want that coming out in court? Is that what your father wants?"

"You can't prove he sent this." My mind, however, had flown back to my father's near admission that he'd blackmailed Bell, and to his earlier attempt to get out of prison by falsely accusing Santorez of having my brother shot.

"You can't prove he didn't."

"This can't come into evidence. It was sent from an anonymizer website, untraceable." At least not without a court order, but I didn't want to think about that. My father, having spent the last twenty years in prison, would have no inkling about IP addresses, cookies, Internet history folders, the invisible trail that every online action leaves.

"Where's the picture? What does it show?" I wanted to know.

"Never mind," Eric said. "Just pass the message to your father. He needs to back off if he doesn't want this coming to light."

Chapter 11

Whatever Gainer was hiding, it must be worse than what he'd told me—something in the present, involving the anonymous threat he'd been sent. I drove straight from his place to my office, needing to reassure myself that the police would find no proof that the e-mail had been sent to him by one of us.

We had an open network, meaning that from my computer I had full access to the hard drives of the other machines in the office. I started by searching the whole system for the file name, typing in the numbers I'd remembered and written down as soon as I was out of Gainer's house. There were no hits, but all that proved was that whoever had sent the file attached to that anonymous e-mail hadn't been dumb enough to save it locally. Or so the police would say.

I widened the search to include all picture files, which led me to a trove of pornography in Teddy's Internet cache. I clicked through some of the pictures. None of what I saw struck me as potential blackmail material or as having anything to do with Eric Gainer.

I felt a momentary relief. Whoever had sent that e-mail, it didn't appear that it could be traced back to this office. On the other hand, I wasn't so naïve as to believe that the lack of an obvious connection put us in the clear.

I typed the file name into the search bar of my web browser, and my breath caught, a jolt of adrenaline going through me as the result appeared on my screen. The picture showed Eric Gainer with a wide smile, sitting on an Adirondack chair on a balcony over the ocean at night. A woman sat on his lap, her legs over his legs, her arm around his neck. She was a tall woman, big-breasted but with a small pixie's face, teeth that had never been fixed, and an attractive mop of curly brown hair. She looked straight at the camera, her face seeming to glow with pride of possession and something else, like she was keeping a secret from him. Another girl knelt beside her, holding the camera out before her to take the shot.

The picture was on a photo-sharing website. There was no clue as to the women's identity, no way to contact the poster. We could send a subpoena, but it was doubtful that the person who'd set up the account had used his or her real name. I could go to Car and ask him to try his contacts with the police to identify the woman. But I couldn't see him getting anywhere without telling more than I wanted him to know about the blackmail allegations Eric Gainer had made against my father.

There was another option, but I didn't like it. Something about the woman made me think she might be a prostitute. The next day, after Lawrence had gone for his afternoon nanny duties at Tamara's, I walked across the reception area and leaned in my brother's door. Teddy was absorbed in his work, three different binders open before him as he laboriously typed and rearranged his sentences.

"Hey." He didn't look up.

"Dad at your place?"

"Yeah."

"Tam's okay with it?"

"He gets over there, grabs the laundry basket and runs a load, cleans up the kitchen, takes out the diaper pail, whatever needs to be done. He'll sit with Carly while Tam works or goes to her therapy group or yoga class. He's good with her, Leo. You saw them together. He even made dinner the other night. Mac and cheese. Even Debra doesn't seem to mind having him around."

"Look, you want to help me out on something tonight?" I asked him.

He gave me a regretful look that took in the loaded desk, the boxes and boxes of documents. "I've got just about as much work as I can handle."

"It's not a brief. I want you to come with me to see someone. I need information, and there's only one person I know who might be able to give it to me. Trouble is, I need your charming personality to ease my way."

He laced his hands behind his neck, cracked his knuckles. "Yeah? Who?"

"Tanya." Teddy's old secretary, who'd run a small-scale prostitution ring under his nose for years and now had made pimping her livelihood. "She might be able to help me identify a potential witness."

He frowned. "I don't have a clue how to find her, but Car would know."

I called Car and asked for her address. I didn't tell him why I wanted it; uncharacteristically, he didn't ask. Usually, getting information out of him required paying a toll of petty humiliation, but tonight he just said he'd call me back.

The address he wound up giving me was a condo overlooking Buena Vista Park. As we drove into the city Teddy studied the picture of the women with Eric Gainer. Finally he said, "So what's the connection between this picture and Lawrence?"

I hesitated, wondering how much to tell him. "I met with Eric Gainer the other night. He's being blackmailed, according to what he told me. He thinks the person doing it is Dad."

"And you think that whoever's blackmailing Eric may be the same one who killed Russell, or had him killed?"

"Maybe." I hesitated. "On the other hand, if Lawrence has been lying to us, then we need to know the truth before we get any deeper in it than we already are."

Teddy was shaking his head. "You've always thought the worst of him. You've always assumed he was guilty, that he was this contriving manipulator."

He meant conniving, but it was a close enough miss. I didn't correct him.

Teddy went on. "But I was right about him, wasn't I, Leo? I've always been right about him. Just one time, you might want to think about reserving your judgment."

I just gave a grunt that might have been agreement and might not, not wanting to fight with him, avoiding the issue as I'd always done, as I'd preferred to do for the last twenty-one years. I was tired of being the one who was always in the wrong.

We parked on the street, went to the front entrance, and buzzed the intercom. "Who is it?" Tanya's voice said from the box. A voice as rough as the streets where she'd once walked nightly, before Teddy had hired her. I prodded him. "It's Teddy," he said with a husky depth of feeling, making me wonder again at the mystery of him keeping Tanya employed for so many years, giving her so much of himself. Their relationship had ended with the bullet that changed his life. But why it hadn't ended previously, when she'd stolen money from the trust account of Ricky Santorez, Teddy's most feared and dangerous client, I'd never understood.

We took the elevator to the third floor. I expected wariness, hostility, but Tanya embraced Teddy in the hall. She was short, barrel-shaped, and immodest, ugly but appealing in her refusal to acknowledge it. With a reluctant glance at me, she led us into her apartment.

"You've been doing well," I said, taking in the tasteful décor, the city view.

She gave me a look like she wished she could blink and make me disappear.

"Forget it, Leo," Teddy told me. Again I was struck by how my brother had changed. When someone had fucked him, the old Teddy never rested until he'd found a way to fuck him back.

I could tell that she also perceived the difference in him. "So what's this?" she said. "He finally lets you see me, but you have to bring him as a chaperone?"

An awkward moment. "Leo never stopped me from seeing you, Tanya."

She turned to the kitchen, her feelings hurt. "You still drink Manhattans, at least?"

She mixed two of them, adding to each a cherry on a plastic spear. She brought me a beer, like I was a child at the grown-ups' table. But then, for so long, she'd known me only as Teddy's kid brother.

"We're here for me, not him," I said. "I asked Teddy to come along. But if you two are ready to bury the hatchet, now's fine."

"I never had any gripe with Teddy."

I'd told myself I'd keep quiet on the subject of old grudges but couldn't. "You had a gripe with his old client Santorez, though, didn't you? And because Santorez had some money go missing, and because Teddy was the one who was supposed to be holding that money, Santorez had a gripe with Teddy because of you."

Her mouth barely moved as she spoke. "Santorez made an investment and he's getting a good return."

"So Santorez owns you." Santorez was in prison, and he would remain there for the foreseeable future, but this didn't stop him from operating a criminal enterprise. One that evidently included Tanya and her girls.

"No one owns me."

"A piece of you, then. And in return, you have access to all the muscle you need."

"I got my own muscles." Tanya's cell phone rang. "Excuse me."

She went into the bedroom and closed the door, but not all the way, so that we could hear her end of the conversation. Tanya mentioned an address in the Sunset, a house number, a high price. She'd come a long way from the drug-addicted streetwalkers my brother had once represented.

I glanced at him, trying to gauge his reaction. The old Teddy had thoroughly despised pimps of all shapes and sizes. I wondered what his feelings were now about how Tanya earned her living.

She returned. "A busy night. Now what was it you wanted?"

I'd made a blowup of the picture, blacking out Eric's face. By way of answer I handed it to her. "I need to know if anyone recognizes these girls. I've got a stack of these photos with my contact information. I was hoping you could hand them out."

"One of these women is dead, isn't she," Tanya said, and I felt a chill. As she looked at the photo I studied her. I'd seen emotion there only once before, the day Teddy was shot, when she found me covered in his blood. Now for the second time I saw feeling in her eyes. She looked confused. Then her eyes narrowed and her empathy turned to offense. "What's this got to do with me?"

"You're in the business," I said.

She thrust the photo at me. "You can't blame me. These aren't any of my girls. Even if they were, you can't hold me responsible. I do all I can to keep them safe, but I can't go with them through those doors. They choose this life."

And you take the profits, I wanted to add. I took the picture back. "It's just that we're up against a dead end. You don't need to get involved. You can just ask your girls to hand out the fliers. Someone recognizes them, they call, or they don't."

She thought for a moment, then said, "Okay. If she's been in the game, maybe I'll find out. Maybe I'll even find her if she's still around. But I'm doing this on one condition, and that's that you don't go out and try to bother guys who'd as soon leave you with a hole in your head as answer your questions."

She glanced at Teddy, and her voice softened. "You stay clear of my business, Leo, and I'll stay out of yours."

Chapter 12

The following Friday, two weeks before my father's trial, we met at Nina's office. Car showed up a little before eight, before Teddy and my father arrived. He was unshaven when I met him in the outer office. "Nothing," he said. For the first time since I'd known him, his exhaustion made him look middle-aged. "I got nothing." He was just back from Pelican Bay, where he'd been dispatched to visit Keith Locke.

"He wouldn't see you?"

"He *saw* me," Car said as we went into the conference room. "He talked to me for a good two hours, kept toying with me like he might give me something if I'd just sit there, listen to him long enough. What did you expect? He's not going to confess to murdering your mom back when he was a teenager, not when he's still got a chance of getting out on parole."

"And so the family, the parents, we have to go through their lawyer?" Nina asked.

"You can drop subpoenas on them, sure. But they wouldn't talk five years ago, and I wouldn't gamble on it now."

"Okay," she said. "Cross Keith Locke off the list."

"I could have told you that, saved the trip."

"Fax me your bill. I'll see that it gets submitted with this week's requests for payment." Irony of ironies, the state that was prosecuting my father was financing his defense.

Car checked the time on his phone. "Much as I'd like to stick around for the meeting, unless you've got any actual investigation for me to do . . ."

"I'll have subpoenas for you to serve on Monday morning," Nina said, dismissing him. "In the meantime, rest up."

Half an hour later we met for a long-planned session in the conference room. The four of us—Lawrence, Teddy, Nina, and I—needed to take stock and begin planning for the trial. Dot would not be joining us, Lawrence had announced. The first order of business would be the hearing at which Judge Liu would decide the admissibility of my father's supposed confession.

"I've given some serious thought about how to handle these issues," Nina said. "Obviously, it would be best if we can prevent the confession from coming in. You've got a right to have the jury determine all the facts, but in my opinion it'd be a disaster if the jury were allowed to hear about Bell's murder and your motive for committing it."

"So keep it out."

Nina nodded. "If we mount a vigorous defense at the hearing and prevail, Judge Liu will keep the confession out, which should mean that he dismisses the case. If we lose at the hearing, then our next move would be to file a motion to keep the jury from hearing about Bell's murder or any suggestion that you were behind it. The trouble is, our position on that motion would not be strong. If you, in fact, had had Bell killed to prevent him from testifying, that would be compelling evidence that you'd indeed confessed to him that you murdered your wife."

My father watched her intently. "So it's all the chips on the table."

"Exactly. To put it quite simply, we can't afford to lose this hearing."

"Then let's win," Lawrence said. "Let's win the whole thing right here."

"Well, I always love to fight for a fighter. But we've got to be smart. Right now, we have the ability to choose our ground, to define the battle."

Lawrence frowned. "Now it sounds more like you're telling me to give up without a fight."

"You have a right to confront the witnesses against you. But it's my judgment that if we allow Detective Shanahan to testify regarding Bell's hearsay statement, and if you waive your right of confrontation, then Liu will likely look favorably on a pretrial motion to prohibit the state from arguing that you were responsible for Bell's death. In fact, I would hope to keep out *any* mention by the state of the reason why Russell Bell isn't available to testify."

"Except anyone who's read the papers already knows what happened."

"That can't be helped, but at least this way we can keep it out of the trial."

"So what you're telling me is you think we should just skip the hearing and go to the main event."

"That's my advice."

She hadn't discussed this with me prior to this meeting. At first, I was irritated, despite having agreed at the outset that she wouldn't consult me in matters of trial strategy. But I understood. Like my father, I wanted to take the bold route to victory, yet if we showed our hand at the hearing as we had at the prelim, and if Liu ruled against us, we'd be giving the prosecution crucial days to figure out how to turn our best evidence against us. Preferable to blaming Bell's murder on Eric Gainer was avoiding any mention of the murder at all.

"Advice noted. Now, if you don't mind, I'd like to talk to my sons."

She rose. "Take as much time as you need. I'll be in my office."

When she'd gone, Lawrence frowned. "What do you two think?"

I waited a second for Teddy to speak up. As the oldest, he had the right to speak first. But, when he said nothing, I spoke. "The media's already painted you as guilty of his murder. But the media's not going to be in that jury box."

"We've got to explain why Bell lied. Isn't that what she said? How are we going to do that?"

I glanced at Teddy. It was an awkward moment, one needing to be handled delicately. But, again, he was no help. I said, "I don't want to put words in Nina's mouth, and she and I haven't talked about this. But I think she must be planning on you testifying."

Lawrence had been intently listening to me. Now he seemed to be seeking the deeper meaning behind my words.

"Is that so?" he asked.

"You had a number of conversations with Russell Bell. Some of them quite lengthy. The phone records make that clear. The jury's going to be interested to know what the two of you talked about. Bell's dead, so you're the only one able to tell them. The question is, what did you and he talk about?"

He waited for me to go on, but I only returned his look. He glanced at Teddy, who clearly was unable to follow what Lawrence and I were saying between the lines. After a moment our father said, "And it's my decision whether or not to testify. Not Nina's."

"Right. Alive or dead, Russell Bell is one of the witnesses against you, and unless you waive your right to cross-examine him, they can't use his statement without showing that you had him killed to keep him from testifying. We don't want them doing that, but if you refuse the compromise Nina's recommending, she can't stop you."

"I'd like to see the look on her face if I say I won't go along. We can still win this whole thing if we win the hearing. Right?"

"Sure. But what Nina pointed out is that if you lose the hearing, we'd be in bad shape. The judge's ruling would allow the DA to talk about Bell's death. And we'll have given them a sneak preview of our evidence. On the other hand, if you waive your right to cross-examine, there doesn't have to be any explanation why Bell isn't available. Shanahan just gets up there and tells the jury what he said."

Lawrence nodded, but he'd tuned me out. "I want to hear what Teddy thinks."

Teddy stammered at first, like a swimmer flailing. Then his feet seemed to find solid ground. "Trust the jury. Don't ever put your fate in a judge's hands if you don't have to. That's what I used to tell all my clients. But this judge . . . I'm not so sure. You'd still be in prison now if it weren't for Liu. Most judges wouldn't have granted that petition."

"Never put your head in the lion's mouth," I offered. They both stared at me. "It's something Teddy used to say." I found myself wistful for Teddy's old mastery and grandeur, his self-assurance that only seemed to increase as the odds rose against him, his uncanny ability to always pull a rabbit out of his hat.

I went on hurriedly. "The judge may doubt the prosecution's case, but he's going to let it go to the jury. The point is to keep them from hearing the most damaging allegations against you. I agree with Nina that it would be a disaster if the DA were allowed to argue that you killed Bell to keep him from testifying. The compromise she's suggesting is the only way to avoid that."

"Okay." My father nodded. "Let's have a jury trial."

~ ~ ~

"Your brother and Car are going to have to testify about his investigation into Keith Locke and the shooting," Nina said. "I'll put the witnesses up, but I may need your help preparing those two. And of course, preparing your father and also Dot, if she ends up having to testify."

The others had gone. It was now just the two of us, alone with the mountain of work that remained before the case would be ready for trial.

"Fine." I wasn't sure how much Teddy remembered about the investigation he and Car had launched in preparation for filing Lawrence's habeas brief, or how he'd perform in front of the jury.

She seemed like she was about to say something more, then she shut her mouth with a frown. "This case. I don't feel prepared, or in control." She lifted her chin. "Your father's determined to go to trial."

"What's that mean?"

"You've sat in this chair. What if there were an offer on the table? Manslaughter, second-degree murder? A few years, then a shot at parole? He never had a shot at getting out before."

"For what it's worth, Dot wants him to plead out, if he can get time served. That's why she can't stand to sit through our strategy sessions. She went through all this before, with her son, the one who, when he finally got out of prison, died of an overdose. But I'm telling you there's no way he's going to plead to a homicide."

"At the beginning they all want to fight the charges. They want their day in court. Ultimately this case will come down to Lawrence's credibility. That means he'll need to testify, and he'll have to be very convincing. Will he be ready?"

"I mentioned it to him." I locked eyes with Nina. "You're telling me that you'd advise him to plead guilty even if that means going back to prison."

"He's got Bell's murder hanging over his head in addition to this case," Nina went on. "But, yes, if there were a deal, I might well advise your father to grab it, depending on the terms. At the moment, we don't know what the terms might be. We haven't asked."

"I'm not going to help you talk my father into a guilty plea."

She nodded, her attitude abruptly shifting, treating me now as the son of a client rather than her co-counsel. "No, of course not. Ultimately if there's an offer, your father will have to decide without pressure from you or me. I'm eager to try the case. But I'm not the one who will die in prison if we lose—and neither are you."

I decided that this comment didn't deserve a response, and kept my mouth shut.

She stood. "I'll be in my office. When you're ready to call it quits, just make sure the street door latches behind you."

Chapter 13

I tried to outwait her, but midnight came and went. If I didn't leave, I'd miss the last train back to Oakland.

My phone rang half an hour later as I was starting my truck at the MacArthur BART station. The voice was slurred, without affect. "Her name's Lucy Rivera. She's dead. Russell Bell killed her."

In the background I heard street sounds—engine noises and women's voices. "Please don't hang up," I said.

I waited for the click, and when it didn't come, I went on. "I'll meet you wherever you want. I'll come where you are. We'll find a place to talk."

"Come to Civic Center. Down toward Leavenworth."

She told me how much money she wanted me to bring.

I debated going alone, then called Teddy and woke him up. People seemed to trust Teddy, as if they could sense his vulnerability. More important, he had a right to be involved, since he was the one who'd made possible the meeting with Tanya. I figured he'd want to help me see it through.

He was waiting outside when I arrived at his house. We drove into the city, across Market and up toward Civic Center. I told him about the call as I drove.

Near Leavenworth, a female shape detached itself from a darkened doorway. She wore a long coat with wide lapels. We slowed to the curb as instructed, and I reached across Teddy and opened the door.

The picture hadn't done her justice. Her features were chiseled in the dome light, with an angular beauty that caught my breath. She brought into the truck a smell of city wind and sour breath. She'd changed her hair color from brown to blond and sheared it off, but she was undeniably the woman in the pictures, the one who'd had her arm around Gainer.

She touched my hand. Her fingers were like ice. "You got anything to eat?" she asked, her voice hoarse and weary. I didn't, but I gave her a ten and she came back with a sack of donut holes and a Mountain Dew. Teddy slid over to the middle seat.

"Here are the ground rules," she told me after she'd shut the door. "I'm not testifying or talking to the police. This is a one-time deal. I'll take you to the place if you want to see it, the last place she went. But it's going to cost you a thousand, and after that you're never going to see me again. And you don't get to learn my name."

"I'll pay you when we get back from where we're going, safe and sound."

I wondered if this was how it had started for Teddy, telling himself that he was paying for information, not for testimony.

"Lucy was a hustler, but I'm not. I'm just scraping by. I need this money to get out of town."

I took out my flip phone and showed her the picture of Russell Bell dead in his coffin. "Russell can't hurt you, if that's what you're worried about. Somebody put six bullets in *him*."

"They'd kill me, too, if they got the chance." She brought her knees up, making herself small against the door.

She told me to head north on 101, then cut across to the coastal highway. She might not have remembered the spot, just south of Mendocino, except she'd spent hours hitching before someone finally picked her up, she said. We made the three-hour drive mostly in silence. Every so often the woman stirred to check our progress, then let her head fall against the window again. Teddy slept, too. "Here," she said when we'd been on the coastal highway about twenty minutes. "Slow down."

Moonlight shone on the breakers. The stark shadows heightened the effect of the house perched all by itself at the very edge of land, separated by a sweep of empty pasture from the road. I drove up the long drive and parked. The big two-story dwelling appeared shut up and dark.

On the front porch she bent, felt behind a flower pot with dead flowers, and produced a key. She opened the door. Inside, she punched numbers into a keypad. A light flashed green and a tone sounded. "I didn't steal the code," she said. "It's just that I've got a visual memory. I can see it now like he's standing right here, what his hand did. Don't worry. The guy that owns the place is in China for the year. At least that's what Eric said."

Teddy, visibly uncomfortable, told me that he'd keep watch outside.

The front hall was wood floored, opening into a large living room with a stone hearth and chimney like a pillar. The sky was visible through the windows thirty feet overhead. A balcony edged by a railing of gnarled pine ran the perimeter of the second floor. The doors of the rooms along the balcony were closed. A wall of windows looked out on a spacious deck that at least from the inside appeared to jut out into emptiness with only the vast ocean beneath.

I passed through the echoing living room, went through a sliding door, and stepped outside. At the railing, with the salt wind in my face, I looked down and saw waves breaking white and small far below. I felt suddenly that I was toppling and turned back to face the house. It appeared to be the same balcony from the picture. "What happened?"

The woman spoke out of the darkness beside me. "She fell. She's probably still out there somewhere. They say it can take months for a body to come ashore. Sometimes people drown and they never get found. Maybe the sharks get them, or maybe they just sink to the bottom and they never float up."

"You mean Russell pushed her."

"We were partying, the four of us. Russell wanted to use Lucy to get to Eric. You know the backstory," she said, glancing at my face. "Everyone does. Well, as soon as he got out of prison, he found her again, and there was no one to protect her. No one would have believed her. She was a whore and he was a john. That's how it went down. Try telling the police any different. She told me all this the night she died. She told me everything.

"It was a sick fucking tragedy. Once he'd had her again, it was like she was back there all the way back in the beginning, with a sack over her head and her hands and feet tied. There was going to be a lot of money in it for both of us, he said. But Lucy wasn't in it for the money. She wasn't in it for anything. She told me she knew now she could never escape, and no matter how far she ran, he'd find her. She was a walking dead person, a zombie. Whenever he came into the room, she'd hold her breath. He'd killed whatever he'd left alive the first time.

"Once I realized who he was, and what he'd done to her, I tried to get her to leave with me, but she wouldn't go. We were on this deck, with a fire going. Russell was pushing all kinds of stuff on Eric and Lucy. He kept daring her to do reckless things, and she'd do it just because he said. Like walk on the railing. When Eric passed out in a chair, I thought Russell would stop egging her on.

"I went to the bathroom, and when I came back she was up there again. Standing in space, high as a kite, like she might fly straight to the moon. Russell gave me a look, then he grabbed her ankle and all of a sudden yanked her foot up and made her fall headfirst. Like picking a flower. She didn't even have time to scream, she was just here one moment and gone the next. But she didn't die that day. She'd died weeks before, the day she first saw him again.

"*I* screamed. I tried to run, but he pushed me down and raped me. Like it was a turn-on for him to kill my friend. Afterward, he told me to say Eric pushed her. That he'd been drunk and she'd climbed up there, and he pushed her. Eric wouldn't remember anything, Russell said. If I went along, I'd get more money than I ever dreamed. If I went against him, he'd kill me.

"We were two feet from the ledge. He could have picked me up easy and tossed me over. For a moment I thought that's what he was going to do, even after I agreed. I was sure that he'd see I was lying. But finally he got up and went in to use the phone. 'Jackson Gainer will be here in an hour,' he told me when he came back. 'He doesn't want me to call the police. That means we're golden. Now you just have to do your part. Eric pushed her. Just keep saying that.'

"I waited until I heard Jackson pulling up. I pretended I had to go to the bathroom. I went through the window, dropped out onto the lawn, and ran. It was so far. I thought for sure they'd see me before I got to the end of the driveway, that they'd come roaring out and that would be the end. I was barefoot. I just kept going up that mountain until my legs wouldn't carry me anymore. I stayed there for most of the next day. From where I was, I could watch the house. I saw them coming and going, looking for me. Finally I came down and hitched a ride back to the city. If Jackson finds me, he'll kill me. What else can he do? He covered up one murder already."

She turned toward me and the space between our bodies melted, and I felt the moist heat of tears on my cheek, the warm swell of her breast, every inch of me responding to her. In my arms she made herself seem small and vulnerable. Her lips made a small movement at my neck, and I shuddered.

The deck lights flooded on like the lights in a stadium. She ducked out of my arms, shielding her eyes. I turned, squinting. It was Teddy. I nodded to my brother in thanks for what he might have prevented from happening. "Let's get out of here," he said, and we went back out through the house.

"You haven't asked how I found that picture," I said when we were driving again.

"I'm not like most people," she said, settling against the door, the crumpled bag of donut holes once more clutched in her lap. "I don't ask a question if the answer's obvious. The picture was on the web for anyone to find. I put it there."

"Why put it on the web?"

"Look, I got out of there. I ran. I saved my ass. I wasn't about to bring it to the police. You think they'd have believed me? But not wanting to go to the cops doesn't mean I wanted to let them get away with it."

"But how could you hope to get away with blackmailing Eric Gainer?"

She didn't respond immediately. Then she said, "Get a life, someone told me once. The trick is finding someone who doesn't want theirs."

"Like Lucy."

"Why shouldn't he pay?"

"Maybe because he isn't guilty, from what you said."

"But he thinks he killed her, and he let Jackson cover it up. And what does he think happened to me, the only witness? No, I don't feel bad about sweating him for cash. Because of Eric Gainer, I've got to start over. He has the money to do that and I don't."

Teddy said, "I'd lend you my life, sweetheart, but if you haven't been shot in the head you probably wouldn't want it."

"They'll wish they'd shot me by the time I'm through."

Chapter 14

"We have a number of matters to take up before jury selection," Judge Liu said. "Let's start with the defendant's motion to exclude the confession. Is the state prepared to present whatever evidence it has that the defendant procured Bell's murder in order to prevent him from testifying in this trial?"

Crowder stood. "We are. Detective Shanahan is here at counsel table. He's ready to take the stand. We have a number of exhibits."

"What about the defense?"

"Your Honor, we'd like to offer a stipulation." This referred to a formal agreement as to what evidence would be admissible and what would not. Nina distributed copies to the judge and the DA, the language firmed over several evenings of drafting and redrafting. "Mr. Maxwell offers to waive his right to cross-examine Russell Bell. In return, the state can introduce the confession itself but not the fact of Bell's death."

With a thoughtful look, Liu turned to Crowder. "You still haven't charged him. I'm not going to let you come into my court and prosecute a defendant for a crime he's not on trial for."

"We still fully expect that he will be charged."

"When? After the jury acquits him here? Wait a minute," Liu said, holding up a hand to keep Crowder from interrupting. "I think the defense's suggestion is an excellent solution to our problem. I'm going to approve the stipulation, deny the motion to exclude the confession, and order that any mention of Russell Bell's death be kept from the jury."

"But the state has to be allowed to explain the reason Bell isn't here to testify," Crowder protested. "Otherwise the jurors will blame the prosecution for failing to produce this witness. If we're not allowed to talk about Bell's death, the jurors will hold his absence against us."

"Think about it. We instruct jurors every day not to draw any unfavorable inferences from the defendant's decision not to testify. I can give a similar instruction here telling the jurors not to draw any conclusions from the fact that Bell won't be taking the stand."

Liu turned his gaze to Nina. "The defense will not be allowed to seize the advantage. Any implication, any innuendo that the prosecution is somehow remiss in not bringing this witness into court, and the stipulation goes out the window. You even crack open that door, Ms. Schuyler, and I'm going to let them drive a truck through it."

"Yes, Your Honor."

"Don't even think about asking for another delay so that you can gather more evidence and charge him," Liu said to Crowder as she rose again. "We've got a hundred jurors waiting downstairs—this trial is going forward." He consulted the papers in front of him. "Next motion is also the defendant's, to prevent the state from arguing that the physical evidence concealed from the defense in the first trial would have showed that the defendant murdered his wife."

He looked up. "Now, Ms. Schuyler, do you really expect me to grant this?"

"The point of our motion, Your Honor, is that we'd be able to do a DNA test if we still had the evidence. We've got the man who we think did this sitting there in Pelican Bay, and we could get a sample and make the comparison, except that the evidence we'd want to compare it to was lost and destroyed through no fault of the defense."

Liu didn't even need to hear from Crowder. "The state can argue the facts their way, and you can argue the facts your way, and the jury can decide whether the state has proved its case beyond a reasonable doubt. Motion denied."

They went on to discuss other matters, including our motion to exclude mention of previous instances of violence in our parents' marriage, which Liu denied, and the state's motion to exclude mention of his reversed conviction and the misconduct of the government in the first case. This Liu denied as well, meaning that Nina would be allowed to harp on Gary Coles's transgressions. I wondered again if she was making the right choice by letting the confession come in. It was a judgment call, and it would have been easy to second-guess her either way.

At ten o'clock the deputies brought in the first group of potential jurors, known as a *petit venire*, and the lawyers began the process of selecting those who would serve. The courtroom deputy called the first fourteen names, and the unlucky chosen took their places in the jury box, most of them grim faced at the trap that had suddenly opened in their lives. Nina and Crowder took turns questioning the group as a whole, then followed up with questions to individual jurors regarding their ability to apply the burden of proof, their potential biases, and exposure to the media coverage. Picking twelve jurors and two alternates took the next day and a half.

~ ~ ~

In the past two weeks, I'd spent more concentrated time with my father than at any other time since my childhood, drilling and redrilling him as the examination Nina had structured for us took shape. Fourteen-, then sixteen-hour days, taking the BART over with the early commuters and running to catch the last train home at night, with my own practice on the back burner. I'd spent most mornings preparing the testimony of Lawrence, my brother, and Car. The afternoons and evenings were given over to drafting and researching our motions and proposed jury instructions. My father, by contrast, seemed almost to have withdrawn from our preparations. Except for our practice sessions, he spent his time at Teddy and Tamara's house, no longer making appearances at the office, eating his meals there and riding his motorcycle back to San Rafael in the evening. It was as if he were determined to wring all the life he could out of these few days and nights that might be all the freedom that remained to him.

Late at night, when I'd become too tired to write, I'd pore over the files on the shooting of Russell Bell, looking for something the police might have missed or obscured, something Nina hadn't noticed.

I would be as prepared for this trial as I'd been for any trial in my life, if only it were mine to try. I'd felt like a second stringer on opening day, sitting in Nina's office that morning watching her make her final preparations. I wanted to be helpful but the main thing now was staying out of her way. For the first time since I was a recent law graduate, I'd be riding the pine.

~   ~   ~

Standing beside the podium rather than behind it, her notes lying before her, Crowder began her opening statement. "I want you to picture a scene. June twentieth, nineteen eighty-three. A child, Leo Maxwell, is walking home from school. Normally at this hour his mother is at work. He has his apartment key on a chain around his neck." A detail I'd forgotten. "He's used to letting himself in to the apartment, getting his snack, doing his homework or watching TV.

"He climbs the stairs to the second floor, opens the door with his key. This is what he sees." Crowder picked up a poster board blowup of the crime scene photo. Seeing it in the courtroom along with the crowd of spectators, it was hard to believe that this was my real life. It was like something that had happened to someone else. "His mother, Caroline Maxwell, crumpled on the floor in the front hall in a pool of blood, her body half nude. She'd been savagely beaten with the child's aluminum baseball bat, which lies nearby, covered with blood, clumps of hair. Standing in the hall, he wets his pants. Then he picks up the phone and dials the number that he's been taught to dial.

"You'll hear that child's nine-one-one call. You'll also hear that in the six months preceding Caroline Maxwell's death, police had been called at least four other times to the residence. Emergency calls, domestic violence. Two of those calls were placed by Caroline Maxwell, the other two by her oldest son, Teddy. On each of these occasions, Caroline changed her mind by the time police arrived. Each time, she decided that she didn't want her husband arrested after all. Each time, police complied with her wishes. You'll have the chance to examine the police reports, and you'll see that they reflect a pattern of escalating violence, a rage building in Lawrence Maxwell. A rage that kept swelling until that fateful day in June nineteen eighty-three, when Lawrence Maxwell decided to do what, as he'd later say, 'had to be done.'

"He came home from his law office in the middle of the day. Around one or two o'clock, judging by the coroner's estimate of time of death. A Wednesday afternoon. We don't know what happened between them, whether words were exchanged before he did what he'd planned. He beat her to death there in the hall. Afterward he wiped the handle of the bat, but his fingerprints were left on the barrel. He dropped the bat and simply walked out of his own home, leaving her there for his ten-year-old son to find. Later, Maxwell was located in a neighborhood bar not far from the scene of the crime. No alibi. He was arrested, tried, and convicted of his wife's murder and sent to prison. But I'm here to tell you that twenty-one years ago justice was not done. That failure to do justice is the reason we're here in this courtroom today.

"The next chapter is one that I'm not proud to tell. The prosecutor on Mr. Maxwell's case was a man named Gary Coles. Coles, at some point in his career, came to believe that rules were for other people. They certainly didn't apply to him. What the rules say is that whatever evidence there is, good or bad, the prosecutor has to share it with the defense. Everything must be turned over.

"Gary Coles didn't like that rule, and he broke it. Not just in this case but in others. He broke our golden rule, hiding evidence that he thought was unfavorable to the people's case. What this evidence showed was that Caroline Maxwell had had sexual intercourse with another man on the day of her murder. She had another man's semen in her body, type A blood rather than type O like her husband's.

"Gary Coles didn't like that fact, and when he got the report he threw it in the trash, sat down at the office typewriter, and made another one. Thus, that evidence never saw the light of day. The medical examiner, when he testified, inexplicably failed to notice that a change had been made.

"In short, Gary Coles cheated. And this evidence was never turned over to the defense. Over the years, the samples were destroyed as a matter of routine practice. The defense never had a chance to test them. Gary Coles is dead, and so he can't explain why he did what he did. In the end his intentions, good or bad, are irrelevant. What matters is that it happened. As a result of Gary Coles's long-ago misconduct, Lawrence Maxwell's conviction has been overturned. He deserves a new trial and that's why we're here. But Caroline Maxwell deserves justice, too.

"Don't get me wrong. Mr. Maxwell killed Caroline Maxwell viciously and in cold blood. I'm telling you now to look hard at all the evidence, the good and the bad. And at the end of the state's case, I'm going to ask you to give Caroline the justice she deserves and convict Mr. Maxwell of the crime of first-degree murder. Twenty-one years is a long time, but it's not too late to do the right thing. The only way to fix the injustice that was committed is by convicting Mr. Maxwell based on all of the evidence. Not just the evidence that one side or the other wants you to hear." This last comment said with a warning nod toward the defense table.

So far Nina hadn't objected, and she didn't rise to the bait now.

Crowder went on. "In the original trial there were unexplained questions. Why did Maxwell come home when he did? Why did the assault happen in the middle of the day, rather than late at night, like the others, after he and Caroline had been drinking? The answer's simple. She'd been with another man that morning, and he knew about it. He didn't catch them in the act, but he came close. Close enough that his suspicions became certainty, like a bomb going off in his brain. I guess Gary Coles didn't think the jurors would understand that."

"Objection," Nina said at last. "Who knows what the man was thinking?"

"Sustained," Liu said. "Keep to the facts you can prove at trial."

Crowder continued, barely chastened. "Unlike the jurors who convicted Mr. Maxwell twenty-one years ago, you'll have the benefit of understanding why Mr. Maxwell did what he did. Unlike them, you'll see evidence showing that jealousy was his motive. He couldn't tolerate knowing that his wife had slept with another man.

"You'll have the benefit of other evidence that the jurors in nineteen eighty-three weren't able to consider. Not because Gary Coles kept it from them, but because the evidence did not then exist. The most powerful evidence you'll hear won't be the nine-one-one call or the physical evidence, the fingerprints, but rather Mr. Maxwell's confession to a fellow inmate at San Quentin. Mr. Maxwell, at the time, was a prisoner serving a life sentence with little hope of parole. He had precious little to lose by bragging, building up his 'cred,' as they call it.

"The confession came about during a conversation about Mr. Maxwell's younger son, who was graduating from college. Leo, the very boy, now grown, the one who'd come home to find his mother's corpse on the floor. 'The boy hates me. I killed his mother,' Lawrence Maxwell said. 'It was a terrible thing, but it had to be done.' That's what he told a fellow prisoner. And to show you what kind of man this is, he admitted that he felt no remorse. 'I just wish he hadn't been the one to find her. I'll have to live with that for the rest of my life.'"

Crowder looked up from the notes she'd been reading. "'I just wish he hadn't been the one to find her.' I want you to remember these words as this trial progresses, as you hear all the evidence in this case. 'It was a terrible thing, but it had to be done.' I want you to ask yourself what kind of man could say that. I want you to keep those words in your mind as you consider justice for Caroline."

~ ~ ~

Crowder spoke for about two hours, but the introductory summary packed the most wallop. Each time she described me finding the body, I felt pinned for dissection, the air seeming to enter my lungs through a straw, as if breathed across that gulf of years. The child she spoke of was me. Despite the presence of Teddy sitting on one side and Dot on the other, I felt or imagined that everyone in the courtroom was looking my way in hostile judgment.

Finally she sat down. Judge Liu checked the clock, instructed the jurors not to discuss the case, and told them to return at 9:00 AM.

~ ~ ~

After court, my father, Dot, Nina, and I went back to her office, and Teddy went home to spell Tamara, telling Lawrence that he and Dot should stop by on their way back to San Rafael. He just nodded, his mind elsewhere. Nina went to her desk to return phone calls and e-mails, while my father and Dot went to sit in the conference room. I joined them, using the long table to go through the exhibits Crowder was likely to introduce tomorrow afternoon when she called Shanahan to the witness stand.

My father paced distractedly. Again and again I glanced up at him, but he seemed not to notice my gaze.

Finally he said, "They're going to come after me for Russell even if I beat this."

"They're likely to."

Closing his eyes, he nodded, as if he saw his fate playing out through the windows and couldn't bear to follow it. He glanced at Dot, then back at me. "What about that deal? I plead guilty to Caroline, time served. And they agree not to prosecute me for Russell."

Dot looked away as my eyes sought hers. Her face was ashen with regret and fear, and I saw that she knew, as I did, that it was too late. I was stunned, though I shouldn't have been surprised. Not only had Nina warned me that his courage might falter, but I'd been in the same situation time and time again with clients who'd turned down reasonable deals when they had the chance, then on the eve of trial had suddenly gotten cold feet and wanted to plead out. But, by then, it was always too late. It would be no different here.

"There was never an offer not to prosecute you for Bell. The time served offer was for this case only, and it was only good until the probable cause hearing," I said as gently as I could. "And that was before Bell was killed. The DA's ready to try the case, and

129

Crowder's in a better position now than she was when she initially made the offer. At this point, I'd be surprised if she'd agree to any deal that didn't involve you going back to prison."

"He's not going back in," Dot said. "You're not, Lawrence." She turned to me. "He's been waking up every night with nightmares. 'It's happening again. It's going to be just the same.' I keep telling him that it's not. You've got a good lawyer this time. You've got your sons, standing behind you. And *me*."

He seemed not to hear her. "You've never even asked if I killed her. Over and over again you hear all these terrible accusations, and you don't say anything. Are you afraid?"

"Even if you had murdered her, I'd still love you. I wouldn't like it, but I'd have no choice." Her voice was quiet. She stared him down. "I'll marry you tomorrow if you want me to prove it."

He returned her stare, then, as if seeking an easier target for his insecurity, he turned to me. "What about you, Leo? What would you think if I pleaded guilty?"

"I'd think you were making a decision you'd regret."

He responded to my tone. "You secretly despise any defendant who'd even think about taking a plea, don't you? Surely you must have had innocent clients plead out before."

"So they said. I didn't believe them. Look, the trial's just started. Teddy always told me that when you start acting from weakness, the jury can smell it. And once they smell weakness, they usually convict. I'll talk to Nina if you want, but in my opinion you need to give her a chance to do her job."

He gave a nod. Dot turned with a chagrined look and went to the window. I crossed the hall and knocked on Nina's door. "He wants you to ask for a deal."

She pushed back from the desk, her shoulders slumping. "But he hasn't even heard my opening."

"He's having flashbacks to the first trial. *She* wants him to fight, even though she was all for him taking a plea before. I told him there's no offer on the table. He wants to know if he can get time served and a nonprosecution agreement for Bell."

"Snowball's chance."

"That's what I said. But he wants you to make the call."

She picked up the phone, dialed. "Angela, it's Nina Schuyler. Look, my client's out on the window ledge. I guess your opening was pretty good, because it even convinced him. He's worried that even if he wins, you're going to try to nail him for the Russell Bell thing. He just wants to be done. How 'bout he pleads guilty and you let him walk away, time served, no prosecution on Russell Bell."

Nina listened, clicking through her notes on the computer. Finally she broke in. "Listen, Angela, I get all that. Just tell me how much time he needs to do, so I can tell him." Rolling her eyes. "I'll pass the word. And hey, great job today."

She hung up. "Ten years on this case, he takes his chances on Bell. Actually, a better offer than I thought we'd get. He has a chance to get out of prison before he dies."

"I'll tell him." I went back across the hall to the conference room where my father stood at the window, his arm around Dot's shoulders, and told them.

He nodded in resignation, as if he'd known all along that this was how it would be.

Chapter 15

Nina began by describing the crime from the point of view of the defense, telling of the "male intruder" who, after entering the apartment, had raped Caroline Maxwell. "She had bruising on her thighs, wrists, and neck, a skinned knee. The autopsy found a broken nail.

"Afterward, the rapist seized a nearby baseball bat and savagely beat her, focusing his blows on her face. The first few would have been fatal but he dealt her many more." She gave brief treatment to the fingerprints wiped from the baseball bat and my discovery of the body.

I gave a tiny nod of acknowledgment but kept my gaze focused on Nina. "Despite evidence showing that this murder must have been committed by a stranger, the police from the start focused their energies on Lawrence Maxwell. Within hours, they arrested him. They never considered any other suspect for this crime.

"The presence of the intruder was immediately written out of the story the police and prosecution chose to tell. Mr. Maxwell was inserted in the rapist's place, the easiest answer for the least possible effort. But an answer without any regard for the actual facts of the crime, and without any thought for the safety of the community in which a killer continued to roam at large.

"In Mr. Maxwell's first trial twenty-one years ago, there was no mention of the physical evidence showing that Caroline Maxwell had been raped. That evidence, as you've heard, was withheld from the defense. The biological evidence, the semen that was found in her body, was subsequently destroyed. We can't know whom that evidence would now have pointed to.

"We know for certain that the person who raped Mrs. Maxwell was not her husband. The blood type of the individual who left the semen in her body was recorded in the original lab report that was hidden from the defense. Unlike the jurors in the first trial, you'll have the chance to examine the carbon copy of the original report that was discovered in the medical examiner's files, and you'll see that the man who left the semen in Caroline Maxwell's body is blood type A. Mr. Maxwell's blood type is O. You don't need an MD-PhD to see that's not a match.

"Twenty-one years ago, of course, Mr. Maxwell couldn't show that the blood types didn't match, because he didn't have the evidence or the report. It was hidden from him intentionally by Gary Coles, the DA, who saw that it would undermine his case. The result was that Mr. Maxwell never learned that the semen of another man had been found in his wife's body, that she'd been raped before she was murdered. Mr. Maxwell was convicted. Of course he was. He was convicted as a result of the worst kind of cynical abuse of power, the kind of miscarriage of justice that simply isn't supposed to happen in the United States.

"Well, it happened here."

Next, she summarized Lawrence's relationship with Bell in prison, including his role in helping free him and the state's decision not to retry Bell. "But there's one problem. Bell confessed to Mr. Maxwell that he'd committed the crime he was in prison for. Upon Mr. Maxwell's release, he learned that Bell had gone to work for a prominent public servant.

"Mr. Maxwell, feeling responsible, attempted to alert Bell's employer of the danger of harboring such a man. In response, Bell invented a story about Mr. Maxwell supposedly confessing to *him* in prison. This was a blatant attempt to discredit Maxwell so that Bell could go on enjoying his freedom without interference. So far, it has worked. Bell is an opportunist and a liar who will say anything to avoid facing the consequences of his crimes. This includes telling the worst kind of lie against the man who gave him the freedom he now abuses."

This was the weakest part of Nina's opening, the Achilles' heel of our defense. We still lacked a satisfactory motive for Bell to invent the confession, unless you counted my father's near admission that he'd blackmailed Bell, but of course we couldn't use that.

Crowder sat frowning on the edge of the chair, her jaw tight and her eyes on Nina. It wasn't lost on her, or on me, that at every opportunity Nina was speaking of Bell in the present tense, as if he were alive and would be testifying in this trial, setting the stage for the jurors to blame the DA for failing to bring him into court. Nina walked right to the edge, never quite crossing the line the judge had drawn.

"Finally, you'll hear that in seeking to retry Mr. Maxwell, the police and the district attorney's office did little more than pick up the case Gary Coles had prosecuted and run the old film back through the projector. Mr. Maxwell was the only suspect they considered. From the moment of his exoneration and release, the focus of the investigators was to build a case against him so that they could put him back behind bars. Just as in nineteen eighty-three, the police disregarded the possibility that someone else might have committed this murder. Recognizing that it was too late to solve this crime, they went for the low-hanging fruit.

"It wasn't an investigation at all. It was a setup. They had their answer before they started. The goal was to drum up just enough evidence to bring this prosecution, save face, and cover up the true seriousness of what Assistant District Attorney Gary Coles did. Gary Coles may be dead, but he charted the course we're following. Detective Shanahan will tell you that he didn't have much time to investigate, that he had to choose his priorities. When you listen to his testimony today, ask yourself what those priorities were.

"I expect Detective Shanahan to testify that he began with the assumption that Mr. Maxwell was guilty, and proceeded from there. He focused his efforts on interviewing people who'd known Mr. Maxwell in prison, inmates and corrections staff, asking them each, did Maxwell ever say anything about murdering his wife? Did he confess? He went down a long, long list of those who knew my client during his more than two decades behind bars, until he found someone who had a motive to answer *yes* to his questions. That was Russell Bell.

"The evidence is going to show that Detective Shanahan didn't have to spend his valuable investigative time trying to dig up a snitch. The police had other options." She spoke of Keith Locke, the son of our mother's lover, now serving a sentence in Pelican Bay for gunning down Teddy in a crowded restaurant a few blocks from city hall just as Teddy was assembling evidence that suggested he'd raped and murdered Caroline Maxwell twenty-one years ago.

"Detective Shanahan didn't for a single moment entertain the possibility that the man who shot Teddy Maxwell in the head just as he was about to file a habeas petition implicating him in Caroline Maxwell's murder might be the killer. Instead, he set about repeating the mistakes and reliving the deceptions of Gary Coles. Detective Shanahan went looking for a snitch. Lo and behold, he found one.

"As to this supposed confession, you'll hear Mr. Maxwell testify that he never spoke those words. Rather, he has steadily maintained his innocence. He'll tell you that he did not commit this crime, and he'll tell it to you in his own voice."

A toe over the line, but she went on before Crowder could object.

"Russell Bell is a liar, and when Mr. Maxwell gets through testifying, you'll understand Bell's motivation. When you've heard the evidence, you'll see this prosecution for what it is: a sad refusal to acknowledge the mistakes of the past, a waste of resources, and a destructive misuse of the state's power. When you've heard all the evidence in this case, I'm confident that you'll give Lawrence Maxwell the justice he deserves and find him not guilty of this crime."

~ ~ ~

"Please state your full legal name for the record."

"Lieutenant Neil James Shanahan."

Crowder proceeded crisply through the preliminary steps of her examination, Shanahan, for the most part, repeating the testimony he'd given at the prelim. His manner, however, was quite different from that of his testimony then. At the prelim, with only Judge Liu as his audience, he'd come across as stiff, a little arrogant. Now, with each answer, he glanced at the jurors as if seeking their permission and approval, speaking as if to them rather than to Crowder. Within a few minutes, I knew that on cross Nina was going to have her work cut out.

Crowder used him to lay out the case from beginning to end, starting from his review of the old investigative file and the documents it contained, the police reports, the crime scene photographs blown up to poster size, the autopsy report and forensics analysis, and finally, the evidence that had been withheld from the defense. Like any competent trial lawyer, she was careful not to gloss over the bad facts. She had Shanahan go through the details of Gary Coles's misconduct and the evidence he'd withheld, all with the goal of showing that it didn't matter, that the new evidence also established Lawrence's motive of jealousy.

She also sought, point by point, to rebut Nina's opening statement, especially the accusation that Shanahan's investigation had focused single-mindedly on my father. "Do you agree with Ms. Schuyler's characterization of your investigation as a sham designed to drum up evidence against this defendant?" Crowder asked.

"I do not."

"What suspects did you consider?"

Shanahan spoke to the jurors. "I made a point of starting from zero, as if this crime had happened yesterday. I didn't want to be tainted by any assumptions or mistakes from the past."

"What evidence, if any, did you have that was not available to the investigators twenty-one years ago?"

"From the start, I knew that Mrs. Maxwell had been having an affair with a married man at the time of her death. I had a set of pictures that were taken of them together, which had been filed by Maxwell's lawyers as newly discovered evidence. Evidently he'd gotten these pictures from the family of the woman who'd had them taken. These pictures were never brought to the attention of the police at the time of the original investigation."

Crowder introduced the pictures into evidence, solving what otherwise might have been a thorny problem for Nina, and one that had occupied several hours of research time for me, since the private investigator who'd taken the pictures was untraceable and we had no other way of proving that the pictures were what we said. However, as long as Nina didn't object, Crowder could introduce whatever evidence she wanted. These pictures had come to Teddy from Keith Locke's sister, and both sides had agreed that they'd be admitted.

"Were you able to identify the man with whom she'd been having the affair?"

"I was. He's a physician at UCSF."

"Did you consider him a suspect?"

"Initially, yes, but the physical evidence ruled him out. The semen collected from the victim's body at the crime scene has been destroyed, but the results of the tests they ran on it are still available. Although these tests can't make a positive confirmation of the killer's identity, we can use the results to rule out suspects whose blood types don't match the blood type of the donor."

"How were you able to determine that the semen in her body didn't belong to this man?"

"I went to his lawyer and asked if he would give a blood sample. He readily agreed. The semen collected from her body at the crime scene didn't match his blood type. He's O negative; the donor was type A positive. Simple as that."

"Based on your experience, is there any way that a DNA sample would have turned up a different result?"

Nina objected that Crowder hadn't established Shanahan's expertise in DNA testing, but Liu overruled her. The point was obvious.

"No chance," Shanahan said. "If the blood types don't match, then we're dealing with two different people. I don't need DNA to tell me that. Even so, I asked the doctor's attorney if I could interview him. He'd been in an intimate relationship with the victim at the time of her death, and I thought that he might have relevant information. Of course, twenty-one years had passed. As it turned out, however, his memory was quite clear."

"What conclusions, if any, did you form based on the fact that the DNA didn't match?"

This was the weak point of Crowder's case, and she was not going to make the jurors wait for her answer to what ought to have been a thorny dilemma. Shanahan's answer was audacious and cunning: "I concluded that the victim must have had multiple boyfriends."

"What was the focus of your investigation after speaking with the physician?"

"After that conversation, my focus was on the defendant, Lawrence Maxwell."

"Why was that your focus at this point?"

"Because of information I received from my interview. The doctor told me that Caroline was deathly afraid of her husband, that she was convinced that sooner or later he would find out, and something terrible would happen. He also told me he was convinced she'd been unfaithful to her husband with other men." Nina interrupted with a hearsay objection, an objection that I'd been itching for her to make ever since the previous question. Liu overruled her on the shaky ground that she'd attacked Shanahan's investigation and the state was entitled to rehabilitate it.

Shanahan went on. "He didn't take her seriously. She was a dramatic woman, and he thought it excited her to pretend that the danger was greater than it actually was. After speaking with him, I felt certain that the motive was jealousy."

"What did you do next?"

I felt relieved as I realized that this was all they had, their only answer. Under the state's theory, it seemed equally probable that Caroline's other lover, and not Lawrence, had killed her, if such a man even existed. I hoped that this point was as obvious to the jurors as it was to me.

"I began tracking down and interviewing men who'd known Maxwell in prison. Twenty-one years is a long time to spend behind bars. In all that time, I figured he might have opened up to someone."

"Whom did you speak with during this part of your investigation?"

Shanahan repeated the testimony he'd given at the prelim about his conversation with Russell Bell in which Bell had related Lawrence's alleged confession behind bars, concluding with my father's alleged statement about his only regret being that I was the one who'd found her body.

"Did Maxwell say why his younger son hadn't been to visit him in all those years?"

"It was obvious. His father had murdered his mother and the kid knew it. He'd found the body."

As if from far away, I heard Nina's objection. But my eyes were on Shanahan, who'd turned his own gaze on me as he made this statement. I felt the jurors' eyes follow his.

Angela Crowder chose this moment to introduce the 911 call I'd made, and before I knew what was happening she was playing it. The child's voice that had once been mine filled the courtroom. *It's my mom*, the small voice said. *She's hurt.*

The light in the courtroom seemed to change. It was as if an actor had stepped off the stage and taken my hand against my will.

After the recording, Crowder went through the confession a few more times, fleshing out all the details, getting Shanahan to repeat the crucial parts, asking questions the only point of which was to burn Bell's words into the jurors' brains, emphasizing the past tense just enough to beg the question of where Russell was and why he wasn't here to testify in person.

Shanahan's testimony was simple, to the point, and devastatingly effective in establishing my father's guilt. Sooner than I expected, Crowder's examination was finished.

We broke for lunch, and then it was Nina's turn.

Chapter 16

She stood at the podium, her hair swept back and held in a tight knot with a comb, the light finding the tender place at the side of her jaw. I was almost as aware of the jurors looking at her as I'd been of them looking at me, and I felt a stirring of pride at the relaxed set of her shoulders, the way she stared Shanahan in the eye as if he were a captive animal and she knew how to handle him.

"You just testified about a set of pictures filed as newly discovered evidence. Who took them?"

"My understanding is that they were taken by a private investigator hired by the wife of the man Caroline Maxwell had been having her affair with, but I don't know that for certain. They were discovered by Teddy Maxwell, the defendant's oldest son. I understand that he received them from a family member," Shanahan said, repeating the testimony he'd just given.

"The doctor's wife was angry at him for having an affair with Caroline Maxwell. Would that be fair to say?"

"I think that would be fair. The doctor told me that he'd wanted to call it off, but he couldn't bring himself to end it."

"So even after his wife discovered the affair and confronted him with the photographic proof, this man went on seeing Caroline?"

"In my understanding."

"Did the doctor's wife know that he was doing this?"

"I can't say what she knew or didn't know," he said.

"Did you ask the doctor's wife that question?"

"I haven't spoken with her," Shanahan replied.

"So you made no attempt to interview this woman to determine whether she harbored feelings of jealousy and rage toward Caroline Maxwell for intruding on her marriage?"

"I felt that I'd already intruded on the family enough."

"And to be clear, you never considered the possibility that this woman, motivated by jealousy, murdered her husband's lover, did you?"

Shanahan blinked. "No, I never considered it. She couldn't have left—"

"Couldn't have left the semen in her body. That's what you were about to say."

Shanahan didn't answer.

"That's what you were about to say, isn't it, Detective?"

"Yes," he admitted. Watching from the gallery, I was elated at his unforced error and her deftness in catching it. Maybe the jurors had seen *Presumed Innocent*, or read the book.

Nina stepped back from the podium and turned to the jurors, driving home her point. "But Mr. Maxwell couldn't have left that semen, either. We know from the lab reports, the ones that were withheld from the defense years ago by Gary Coles, that the semen in Caroline Maxwell's body didn't match his blood type."

"That's right. She probably had multiple lovers."

Nina circled to establish that this was pure speculation, then said, "You've just testified that your belief is that Mr. Maxwell was motivated by jealousy to murder his wife. Wouldn't the wife of the man whom Caroline Maxwell was sleeping with have had a similar motivation?"

"Possibly. But that doesn't mean she acted on it like he did."

"How about this other man or men she was supposedly sleeping with? Couldn't he have killed her?"

"The circumstantial evidence pointed to the defendant."

"But not the *physical* evidence," Nina said. "Or at least Gary Coles didn't think so."

Crowder objected and Nina moved on, next getting him to admit that there was no evidence that my father had known Caroline was having an affair, that unlike the doctor's wife, Lawrence hadn't hired a private investigator. This was just warmup for the main attack, I knew. We didn't intend to argue that the jilted wife was the killer. The point was that Shanahan hadn't bothered to eliminate her as a suspect. "The man confessed," he finally said. "That's good enough for me."

Now Nina turned to the real focus of our defense. I rested my elbows on my knees, inwardly urging her on. She briskly established the facts of Keith Locke's attempted murder of my brother, his guilty plea and subsequent imprisonment, and that this crime came as the culmination of a long criminal career. "And despite this extensive criminal history, including sex offenses, you never considered Keith Locke a suspect in Caroline Maxwell's death."

"No, I didn't."

"Instead you focused your energies on trying to find a snitch."

Shanahan was growing frustrated. "It seemed logical to me that in all those years, Maxwell might have confessed."

"Do you even know if Keith Locke's blood type matches the semen that was left in Caroline Maxwell's body, according to the report we have?"

Shanahan admitted that he hadn't looked into whether the blood types matched. I allowed myself a fist pump behind the back of the bench in front of me, where the jurors couldn't see it. My face was as impassive as a choirboy's.

"It wouldn't be difficult to check, right? All you'd have to do is get his Department of Corrections medical file. In fact, I have it right here." She'd walked to the defense table and picked up a folder. Now she approached the witness stand. "Do you want to look at it, Detective, and see if Keith Locke's blood type is consistent with him being the person who left that semen in Mrs. Maxwell?"

"Do I *want* to?"

"You don't really want to do that, do you?" She picked up one of the DA's exhibits from the clerk's table. "Here's the old lab report that Gary Coles didn't want the defense to see. Here's Keith Locke's medical file. I've got the page marked for you. Just turn to the red flag. Don't you want to look, Detective, just to check?"

At the witness stand, the man's body language betrayed his deep reluctance and loathing. "Sure, I'll take a look."

Nina offered the medical file as an exhibit, handed a copy to Crowder, gave another to the clerk to be marked, and passed a third to Judge Liu. She retrieved the marked copy and handed it to Shanahan. "Turn to the tabbed page, if you will. What can you tell us?" She turned to the jury. "Do we have a match?"

He glanced at the exhibit, then set it aside. "All this shows is that Keith Locke's blood type is the same blood type as the person who left the semen. But that doesn't prove anything. A sixth of the world has the same blood type."

"So you're telling me it's just a coincidence?"

"Sure. You pull up enough possible suspects, sooner or later you're going to get a match."

"And we've got one here, don't we, Detective?"

"Sure we do," he said. "Doesn't mean anything. It's not DNA."

"No, the DNA evidence was lost by the police, wasn't it, Detective? But if we had that DNA evidence, we could tell to a certainty whether there really was a match, correct?"

"It would prove that there wasn't, yes."

She came at him and made him admit that he couldn't know whether the DNA matched or not, driving home her point that Shanahan's mind was closed to any possibility other than my father being the guilty one. Then she said, "Today in this courtroom is the first time you became aware that Keith Locke could have been the donor of the sperm found in Caroline Maxwell's body, correct?"

"Like I said, anyone with the same blood type could have been."

"Exactly. Anyone other than Lawrence Maxwell, because we know his blood type didn't match, right?"

"Yes," Shanahan admitted.

Nina next established that the SFPD had done no investigation into whether Keith Locke might have had an alibi for the murder, that Shanahan had made no attempt to account for his whereabouts at the time of the murder twenty-one years ago. "The reason you didn't ask the doctor any questions about his son is that you already believed Lawrence Maxwell was guilty, correct?"

"Let me put it this way. He was my primary suspect. I was trying to keep an open mind. But at that point, and especially after what I'd already learned in that conversation with the doctor, I felt that Maxwell had committed this crime."

"Because in your mind, Russell Bell's story about Mr. Maxwell confessing is all that counts."

"I found Bell very credible. And he was genuinely terrified. He told me about a number of attacks that he believed Mr. Maxwell had orchestrated behind bars, one of them resulting in a death. Bell believed he was risking his life talking to me. The fact that he was taking that risk told me that he was telling the truth."

"Objection, our stipulation," Nina was saying as Shanahan spoke over her.

"Sustained." Liu addressed the jury. "The jury is to disregard the witness's last answer."

In the gallery I felt murderous myself, my anger multiplied by my powerlessness. I shared a glance with Dot. Shanahan had clearly decided to throw aside the rules and fight dirty, stinging Nina whenever he had the chance.

"And if Bell is lying, your whole case falls apart, doesn't it, Detective?"

He wouldn't go that far, but she'd made her point. Nina sparred with him for a few more questions, then tightened the leash and ran quickly through Shanahan's first contact with Russell Bell, frequently referencing the transcript of the preliminary hearing. She established that Bell had approached Shanahan rather than the other way around. She made the detective admit that Bell had failed to divulge key facts, including that Lawrence had drafted the habeas brief that had earned Bell his release from prison. She also had Shanahan admit that Bell had given him no information that had not already been publicized about the murder itself.

Finally Nina asked, "Does Russell Bell have a source of income?"

Payback, I thought. At her use of the present tense, Shanahan's mouth gave an angry twitch. "Not at present."

Nina simply waited. Finally Shanahan said, "When I talked to him he was working as a driver for City Supervisor Eric Gainer."

"Did you do anything to determine whether Russell Bell might have had a motive to get Lawrence Maxwell off the street and back in prison?"

"If he did, he never told me about it."

"Did you ask Bell if he'd talked to Maxwell since his release?"

Shanahan hadn't asked that question.

"Why not, Detective? If there was some recent conflict between them, wouldn't that be important information for evaluating the truthfulness of Bell's story?"

"Why don't you ask Bell yourself?" Shanahan said, biting back. "I'm sure he'd be happy to fill you in."

"That's enough," Liu told him. "Counsel, are you finished with this witness?"

Nina consulted her notes. "For now, but I may wish to recall him."

"The witness is excused," Liu said. "We'll adjourn until nine AM."

Chapter 17

We had pizza in the conference room at Nina's office, Lawrence studying the newspaper, me going through my notes. Teddy had gone home, but Lawrence had hung around, even though I kept urging him to leave. He was nervous about his testimony tomorrow and wanted to practice his direct examination one more time, but I rebuffed him. "Go home to Dot, have a beer, and go to bed," I said. "It's time to let tomorrow take care of itself."

He seemed to accept this, but first asked if he could borrow my laptop. He wanted to see if a story recapping today's events was posted on the *Chronicle*'s website yet. I gave it to him. He clicked a few times, then studied the screen, remaining motionless. At last he looked up. "I thought we'd agreed to trust each other."

"I thought so, too." I met his gaze.

"Then why am I, just now, learning about this?" He turned the laptop around to show me what he'd been staring at. It was the *Chronicle* site. Prominently displayed there was a copy of the picture I'd found online, the one with Eric and the two girls. "Teddy told me that you'd found something. I've been trying to be patient, trying not to second-guess. I figured that you must have wanted to do your homework before you talked with me about it. But don't I at least have a right to be consulted before you decide to leak something like this?"

"We didn't leak it." I was as shocked as he was. "We wouldn't have."

I clicked on the story that accompanied the picture. The text stated that the paper had obtained, from an anonymous source, the photo and the e-mail it had been attached to, sent to Eric Gainer's official account. It was the same one he'd showed me: *You've been a very bad boy, Eric, and I know all about it. Now will you follow my instructions? Keep ignoring me, and you'll get what Russell got.*

The source evidently hadn't given the reporter any information to go with them. The article could only point out the obvious: that someone appeared to have been blackmailing Eric Gainer after Bell's death. The identities of the girls in the photograph were unknown, as were their whereabouts.

"Crowder leaked it?" Lawrence asked when I'd finished reading.

"Maybe. Then tomorrow she can come into court, pretend to be shocked." But I had a better guess about who'd done the leaking. It'd been the same person who'd put the picture online, no doubt. The girl who'd taken me to the house on the coast—Lucy's friend.

If the DA could show that the person who'd sent the e-mail was my father, we were in trouble. In the absence of such proof, however, the leak of these documents only muddied the water, and possibly worked to our benefit, since it gave us the opportunity to portray Eric Gainer as a man with a hidden motive for employing Russell Bell. If the e-mail was genuine, it strongly suggested that the person who'd sent it had been the one who'd killed Bell.

I went across the hall to Nina's office. "I just saw it," she said, scrolling down the website on her desktop. She was furious, convinced Crowder had been the one to leak the photo. "It won't get them anywhere," she assured me. "They can't lay a foundation to introduce the e-mail or the photo into evidence. They can't show that it has anything to do with your father. Still, we need to be prepared to deal with it, in the unlikely event Judge Liu lets it in."

My father had followed me and stood in the doorway. With a glance at him, I reminded her I'd put copies of that picture all over town with my name and number on them. "We've got to be careful," I told Nina. "Because where would I get the picture other than from him?"

"Where *did* you get it?" Lawrence asked.

I told them about Eric Gainer's showing me the e-mail and blaming it on my father, then about the search I'd conducted for the file name, turning up the picture on a popular photo-sharing site. The silence as I spoke grew deadly. As I was talking, Nina called up the website again. "It's not there now," she told me. Whoever'd put it up had taken it down.

"You'd better get home," I told my father. "If Dot's seen this, she'll be worrying."

He nodded and went out, strangely silent, as if his fears had grown too weighty for words.

"Be ready to testify if you have to," Nina said to me when he was gone, her voice cold.

When I walked out to the sidewalk ten minutes later my father was still there, straddling his bike, his helmet crooked over one elbow. He seemed to be waiting for me, but there was a settled heaviness in his limbs, as if he lacked the energy to move.

"Where are you going?" he asked.

"I have to try to do something about this," I told him.

"I was thinking I'd head over to Teddy's. I can crash on the couch there, meet you in court tomorrow. Could be the kid'll wake up screaming in the middle of the night, need someone to rock her."

"Dad," I said. "Dot's going to read that story tonight. She's going to wonder what it means. Shouldn't you be with her?"

"I know I should, son. But some nights I just can't bear it."

"You've got to try to bear it," I told him. "She needs you. And you need her."

"That's the part neither of us can stand. Because what we've figured out, see, is that needing and having are two different things, and having's not all it's cracked up to be." He pulled on his helmet, kicked the engine to life, and rode away, leaving me to ponder what he meant. Tomorrow he would testify, taking his fate into his own hands.

I rode the BART back to Oakland, then drove to my office. Once there, I called Tanya. "I was wondering if you'd heard anything about that picture I asked you to show around."

"You mean the one that's all over the news tonight. I'm not the one who gave it to them. I haven't said a word."

"I didn't think you had. I was just wondering if you'd had any results."

"No one's called you?"

"Just some crank calls," I lied. If I ended up testifying, I'd have to make up my mind what to say about my visit to Mendocino. If asked a direct question, I wouldn't lie, but it didn't mean I'd volunteer facts. That I wouldn't lie under oath didn't mean I'd tell the truth to Tanya, however.

"Someone I talked to, one of my girls, recognized one of those girls from the picture. I'm not saying who, 'cause if my girl doesn't want to talk to you, she doesn't have to. But she gave me a name. Sherrie. No last name, just Sherrie. She pointed me to an ad on Craigslist. I got a phone number."

"I want to talk to her," I said.

"So call her. I'll give you the number."

I couldn't do that. Sherrie, if that was really her name, had told me not to try to find her. "I'll only get one chance at this. I don't want to blow it."

"Is there anything in it for her? Anything she'd want, I mean?"

"I'm not trying to get her in trouble, if that's what you're asking."

"You need my help again, you're telling me."

I wasn't going to beg. "What did you have in mind?"

"I can set it up like a trick. I'll tell her your regular girl left town, and someone recommended her. You can use one of my places. This way, Leo, if she doesn't want to talk to you, at least you can get laid and she can make a buck."

"Getting laid is the last thing on my mind."

"You'll have to pay her anyway. And me for the room. Let's say an even six hundred."

I'd figured she'd only be helping me because she'd seen an opportunity to turn a small profit, so I wasn't surprised. "You don't even know who she is, what she charges."

"I'm in business, Leo. Think of this as a professional courtesy on my part. Or would you rather owe me a favor?"

She was right. Best to keep the books clear. "Set it up. Six hundred."

"No promises," she said and ended the call.

~ ~ ~

I thought of calling Eric before I drove over there, then decided against it. After that article in the paper, I doubted he'd be anywhere but home, nursing his wounded reputation.

I drove into the city to his neighborhood and parked half a block from his house. Lights shone in the upstairs windows. I sat watching the house for a few minutes, still unsure how to play my approach. As I waited, the garage door swung up and a black Porsche 911 backed out. Jackson was at the wheel.

The garage door remained open; I waited until the car turned the corner, then pulled into the spot. Eric stood with his arms crossed in the entrance. "I can't talk to you," he said as I got out.

"Why, just because you're listed as a witness for the prosecution?"

"You know the rules. You have to contact me through my lawyer. And you know what he'll tell you. You might as well just turn around and go."

"I'm not here to talk about the case."

He stood for a moment, visibly torn, then punched the button to lower the garage door. "Fine. Want a beer?"

"Sure."

Wordlessly he took two Stellas from the fridge. Evidently I didn't merit the top-shelf stuff anymore. "You must have seen the papers today."

"Ah. So you're here to apologize, to tell me that it's all part of the adversarial system, smearing my character, meaning I'm not supposed to take it personally. Well, don't worry. I don't. That's my lawyer's job. In any case, this will pass, and in a few years, when I'm in Sacramento, or maybe even Washington, no one will remember a thing."

"I didn't leak the picture."

"That's not what Jackson thinks. Anyway, you told me you weren't going to talk about your father's case, and now we are. You know as well as I do that your father sent me that picture, that he's been the one who was blackmailing me."

"I know what happened at George Chen's house." I'd checked the property records and put a name to the owner of the Mendocino house. Chen was a Silicon Valley entrepreneur who'd contributed the maximum each election cycle to Eric Gainer's campaigns. He'd also underwritten a number of Gainer's pet causes, including a highly successful program to keep at-risk kids in school. "George's in China. He's opening his firm's Beijing office, but he left you a key and the use of his house. I've been there. I've been inside. It's a great place to bring girls without the risk of someone snapping a photo. Except that's exactly what happened, isn't it?"

"I don't know what your father thinks. Ask him."

"He couldn't be the blackmailer, because he doesn't know anything about your having pushed Lucy Rivera off the railing when you were drunk. He also doesn't know what happened to the other girl in the picture. Sherrie. The witness."

Eric sank into a chair. I saw by the look on his face that as far as he believed, both girls were dead, and that he hadn't thought it possible that anyone still living could know about his crimes. "Russell told his lies to your father," he said. "That's where you got this."

"There's no question in my mind that Bell deserved what he got," I continued, ignoring him. "If he'd lived, he'd own you."

Eric tilted his head back, gazing at me with shock and understanding. "I won't testify. I'll tell them I changed my mind, like I did when they wanted to retry Russell."

"You can delay things by not taking the stand tomorrow, but eventually it's all going to come out. The question is who's going to tell it?"

"Or rather, will the person telling it be believed?"

"Oh, I think so. This photo's just the tip of the iceberg. They haven't found Lucy's body yet. I took a look over the railing while I was at Chen's. There's a shelf of rock about a hundred yards down. Russell wouldn't have left her there, but he knew better than to get rid of the body like he promised you and Jackson. Nobody would have believed him unless he could show a corpse."

Eric looked me in the eye. "Okay. If that's how you want to play it, she's in the freezer at Chen's. At least, that's what Russell told me, when he revealed who she was, how he'd corrupted her. Made her into the perfect victim. He bragged to me that he could give her a knife and tell her to cut herself, and she'd do it. I haven't looked in the freezer for myself. I haven't been out there since that night, and I don't intend to go back. Is that what you wanted to know? I didn't sleep with her. I didn't know who she was. That part, at least, wasn't my fault."

His guilt was devastatingly simple, and his surrender far too easy. He was calling my bluff, the only thing he could do. "Bell *was* blackmailing you."

"You could say the mask came off. He had a hold on me and he wasn't going to let go. It wasn't about money. It was hatred. Revenge. Gary Coles was dead but I was still alive. He set out, step by step, to tear away the foundation of my life, of my success, by re-creating his crime and then completing it as he hadn't managed to do the first time. He found a way to get his hooks into Lucy again, and then he used her to have his revenge on me. She was an addict, and I think mentally ill. By the time he brought her to me, Russell had her completely under his control."

It was almost like he was trying to persuade himself that she was better off dead. "You went to Jackson with your problem."

"I didn't have to. Your father took care of it for me."

"I can see how you'd prefer believing that to accepting that Jackson had Russell murdered. But don't you see, someone's been playing us both?"

"Call the police. Tell them where to find the body, if you really think it's there. Because I'm not going to be blackmailed again. Not by your father, not by you. If you think you're going to turn the focus of this trial on me and my brother, blame us for your father's situation, it's going to backfire. You have to understand, Leo, that I'll do anything to protect my family, and my brother will do the same. You of all people ought to know where I'm coming from on that."

"My concern's defending my father, not causing more problems for you."

"That's what I thought. So far I've been keeping out of the way. But if I have to, I'll testify that your father was blackmailing me. He'd gotten hold of that photograph and was accusing me of murder. Maybe he and Russell were working together. You know these criminal partnerships often end badly, especially when one of the partners decides to testify against the other. And I'll also testify that your father threatened Russell, according to what he told me."

"So it's Gary Coles all over again."

Eric picked up the beer I'd left on the counter and poured it in the sink. "You want a shot at me, then take it in court. Or call the police tonight. We can even call them now, together. I've spent enough sleepless nights wondering whether there's really a body in George's freezer. I'm ready to bet that the whole thing was a lie, cooked up by Lucy and Russell to shake me down, then picked up on by your father. She wasn't Lucy anymore, you know, not when I met her. To her, that person had ceased to exist." Again, he seemed on the verge of rationalizing her death. "You'll have egg on your face, and I'll be safe on the road to the state assembly or the governor's mansion, and I'll be done with people like you and your father forever."

He stared me down, his uncertainty betrayed by a twitch of the eyelid.

"I'll see you in court tomorrow," I told him. "Thanks for the beer."

Chapter 18

My phone rang an hour or so later, as I was gazing at my reflection in my office window, trying to summon my mind back from the brink of exhaustion. In an effort to focus my thoughts, I was going over my notes and composing an e-mail to Nina with bullet points, as I'd done every evening during the trial.

I hadn't called the cops about Eric. I'd never intended to, and I could only hope that my visit to him tonight wouldn't backfire. If the DA learned of my visit, it might be portrayed as an improper attempt to influence his testimony, particularly if he called my bluff and there was no body.

I'd begun to question all my assumptions about the case. Despite all that I'd learned, I felt that we were no closer to pinning down Russell Bell's killer. Instead of answers, I'd only succeeded in broadening the field of questions. For a defense attorney, that typically was good enough, but I wasn't looking at the situation as a defense lawyer might. I needed to know who killed Bell. The ringing phone jarred me back to the moment.

"Hey," Jeanie said when I answered. "I'm at your brother's."

Because neither my father nor Teddy could be there, Jeanie had been playing the role of surrogate nanny during the trial, checking in on Tamara to see if she needed anything. Debra had planned to be there with her, but a chronic foot problem had flared up two days ago and she hadn't been able to leave home.

"I only meant to stop by for a few minutes. I'm sitting outside in my car."

"What's going on?"

"Carly and Tamara are both sick, and Tam hasn't been keeping up her baby log. The baby's been having diarrhea. Tam says she nursed earlier, but it's not in the log. You know how she is, Leo. She'll never admit she can't remember. Your dad's here, and he's freaking out. He thinks Carly needs to be in the ER."

"What do you think?"

"If your father hadn't been here, I'd have just thought she was sick. Do I think she needs to go to the ER tonight, as opposed to waiting until the pediatrician's office opens tomorrow? I don't know."

"Great. How am I supposed to know if you don't?"

"Leo, I don't want to be in the middle of this. Teddy's no help. I know you're in trial, but you really need to be here."

"Fine," I told her, realizing there was no other choice. "I'm on my way."

I sent an e-mail to Nina letting her know I'd be out of pocket for a while. Half an hour later I pulled up in front of Teddy's house. I heard the baby crying from outside. Jeanie and Tamara were in the front room. Tamara was trying to nurse the baby, but Carly wasn't having any of it. Her skin looked yellowish. As I entered, Tamara thrust Carly at Jeanie and hurried to the bathroom.

"Some intestinal thing," Jeanie said. "Carly seems to have it worse than Tam does."

In the kitchen Teddy sat propped on a stool. Our father was pacing. "Leo," he said, turning to me as I came in. "God knows

I'm not trying to step on Tam's toes. I'm just concerned about the child."

Teddy wouldn't meet my eyes.

"She was having diarrhea earlier, judging by the state of the diaper pail, but now she's stopped," Lawrence continued. "That's a very bad sign."

I turned to Teddy. "Do you agree?"

He nodded. I could see how hard it was for him to admit that something had gone wrong. "Tam and the baby started feeling sick last night. Debra was supposed to be here but she couldn't come. We put a call into the doctor's after-hours line. They say take her in."

"Then what are we waiting for?"

Teddy went out into the other room to talk to Tam. My father and I waited in the kitchen. After a moment Jeanie came in. "We're going. You and I just need to get the baby's car seat installed. We can put it in my car, I guess." Teddy and Tamara didn't own a vehicle.

It was in the corner of the kitchen. In the front room Teddy and Tamara sat on the couch, Teddy's arm around his wife, her head on his shoulder, the baby in Tam's arms, Teddy talking in a low voice while Carly snuffled and cried. I carried the car seat out to Jeanie's Prius.

"Sounds from the papers like Nina's doing okay," Jeanie said as we worked to fit the car seat into the back.

"We had Shanahan on the stand today." I summarized his testimony. "Nina sounds good when she's working on him, but we don't have any hard evidence. It all happened twenty-one years ago. So basically it's Nina trying to poke holes in Shanahan's investigation, and then you've got this snitch Russell Bell in the mix. It's going to come down to which side the jury believes."

"Meaning your dad's testimony is crucial. He testifies when?"

"Likely tomorrow. Depends on whether the state plans to call more witnesses."

"That would explain why he's so hot to stir up trouble tonight."

Teddy and Tamara came out, Teddy carrying the baby. Our father took Tamara by the elbows and tried to speak to her, looking her in the face, making some apology for whatever tense exchange had passed between them before I arrived. Without seeming to hear him, she pressed her palm to his cheek, then turned and got in back beside the baby. Teddy sat in the passenger seat beside Jeanie. Lawrence and I followed in my truck.

At Children's, time slowed to a crawl. I tried to talk our father into letting me drive him home. "I'm staying until we know she's all right," he said, though it was obvious to me, to Jeanie, to everyone that Carly was just dehydrated, that she was going to be fine. Or so we kept telling ourselves. Sitting in the waiting area, I found myself flashing back to those weeks when Teddy had lain between life and death.

It was nearly 1:00 AM before they had Carly hooked up to an IV in the triage area. Teddy and Tamara were back there with her, my father and Jeanie and I slumped in the waiting room chairs, surrounded by anxious families whose children were probably in far worse shape than Carly. Around 3:00 AM, the doctors made the decision to keep her overnight, having diagnosed her with severe dehydration due to an intestinal bug and diarrhea.

We'd done the right thing by bringing her in, they assured Teddy and Tamara. Another six hours and her kidneys might have been damaged. Hearing this secondhand from Teddy when he came out to tell us that Carly was fine and we should head home, my father seemed to draw himself up straighter. Teddy pumped his hand.

I told my father that he might as well stay at my place rather than make the drive back to San Rafael. He and I made it home around 4:00 AM.

~ ~ ~

In the morning, over Nina's objection, the state called a physician from the medical examiner's office to interpret the old medical examiner's report and testify to the cause of death, establishing beyond a doubt that a homicide had occurred. In her cross-examination, Nina sought to establish that Caroline had been raped, and that the unknown rapist was the source of the semen in Caroline's body, but the witness wouldn't go where Nina wanted to go, insisting repeatedly that the evidence of forced sex was nonconclusive.

"In other words, you can't rule out that the physical evidence withheld from the defense in the first trial was left by someone who raped Mrs. Maxwell and then murdered her, correct?" Nina said, settling for what she could get.

"Can't rule it out, and can't testify that it happened, either," the doctor said. "I will say that if this were a rape prosecution, the fact of nonconsensual sex would have to be established in some way other than through the physical evidence."

In the end, Nina had to sit down, clearly frustrated at getting nowhere with this witness. This was the first tactical error of the trial. In a classic defense lawyer's gamble, Nina had counted on being able to use the various injuries detailed in the autopsy report to develop evidence of rape through the DA's own witness, so we hadn't retained an expert of our own. This gamble had failed.

After the medical examiner, Crowder rested without calling Eric Gainer or any other witness. Sitting in the gallery, I felt little relief, knowing that the danger of Eric's testimony had only receded, not disappeared. Nina made a motion for a verdict of acquittal, a pro forma move at this point. Judge Liu denied it, as judges almost always did.

"The defense calls Lawrence Maxwell," Nina said, and any suspense regarding whether my father would testify was dissolved.

Lawrence wore a gray suit over a white shirt and red tie. His mustache was trimmed, his hair wet combed. When he raised his hand to take the oath, the suit coat lifted like an awning across his shoulders. He'd never gone to bed last night. This morning I'd found him on the balcony of my condo with a full ashtray beside him, another cigarette going between his fingers.

"Mr. Maxwell, I'd like to bring you back to June twentieth, nineteen eighty-three."

They walked through it, sticking closely to his testimony from the earlier trial, establishing Lawrence's explanation of his whereabouts that day and his claim of innocence. He spoke without emotion of his shock upon learning of the murder, and when prompted by Nina, he denied killing Caroline.

Under further questioning, Lawrence admitted that at the time of Caroline's death, their marriage hadn't been right for a long time, that she'd often seemed consumed by frustration, and that their arguments had occasionally turned physical. "At the time of her death, were you aware of your wife having an affair?"

"No. It wasn't until just a few years ago that I learned that."

"How did you discover this?"

"My older son, Teddy, was acting as my lawyer, trying to get me a new trial. This one. He's the one who found the pictures that the man's wife had taken of them together. Good for her, I thought when he showed them to me. I'm glad she had someone. God knows I wasn't bringing any joy to her life."

Again I had the sense of my mother as still present for him in a way she was for no one else. The way he spoke of her, it was as if they'd parted a few minutes before, as if he expected to see her again soon. Dot, beside me, looked as wan as if she hadn't slept at all last night. She'd barely spoken to Lawrence this morning, arriving in court rather than meeting us at Nina's office. I didn't know if he'd made any effort to explain his absence last night. Watching Lawrence, I had the sense that the ghost of Caroline, my mother, having grown stronger day by day throughout the trial, had finally stepped forward and pushed her replacement and rival aside.

He didn't love her, I realized—not the way he'd loved Caroline. Their marriage, coldly anatomized here, had been a burning thing, flaming out in murder. His engagement to Dot, by contrast, was tepid, provisional. He'd been avoiding her not because he was afraid of being convicted, but because with each passing day of the trial he was delving deeper into the past, which, for all its horrific consequences, he somehow preferred to the present. Now, when at last he'd taken the stand, the more powerful hold Caroline had on him must be obvious to Dot.

Nina moved on quickly. "Did you ever make any comment that any other person could interpret as a confession that you murdered your wife?"

"No," Lawrence said. "From the day I was arrested, I've been telling anyone who'd listen that I didn't do this."

"Did you ever tell Russell Bell or anyone else, 'It's a terrible thing but it had to be done'?"

"No. I would never have said anything like that."

"How about that your only regret was that your son was the one who found her?"

His eyes found me in the gallery. "I never said that to Russell Bell or to anyone."

She next had him talk about Bell, recounting how he'd written the brief that had gotten Bell out of prison. Lawrence testified that at one point he'd considered him a friend, but that his feelings toward Bell had changed. "When I got out of prison, I called Russell," Lawrence said. "I knew he'd done well since his release, and he owed his freedom to me. He was working for a San Francisco city supervisor, Eric Gainer. I thought he might give me a lead on a job, but the third or fourth time I talked to him, he told me something I wish to God I hadn't heard."

Nina paused. This wasn't in their script. However, she had no choice but to go on. "What did he tell you?"

Lawrence spoke softly. "The girl he'd raped, the one who was fourteen when he grabbed her off the street, the one he went to prison for. He said that he'd had her again and that it was even better this time than it had been the first time."

My surprise was followed by a surge that I recognized as an instinctive reaction to the truth. I hadn't shared with my father what I'd learned from Sherrie and Eric. The only question was why Lawrence hadn't told me this before.

Crowder was on her feet, crying, "Objection. Hearsay, the stipulation. Move to strike this testimony from the record and instruct the jurors to disregard."

"We'll take a fifteen-minute recess," Liu said, his thoughtful tone giving nothing away. He asked the deputy to clear the courtroom. As the jurors filed out, Nina shot me an urgent question of a look. I nodded to her, trying to convey confidence, but she just looked angry, like I'd conspired with Lawrence to sandbag her. I couldn't ask him about this now, as court rules forbade any communication with a witness while he was still on the stand. I couldn't meet the eyes of Teddy or Dot. Each of us sat staring straight ahead, trying not to betray fear or any other emotion. But if we got through this with Lawrence's credibility intact, then we'd have the missing piece of our defense, Bell's motivation to lie.

It was a mystery and a shame that we hadn't had this piece of the puzzle before.

"I don't need to linger over the hearsay objection," Liu said when the jurors were out of the courtroom. "I presume that the defense doesn't necessarily intend the jurors to consider these statements for their truth. My bigger concern is where this line of questioning leaves the agreement we made before trial."

Nina took a breath like someone about to dive into cold water. "The district attorney violated the agreement first," she said. "Yesterday, Detective Shanahan testified that Russell Bell feared for his life, that he was afraid of being a witness, and that Mr. Maxwell had carried out reprisals in the past. All through Ms. Crowder's examination, the state and its only witness pointedly referred to Mr. Bell in the past tense. In making the agreement, I trusted that the state wouldn't resort to the kind of innuendo we've heard. We need a certain leeway to repair the damage."

Crowder blew up. "What innuendo? The reason we're using the past tense is because the conversations we've been discussing occurred in the past. We're supposed to use the present tense? Bell says this, he says that?"

"So you made a bad deal and now you want out," Liu said to Nina.

"We have to be allowed to mount a defense. *This* is our defense."

Crowder said, "They're doing exactly what you said they couldn't do. Trying to take advantage of Bell's absence from this trial. This testimony has clearly been invented. Clearly, he knows Bell can't come into court and contradict what he says. He's broken the agreement by taking advantage of the fact that we can't put Bell on the stand. We need to be able to ask him about the murder on cross-exam."

"It does seem to me that you've opened that door," Liu said to Nina. "Let me ask this. Do you intend to continue in this vein?"

Nina punted. "That depends on Your Honor's ruling as to whether the agreement is still in force. As I've said, we need a certain amount of leeway so that we can develop Bell's motive to invent the confession. We need some room to maneuver here."

"I'll let you choose. Either I can shut you down, command the jury to disregard this testimony, and hope for the best, though we all know there's no unringing the bell. Or I can rule that you violated the agreement, meaning the door's now open for Ms. Crowder to cross-examine your client about Russell Bell's death. Pick your poison. You're the one who crossed the line, Ms. Schuyler, so I'll leave the choice to you."

Nina glanced at Lawrence, still sitting in the witness stand, clearly wanting to pull him aside, but knowing that the judge would allow no private consultation. Lawrence nodded to her, and she took a sharp breath of frustration, then turned toward Liu again.

Crowder didn't know to quit when she was ahead. "They made a deal but they never meant to abide by it. You ruled that this wasn't going to be a surrogate trial. Now, evidently, it is, and that's what they've been planning all along. We're not prepared to try Mr. Maxwell for a murder he isn't charged with."

"That's your own fault, though, isn't it?" Liu said, turning his frustration from Nina back to Crowder. "You had every opportunity to charge him, if you'd had the evidence. Now you're claiming you could have had more evidence with more warning? Well, I don't see any indication that there's any evidence to be had."

"I don't believe we've violated the agreement," Nina said. "The issue of what Russell Bell told my client isn't a topic that we addressed before trial. If you're going to let them talk about Russell Bell's murder, then we'll renew our motion in limine and ask for a mistrial, because I don't think there's been a proper foundation laid for the accusation that my client was involved in procuring Bell's death."

Liu pondered this, frowning toward the back of the courtroom. "I'm going to give you latitude to conduct a limited cross-examination, Ms. Crowder. I agree with the defense that the state hasn't laid the groundwork to accuse Mr. Maxwell of murdering Bell. I'll allow you to establish that Bell is deceased and that his death is the reason he isn't here in court, so that the jurors realize that Bell can't contradict anything Maxwell says. However, if the state implies that Maxwell was somehow involved in Bell's death, I'm going to favorably entertain a motion for a mistrial."

"In that case, Your Honor, we request a day's recess to further prepare for cross-examination on this subject." Crowder's voice was subdued. "We've kept to the agreement in good faith and assumed that the defense would do the same. We've been sandbagged."

"Denied," Liu said. "We're still on the record. Let me just observe that the defendant, through counsel, attempted to take advantage of Russell Bell's death to introduce statements not addressed in our agreement before trial. The defense's characterization of the state's direct examination of Detective Shanahan is unfounded; there was no improper innuendo. The use of the past tense was appropriate, given that these conversations occurred in the past. Even so, I'm going to allow the defense to withdraw from the agreement. I'm also going to allow latitude to the prosecution to introduce Bell's death on cross-exam. Just so the record is clear, the trial is taking this turn because of the actions of the defendant and his counsel."

Nina accepted this abuse stony faced. Never put your head in the lion's mouth, I thought. With this speech, Liu was sending a message in a bottle to the appeals court, making sure that we wouldn't be able to point to the unfair effect of any testimony relating to Bell's death as grounds for overturning a guilty verdict.

With the jurors back in their places a few minutes later, Nina returned to the podium. "Mr. Maxwell, before the break, you testified that Russell Bell told you that he'd 'had her again' and that it was even better than it had been the first time around. Did Bell explain to you what he meant by this statement?"

"Those are the words he used. He knew that I knew he was guilty of the crime he was in for, which was kidnapping a fourteen-year-old girl off the street in San Francisco, holding her captive, and raping her for three days. He'd told me as much while we were still inside. He wanted to gloat, I guess, show me how he'd beaten the system. He was an evil man, Ms. Schuyler."

The courtroom was still, the jurors frowning, staring at my father. It was impossible for me to gauge whether they were buying his story, whether they believed him or not. Every word from my father's mouth fell now with the impact of stone on glass.

Nina was working without a net, feeling her way forward, but it was crucial that she not betray her discomfort to the jurors. They had to believe this was all part of the script, not the monumental fuckup I knew it was. I alone knew that Nina had no idea what was coming next. "Did Russell tell you that he'd killed this woman?" she asked with apparent confidence.

"No," my father said. "He just told me that he'd had her. I took that to mean that he'd tracked down the victim of the first crime and had sex with her, probably raped her again. That was all he said. Then he laughed, told me I couldn't repeat it to anyone, because I was his lawyer and anything he told me was privileged."

At the DA's table Crowder sat shaking her head, making notes on a legal pad, trying to keep up but clearly not equal to the torrent of perjury she believed my father was unleashing against her prosecution. Sitting in the gallery, I felt myself shrinking into a cold dead center the size of a pea, wanting to beg with him to quit while he was ahead, just play it straight and stick to the script.

Nina kept her equilibrium. "And how did you react to that?"

"I said no way. I'm not a lawyer anymore. I told him that I was going to go to the police and tell them everything he'd told me. The police and his employer. That being Supervisor Gainer."

"And what did he do then?"

"He tried to backtrack, carry it off like he'd only been joking. I guess it must have been that very day that he contacted Detective Shanahan. Beat me to the punch."

"Did you ever share with the police what Russell Bell told you?"

"No. I didn't think they'd believe me. Not with a case hanging over my head. Also, I was afraid how Russell might react, that I might end up with a bullet in me." This last comment, again out of the script, addressed toward the DA's table, where Shanahan returned Lawrence's look dead eyed. "I had enough problems."

My heart sank. By implying that Bell would have put a bullet in him if Lawrence had gone to the police, he'd opened the door for

Crowder to suggest that this was precisely what had happened to Bell after Bell went to the police about Lawrence. Even if Crowder didn't spot the opportunity, Lawrence had done her work for her, planted a seed in the jurors' minds that would inevitably germinate into suspicion once they learned of Bell's death, as in a moment they would.

That one comment made it much more difficult for us to keep Russell Bell's murder out of this case, as Nina couldn't simply trust the jurors not to speculate about why Bell wasn't here and about Lawrence's possible involvement. She had to draw the sting.

With an impressive lack of reaction to Lawrence's blunder, Nina said, "How do you feel now about not coming forward immediately with what Russell told you?"

My father's voice caught. "I regret it very much."

"When was the last time you saw Russell Bell?"

"About a month and a half ago. He was lying dead in his coffin."

"Between your release from prison and Bell's death, did you ever see him in person?"

"No. We just talked on the phone."

Nina flipped through her notes one last time, then turned toward the district attorney. "Your witness," she said to Crowder.

My father swallowed, his eyes taking on a glazed look. His surprise testimony had opened new opportunities for the prosecution and exposed him to tremendous risks.

And now Nina could no longer protect him.

Chapter 19

Standing with her hands braced on the podium, Crowder glared at Lawrence. With each second, the silence in the courtroom grew more charged. Finally, under the strain, my father did what she wanted him to do, what her look was calculated to achieve. He smiled.

"Is something funny, Mr. Maxwell?"

He didn't answer, and the look was on her face again, her eyeballs popping. My father's jaw trembled. Crowder said, "You're smiling because Russell Bell is dead and he can't testify against you, correct?"

"I'm not smiling," Lawrence said.

"You're smiling because Russell Bell is dead and he can't testify against you, correct?"

"That's not true."

Crowder came at him from a slightly different direction. "It must have been very satisfying for you, seeing him dead in that funeral home."

Lawrence leaned forward. "Ms. Crowder, I take offense."

"Before Russell Bell's death, you'd learned that he was going to testify against you?"

"Correct."

"How did you learn that Bell was going to be a witness against you in this case?"

"I guessed."

"You *guessed*?"

Nina stood, making a brazen effort to answer the question on Lawrence's behalf. "Your Honor, I need to advise my client not to answer any question that requires him to divulge what I may have told him. Conversations with his lawyer are privileged."

Crowder turned the look on Nina. Ignoring Nina's transgression, Liu simply instructed Lawrence to answer but not to divulge any confidential conversations.

"I learned that the DA had an informant. We didn't have the name but I guessed who it was. It was immediately obvious to me that Russell had invented the confession."

"You knew this even before your preliminary hearing in this matter?"

"I guessed that Russell was the informant before the hearing. That's right."

"In fact, you even had your investigator serve Mr. Bell with a subpoena."

"I wanted him to testify," Lawrence said. "I wanted him to tell his lies to my face."

"In any event, you never saw him again before his death, and by the time you viewed him dead in his coffin in the funeral home, you knew that he wasn't going to testify against you at this trial as he'd planned."

"Obviously. He was dead."

"Dead men don't tell tales. Isn't that right?"

Nina objected, and Crowder withdrew the question. Instead she asked, "You were relieved that Russell Bell could no longer testify in this trial because he was dead, correct?"

"To tell you the truth, I'd rather have had him here in court so that my lawyer could cross-examine him, so that the jurors could see for themselves that he's a liar."

Crowder went to the jury box, standing just a few feet from the nearest juror, her elbow resting on the rail. "You would agree with me, then, that these jurors are capable of deciding that a witness is a liar and that his testimony should be ignored?"

"I'd agree with that." Lawrence risked a quick glance at the jury.

"Let me ask you this, Mr. Maxwell. Believing in this jury's ability to detect a liar, how can you dare come into this courtroom, sit there before this jury, and tell such shameless lies?" Crowder had turned to face him.

Lawrence's voice rose in anger but he mastered it. "I didn't kill my wife and I never told Russell that I had. I don't know how to answer you other than to keep repeating that."

"And you know that with Russell Bell dead, all I can do to discredit what you call the truth is to stand up here and keep calling you a liar, correct?"

"You can call me whatever you want."

"Are you claiming that there was some other witness, someone else present during these conversations that you say you had with Bell?"

"Just him and me."

"So whatever you say he told you, you expect the jury to believe it because Russell Bell is dead and won't be able to testify for himself and contradict you, isn't that right?"

"They'll believe the truth," Lawrence said. "I hope."

Nina rose and objected to this line of questioning as "harassing."

"You've made your point," Liu told Crowder. "Move on."

Crowder returned to the podium. "Just to be clear, you claim that you never confessed to Russell Bell that you murdered your wife. You also claim that he frankly disclosed that he'd had some kind of sexual relations with the victim of the crime he'd been in prison for, that he told you he'd 'had her again.' Is that right?"

"Yes."

"And you never did go to the police? Today in court is the first time you've revealed these allegations to anyone?" *Including your lawyer,* was the unspoken import of her question. Crowder, at least, must have picked up on Nina's surprise.

He tried to hold his ground, but he was slipping back before Crowder's onslaught. I risked a glance at the jurors and saw they didn't mind her being so rough with him. "When your office decided to reprosecute me for a crime from twenty-one years ago that I didn't commit, that I'd already done twenty-one years of prison time for, I decided that I had enough problems, like I said."

"And just to be clear, there's no other witness to any of these conversations you've testified about?"

"Asked and answered," Nina objected.

"No other witnesses," Lawrence admitted.

"And you also claim that Russell Bell confessed to you when the two of you were in prison together, just as he claimed you confessed to him?"

"He was guilty and he told me as much. That's the difference between him and me."

"And you had no moral qualms about helping to free a man whom you knew to be guilty?"

"Guilty or not, he was entitled to a new trial. It was the state that set him free when Eric Gainer refused to testify in the retrial and your office decided not to retry him."

Again I winced at Lawrence's efforts to outsmart Crowder. She was leading him down a treacherous path that ended at the door he'd opened. Again, I could only hope he saw the danger. "When you heard that the state had decided not to reprosecute Mr. Bell, did you offer to come forward as a witness, seeing how, as you now claim, he'd 'all but confessed' to you?"

"Do you know what happens to inmates who offer to testify against other inmates, Ms. Crowder?"

"Oh, I do, Mr. Maxwell. I'm quite familiar with what happens to snitches. Usually, they turn up dead."

My father paled, realizing the blunder he'd made. "That happens."

"Isn't it known as the code of silence, what you just referenced?"

I saw by the tension in Nina's shoulders that she wanted to object and shut down this line of questioning, but she didn't dare—for fear of calling attention to the implication that Russell Bell had met the fate reserved for snitches behind bars.

"That might be the term you use for it. I've never put much stock in it."

"And even after you got out of prison, you didn't come forward and offer to testify against Mr. Bell, did you?"

"No," Lawrence said.

"That's because you were afraid of what would happen to you if you broke the code, if you snitched on Bell?"

"Like I said, I had problems of my own."

"You were afraid that you'd wind up dead if you told the police that Russell Bell confessed to you in prison that he'd done the crime he was in for, correct?"

Finally Nina rose. "Objection!"

"Sustained," Liu said, glowering at Crowder.

It didn't matter. I doubted that there was a single juror who didn't understand by now that Angela Crowder blamed my father for Russell Bell's death.

Crowder had scored plenty of points, and she hadn't even gotten to the crime my father was on trial for. "You also claim that you had no knowledge of your wife's affair until just a few years ago. Do I have that right?"

"Yes."

Crowder now launched into an exhumation of my parents' failed marriage, retracing my father's testimony from the first trial, when he'd been forced to admit numerous incidents of domestic violence, including a few occasions when Caroline had accused him of threatening her life. Seeking to paint him as a jealous, abusive husband, Crowder succeeded.

"And you never had any argument with her after you discovered her affair, isn't that what you claim?"

"I never discovered it. I told you. I didn't know a thing about it until I saw those pictures my son, Theodore Maxwell, an attorney, uncovered just a few years ago, long after she was dead."

"Then you claim you didn't unexpectedly come home late one morning or early in the afternoon and find evidence that she'd been with another man?"

"No."

"You claim you didn't beat her to death with your son's baseball bat and leave her for the boy to find when he came home from school?"

"No."

Crowder fixed him with that look of hers again. "And you expect this jury to believe you because none of these people, not your wife, not Russell Bell, none of them can come into court here today and say that you're lying. Isn't that true? Because they're all dead?"

"I'm telling the truth."

Again she shot him the look. Five seconds, ten seconds, fifteen. Beside me, Dot seemed to be holding her breath. Finally Crowder turned her back on Lawrence as she moved toward the DA's table. "No further questions."

~ ~ ~

As soon as the five of us were alone in the witness room Nina's composure cracked and she let loose. "What the hell was that?"

"The truth," Dot answered for Lawrence.

I cringed, seeing Nina's sights settle on Dot, who stood behind my father with her hands protectively on his shoulders, like she didn't intend to let him out of her grasp now that he'd been released from his harrowing confrontation with Crowder. Dot returned her stare, clearly prepared to have it out if that's what Nina wanted, seeming even to relish the fight. Teddy sat at the head of the table staring at his folded hands.

"I'm supposed to know the truth before it comes out of my client's mouth for the first time when he's on the witness stand. That's a pretty basic rule of trial preparation." Nina's gaze shifted to me, making it clear whom, ultimately, she held responsible for this failure. I'd been the one charged with preparing my father for his testimony, after all, and for telling Nina what she needed to know. "Why didn't I know about this conversation? It changes our entire defense."

All I could tell her was that I was sorry, but sorry wasn't good enough. If we lost the trial, fault was now established. The loss would be on my shoulders, for having failed to elicit this crucial information from my father before now. Seeing that no explanation was forthcoming, Nina looked again at my father. "You better not have perjured yourself." My father and Dot started to speak at the same time, but Nina cut them both off. "I don't want to hear another word. I don't have time. I need to go back out there and try to pick up the pieces. But if any of you ever does something like that to me again—" She broke off, her eyes on me. "Well," she said, turning away. "You're not going to have the chance. Your father can find a new lawyer to defend him when they charge him with Russell Bell's murder."

She went out, leaving a heavy silence in her wake. "I'm sorry, son," my father said after a moment. "I didn't mean to screw things up between the two of you. You're not a mind reader. There's no way for you to have known about this. I didn't tell you."

I couldn't meet his eyes. "You should have told me," I said. "You should have just told me from the beginning what he said to you."

"I thought you'd blame me for not coming forward sooner," Lawrence answered. "And, to be honest, I thought you wouldn't believe me. You never asked, and you seemed to be making a point of not asking. I didn't want to tie your hands."

"The surprise is what she's pissed about," Teddy said.

"She's one that likes it all to go according to *her* plan," Dot said.

"She's a fine lawyer," I told her. "She's doing a damned good job, and it's not her fault that she just got sandbagged by her own client. If you had any other lawyer, if it had been me, the case would have been lost, because the jurors would have seen that the lawyer was surprised and concluded that the defendant must have been lying. But Nina, she didn't flinch."

"He's right," Lawrence said, reaching up to lay his hand on Dot's. "If we lose, it's not going to be her fault, and it sure as hell isn't going to be Leo's. It'll be mine."

Dot's face crumpled, and she turned, overcome by a mixture of fury and grief, and pushed through the door. Lawrence nodded to me and calmly went out after her, leaving Teddy and me in the witness room to wait for his testimony to be called. Once the absolute master of the courtroom, Teddy now seemed paralyzed with fear. His voice was slurred, halting, as it had been during the first few years after his injury. "Jesus, my whole leg feels dead," he said, rubbing his thigh. At moments of stress, the physical symptoms of his injuries reappeared.

"It's just a matter of listening to the questions and answering them. The jurors either believed Dad or they didn't. Nothing you say is going to tip the balance."

"There was a time when I could have carried a case like this on my shoulders."

"You'll do fine. It's not going to be on you."

"How do you think it's going?"

I saw that he truly had no idea. "You've heard everything I've heard." I didn't want to say what I feared. The judge would later instruct the jurors that if they thought a witness had lied about an important fact, they were free to disregard all of his testimony. If the jurors thought Dad was lying about his phone conversations with Russell, it seemed likely to me that they would also assume he was lying about his ignorance of Caroline's affair, about not having killed her, about not confessing later to Russell. About everything.

"You know, I've been sitting there through the trial, watching Nina, trying to convince myself I could do this again. Try jury cases."

I hesitated, considering my response. "It's remarkable to me that you're even in a position to think of being back in that chair."

"How could I not? You've got a lifetime of trials ahead of you. I'd like to have just one of mine back."

I'd taken for granted that Teddy's role in our practice would be behind the scenes, that he had no aspiration to return to the courtroom. I'd assumed that he would have realized what was obvious to everyone else: that his days as a trial lawyer ended when he caught that bullet.

Clearly, I'd been wrong.

"Back then, there was no room in your life for anything else. You couldn't keep a marriage going. You had no time for a family. You're a lawyer again. You've got Carly and Tam. That's what counts."

"It's just that Dad keeps looking to me like I should know what to do, and I can't tell him anything." He glanced up at me, lines of strain around his eyes. "Do you think he was lying about Russell telling him he'd had sex with that girl again?"

This was a question the old Teddy would never have asked, a question that perhaps would never have occurred to him, though it certainly had occurred to Nina—and to me. And even if the question had entered his mind, the answer wouldn't have mattered as long as it fit in with his strategy in the case.

"I hope not. None of us told him to get up there and invent conversations. But what can we do?" I felt a pang, because hadn't I made a point of reminding Lawrence that he was the only one who knew what he and Bell might have discussed during those phone calls? I hadn't advised him to lie, I told myself. I'd only been pointing out the obvious fact that no one but Lawrence knew what had been said.

The door between the witness room and the courtroom opened. The deputy looked in and nodded to Teddy. It was time.

I went through the other door to the public hallway and came in the back of the courtroom, taking my seat just as Nina started Teddy's examination. It was his first appearance in front of a jury in over five years. The contrast between his newly shrunken demeanor and his former outsize presence couldn't have been starker.

Teddy had once owned this place. Now his brow shone with perspiration. He'd decided that he needed his cane to cross the distance between the witness room and the witness stand. Once seated, he kept dropping it and picking it back up. The point of his testimony was to draw the jury's attention to the old pictures of my mother and her lover and recap his investigation, including the documents exposing Gary Coles's misconduct. Though Teddy had viewed these documents many times during the past few weeks, he had difficulty recognizing them now.

Nina had to lead him, drawing objection after objection from Crowder for using suggestive questioning to elicit the answers we'd rehearsed. With prompting, he managed to describe how, after he'd uncovered evidence pointing to Keith Locke as the killer, he'd been shot in the head while eating lunch at a restaurant near city hall. Nina then introduced the certified copy of Keith Locke's court file showing that he'd pled guilty to this crime.

On cross-examination, Crowder handled Teddy like someone afflicted with a mental infirmity. And Teddy's anger made him into the imbecile that Crowder wanted the jurors to see. Coming at him like a defense attorney, she easily established that his case against Keith Locke was founded on speculation. Then, to my surprise, she moved in on the shooting itself. I'd have thought it was beyond dispute that Keith Locke had pulled the trigger, but she made Teddy admit that he had no memory of the event, that no witness in the restaurant had been able to identify his would-be killer, and that Keith Locke had never confessed.

Locke had several other charges pending against him at the time of his guilty plea, and Teddy had no choice but to concede that defendants sometimes pleaded guilty to crimes they didn't commit.

After Crowder sat down, I was startled to see Nina rise again. "Have you ever been in a courtroom with Ms. Crowder before?"

"I tried about a dozen jury cases against her. Won more than half of them. In about half the others, the jury hung."

"Do you have any opinion about whether or not Ms. Crowder resented your numerous victories?"

"Sure. She's enjoying this a little too much. It shouldn't be about me and her, our history."

"How do you know she resented your beating her in court time and again?"

Crowder objected to Nina's leading the witness, and she re-phrased the question, but Teddy had his cue. "She filed a bar complaint against me after the last one. Completely baseless. I don't want to say that it's a ban—" He broke off, then tried again. "Van—"

"Vendetta?"

"That's the word." His face cracked as he tried to smile away his weakness in this place where he'd once showed only strength.

"No further questions."

Crowder had thrown herself back in her chair, considering Teddy with a deprecating smile. She wisely chose not to rise to the bait Nina had thrown down, probably reasoning that any further at-tempt to cross swords with Teddy wasn't worth the effort.

"The witness is excused," Judge Liu said, nodding toward my brother. Next Nina put Car up to plug the holes left by Teddy's testimony. Car was his usual professional self, testifying crisply and competently, filling in with greater detail his efforts to secure the unsullied version of the forensics report from the medical examiner's office. Crowder didn't even bother to cross-examine him.

"Any further witnesses for the defense?" Judge Liu asked when Car had been excused.

"The defense recalls Detective Neil Shanahan."

Chapter 20

Nina came out swinging. "Detective, what was Russell Bell's cause of death?"

Shanahan blinked in surprise, then glanced toward the DA's table. Crowder made as if to rise, then sat back as if realizing that she'd been outfoxed. However, her look of bemusement suggested she didn't see how Nina might take advantage of what ought to have been an extremely damaging fact.

"Obviously, the state has no objection to letting the detective answer that question," Crowder said. "It was the defense that wanted to keep the jury from learning the truth about Bell's death. We've been ready to share the real story with the jury from day one."

"Ms. Crowder, please remember the rule against speaking objections in my courtroom. That goes for nonobjections as well."

Dot leaned close to me and in a throaty whisper asked, "What the hell's she doing?"

Her hand was trembling, I saw. "You need to be ready to testify. The alibi," I whispered back, and she nodded, a scared look on her face. Whatever Nina was thinking, she hadn't shared her plans with me. I could only guess that she'd made a last-second judgment call that my father's errors on the stand this morning allowing the jury to learn of Russell's death meant we could no longer afford to ignore the issue. If we didn't address it, the jurors would no doubt form their own conclusions as to why Bell was dead and why they weren't allowed to know the cause. Even if the jurors hadn't already learned from the news reports saturating the city that my father was suspected of having Bell murdered to keep him from testifying, then the implications of this morning's testimony might easily lead them to draw that inference. Jurors always read the tea leaves and try to guess what the lawyers and judge are concealing from them, I knew, and nothing was more dangerous than the guesses they might make in a situation like this. No, it would be folly for the defense to carry on as if this accusation weren't part of the case. This meant, of course, that we were now defending him from two murders rather than one. Although Nina's demeanor betrayed no hint of her distress, all her carefully laid trial plans were coming unwoven. It was a desperate move at what could only be termed a desperate moment.

Nina thanked the judge for his admonition, then asked Shanahan if he wanted her to have the court reporter read back the question, but he had his answer ready. "The cause of death was homicide by multiple bullets fired from a nine-millimeter semiautomatic pistol while Mr. Bell sat in a car on a dead-end street near Mission Bay. The gun has not been recovered."

"Are you the primary detective working Russell Bell's murder?"

He said he was.

"Did you ask for the case or was it assigned to you?"

"I'd been working with Mr. Bell as a potential witness in this matter. It seemed natural to me that his murder might be connected with his plans to testify here, so I specifically requested the assignment."

"You haven't charged my client in Bell's murder, but even so, from the minute you learned of Russell Bell's death, you believed that my client was responsible, and you've never seriously considered any other suspect, correct?"

"I approach every case with an open mind."

"Your entire investigation into Russell Bell's murder has been premised on the assumption that my client was behind it, though, right? Wasn't that your reason for asking to be assigned the investigation?"

"I was the best investigator to determine whether there was a link or not, based on my having worked closely with the victim to prepare for the testimony we expected him to give in this trial. Testimony he never got a chance to give."

"And you've never seriously considered any other suspect. Isn't that true?"

"You give me a suspect, I'll consider him. So far, none has come to light."

"Well, let's see if we can help you with that, Detective. Does my client have an alibi?"

"Of course he does."

"Where was he at the time of Russell Bell's murder?"

"Supposedly he was with his fiancée, the woman he met while he was in prison, riding motorcycles down Highway One. Just the two of them, if you believe her. No other witnesses."

"You know for a fact that my client couldn't have been the person who pulled the trigger and murdered Russell Bell, correct?"

"Even assuming she's telling the truth, you can be guilty of murder without holding the gun. You see, he got someone to do his dirty work for him. Whether it was a hire job or an associate who owed him a favor, at this point I don't know. But I have my suspicions."

"What evidence do you have to support your belief that my client hired someone to murder Russell Bell?"

"It's an ongoing investigation."

"In fact, you have no clue who pulled the trigger or what connection he might have had to Lawrence Maxwell, correct?"

"At this point, that's correct," Shanahan conceded. "Like I said, this investigation is still active, and we expect further evidence to develop in the coming weeks."

Nina walked him through the details of the shooting, introducing the police reports, the photographs, and the other evidence, getting him to elaborate on his theory that Bell was waiting to meet someone he knew. She was coolly confident, but I was sweating, and I didn't dare look at the jurors. I kept my eyes fixed on my father's back. He sat motionless, staring down at the table. Here was the evidence we'd fought so hard to exclude, the evidence that was supposed to have been so damning, and now Nina was just giving it to them, since Lawrence had forced her hand.

"You met Bell, you worked with him to prepare for his testimony in this case—and as you've said, you must have learned a great deal about him. We went through this before, but remind me. How had he been occupied since his release from prison?"

"I can't say. All I know is that at the time of his murder he was working as a driver for City Supervisor Eric Gainer."

"How do you explain a man just released from prison getting such a job?"

"I would expect that he applied and he was hired, the way anyone gets any job."

"Was being a convicted felon part of the job description?"

"Well, his conviction had been overturned, so technically . . ." Shanahan shrugged. "I don't know."

"Eric Gainer testified in Russell Bell's trial as a key witness. Isn't that true?"

"So I'm told."

"And he's since recanted his testimony and refused to testify in any retrial of Mr. Bell for the abduction and rape of Lucy Rivera, correct?"

"That's my understanding, yes."

"Who told you that Eric Gainer was one of the witnesses in Russell Bell's trial for raping Ms. Rivera? Was it Bell?"

"No, it wasn't."

"He didn't reveal that information to you?"

"He had no reason to. It had nothing to do with his testimony."

"Eric Gainer must have told you that when you interviewed him, then. After Bell's murder, I mean."

"I haven't interviewed Eric Gainer."

She looked surprised. "Isn't it standard procedure to interview the employer of a murdered man?"

"If I believed the employer might have relevant information, yes."

"Did you determine that Eric Gainer had no relevant information to help you identify who murdered Russell Bell?"

Shanahan looked uncomfortable. "No, I didn't."

"Did you make any attempt to interview him in connection with Russell Bell's murder?"

"I left several messages, but we were playing phone tag."

"At some point, were you instructed not to contact Eric Gainer directly?"

Shanahan sucked his cheeks at Nina's guess. "Supervisor Gainer's lawyer told me that contact should go through him."

"So Eric Gainer refused to talk to you without his lawyer present, is that correct?"

Crowder stood. "Objection, Fifth Amendment."

"Eric Gainer's not on trial here," Judge Liu told Crowder with impatience, letting everyone in the courtroom see and hear it. "Overruled."

"That's correct," Shanahan had to answer.

Nina was pushing hard against Eric's warning, which she knew nothing about, but I didn't see any help for it. Our first concern had to be defending my father against these charges. If the state charged him in Russell Bell's death, we would just have to cope with whatever testimony Eric decided to throw at us.

"And am I correct that you didn't take advantage of the opportunity to question him under those circumstances?"

"It would have been futile. His lawyer told me that Gainer wouldn't be speaking to the police on any subject having to do with Mr. Bell's death."

"So Eric Gainer refused to cooperate in your investigation into Russell Bell's death. Is that fair to say?"

"That would be a fair description, yes."

"And he refused to cooperate on the basis of his Fifth Amendment privilege against self-incrimination. Isn't that correct?"

"I don't know what motivated the man."

"Isn't that what the district attorney was referring to with her objection a moment ago? Eric Gainer's right to remain silent and not incriminate himself?"

"I don't know what she was referring to."

"Well, he has that right, doesn't he?"

"He does," Shanahan admitted.

"And he asserted that right and chose to remain silent rather than answer questions from you about Russell Bell's death. Isn't that true?"

"I don't know what was in the man's head."

"Well, you saw the photograph in yesterday's paper, didn't you, Detective?"

Shanahan waited for Crowder's objection, which came promptly. "This is clearly an improper attempt to influence the jury," she said. "Counsel knows perfectly well that it would be misconduct for jurors to read newspaper accounts relating to this trial, and she's trying to get them to do just that. Lawyers have been sanctioned for less."

"That is absolutely correct," Judge Liu said. "I don't presume that defense counsel had any such purpose in mind, but it would certainly be sanctionable conduct if she did. Approach."

Crowder and Nina approached the judge's bench. Nina wanted to ask Shanahan about the picture, I knew, but Liu wasn't having any of it. She made her arguments, first in a whisper, her voice growing more and more heated as Liu shook his head, shook his head again, then drew back and turned away from her in the middle of a sentence. She'd lost the argument, and it was the first time I'd seen her come close to losing her composure during the trial.

It was playacting. What Nina wanted, I guessed, was for the jurors to go home and look at that picture, even though the judge had told them in no uncertain terms that they must not do so. This was wholly improper, but she was arguably within her rights in bringing up the picture during this line of questioning, trying to use it to suggest that Gainer had much to hide. In any case, she must have guessed that a few of the jurors had seen the picture already. And even if they hadn't, and even if they didn't go home and look at it tonight, their imaginations would fill in the gap.

The lawyers returned to their places, and Liu admonished the jury to avoid all media accounts relating to the trial. In this, again, he was playing into Nina's ulterior motive, indirectly suggesting to the jurors that the picture of Eric Gainer in yesterday's paper had something to do with my father's case, giving the impression of another secret for the jurors to ferret out.

"You're certain that my client murdered Russell Bell, but you haven't made any attempt to determine whether anyone else might have had a motive to want Bell dead, have you?"

"I don't know of any motive anyone else might have had." Shanahan turned to address the jury directly, trying to reestablish a rapport and to cut Nina out of the conversation. "Most likely, the defendant put one of his old prison buddies up to murdering Russell Bell, either hired the job with cash or used intimidation to get what he wanted. I understand that the accused was under the protection of a man named Bo Wilder during the latter years of his imprisonment. Mr. Wilder is known to have an extensive criminal empire, and would have the resources to make a hit like this happen on the outside at the drop of a hat. We're in the process of investigating, and we'll soon know how he did it. At that point, he'll be charged in Bell's death."

Nina asked Liu to strike the answer, was unsuccessful, and was forced to rein Shanahan in with a dogged series of questions establishing that he knew of no money changing hands, no contact between Lawrence and Bo Wilder, no evidence that Wilder was involved, and no connection of any sort between Lawrence and the unknown shooter. He also knew of no leverage Lawrence might have held over such an individual, and he'd made no effort to determine whether the shooter, whoever he was, might independently have wished Bell dead.

This done, Nina renewed her attack. "Well, if Eric Gainer didn't remind you about his role as a witness against Russell Bell, who did?"

"The assistant district attorney," Shanahan said, nodding at Crowder.

"Did you at any point learn from the assistant district attorney or anyone else that Eric Gainer had become aware of Russell Bell having forced sexual contact with his former victim?"

Crowder objected. After a moment's thought, Liu let the question stand.

"No," he answered crisply.

"Tell me, Detective. What was the purpose of your discussing Eric Gainer's role in Russell Bell's prosecution with the district attorney?"

"Just gathering background information."

Nina used Shanahan to run through the facts of the old case, getting him to confirm that Eric had been the star witness, the one to identify Bell as the kidnapper. She also established that Gainer had recanted his testimony after Bell's conviction was overturned, resulting in the DA's being unable to retry him.

"You obtained 'background information' about Bell's case from Ms. Crowder because you believed there might be a connection between the murder of Russell Bell and that old case, correct?"

Shanahan hesitated. "You always want to check those things out."

"And what, if anything, did you determine?"

"That there was no connection."

"At any point in your investigation, did you learn that *Eric Gainer* had recently been in contact with Lucy Rivera, the victim in that old case?"

During the break, I'd quickly briefed Nina on the results of my investigation so far. She'd been furious with me for not sharing my discoveries earlier. That she was running with this new information now was an indication of how precarious she believed our defense was.

"I didn't learn anything like that, no."

"So you didn't learn Eric Gainer had been blackmailed regarding Ms. Rivera?"

Shanahan's expression changed to one of repugnance. "No. I never heard that."

Crowder's objection and Shanahan's answer came at the same time, and Judge Liu instructed the jurors to disregard the question. But my theory of our defense to Russell Bell's murder was before the jurors, out in the open at last. So far Nina had done everything she needed to do with this witness. The question was whether it would be enough.

After another strong admonishment from Judge Liu, Nina continued. "Sitting here today, you can't tell me that Eric Gainer hadn't come to regret his decision to recant his former testimony and employ Russell Bell, correct?"

"As I've told you, I wasn't able to speak with him."

"Detective, I want to be crystal clear. You *refuse* to interview Eric Gainer in the presence of his lawyer to see if he might have had a motive to murder Russell Bell."

"That's up to his lawyer," Shanahan said. "I'm ready to go anytime."

"And the reason you haven't insisted on conducting that interview is because you don't want to do anything that might jeopardize your theory that my client, and not Eric Gainer or someone close to him, murdered Russell Bell."

Shanahan didn't answer immediately. Astutely, Nina didn't press, deciding instead to let the question hang in the air unanswered. She was turning toward the defense table without receiving a response when the detective spoke to her back. "I'll ask him one more time to come in for an interview if you want. Is that really what you want, Counselor?"

She froze, seeming to realize that she'd overplayed her hand. She recovered quickly and turned with renewed attack. "Don't you feel it's a little late in the day to propose such a fundamental step in your investigation?"

"No, because it'll be a waste of time."

"You mean because Eric Gainer is likely to assert his Fifth Amendment privilege against self-incrimination and refuse to answer your questions?"

Shanahan saw his mistake, but it was too late to backtrack. "Anything's possible."

"No further questions."

Chapter 21

Nina had succeeded in planting the barest seeds of Eric Gainer's guilt in the jury's mind, but seeds were all they were. After court, we all went back to her office. During the cab ride I didn't try to talk to her about what had happened, seeing by the pained look on her face that consolation, especially from me, would only set her teeth on edge. I wanted to tell her she'd done the only thing she could after my father dropped his bombshell and then stuck his foot in his mouth. But I knew it wouldn't help.

"Can I talk to you?" I said when we arrived at her building. She nodded and we went into her office. She dumped her file box on the desk and began rummaging impatiently inside it, searching for something that seemingly wasn't there. I told her what Eric had said about planning to testify that Russell Bell had told him that my father had threatened and blackmailed him.

She shrugged, obviously furious with me but too preoccupied with the events of today and the challenges of tomorrow to deal with that now. "I'm not going to let this change how I handle Eric, if they call him. As things are going now, Crowder could afford not to call him and still win. I wouldn't risk it, if I were her, especially now that I've tipped my hand about intending to introduce that picture from the paper. So my attitude has to be that we have nothing to lose."

Nina ran through her plan, which was to force Eric to choose whether to shelter behind the Fifth Amendment, or explain the sordid mess Russell Bell had made of the semi-heroic act that had launched his career. "And he'll confess, I'm sure, and then they'll roll the credits."

Teddy was waiting in the conference room for me to drive him back to Berkeley. My father and Dot had already gone. But Teddy could just as easily take the BART home as catch a ride with me. I asked Nina if she wanted me to stay and help her prepare for tomorrow.

"No," she said, her voice becoming a shade warmer than usual. "You've been a tremendous help. I would never have been so well prepared without you. What happened today wasn't your fault. In the heat of the moment, looking for someone to blame, I lashed out at you, but that was wrong of me. You're a fine lawyer, Leo, and I'd gladly try a case with you again. But now we're coming into the final push. You're a cyclist, aren't you? I know a little bit about the sport. At some point in the big races, the support riders peel off, and ultimately the leader has to go on alone. I need to turn my attention to our closing argument, and that's a mountain I'll need to climb without your help. You'd only be a distraction if you stayed. And besides, you need to get Dot ready. We can't forget to put on our alibi witness."

I didn't mind Nina's thinking of me as a distraction. So I got my pickup out of the parking deck and drove Teddy home.

Talking to her, I'd come to realize what I'd suspected all along—that I never again wished to play the role of bystander in a criminal trial. I didn't want my heart rate tracking another lawyer's examinations, the questions I would have asked constantly leaping to my throat. To be fair, her courtroom performance had been first-rate. She'd leapt into openings I'd have missed, and she'd missed few opportunities to turn the state's evidence in our favor. She'd made judgment calls when she'd needed to make them, and I couldn't argue with her attempt to turn Bell's death to our purposes. She'd had to make that bet.

I dropped Teddy at his house. Tamara and the baby had been back there since early afternoon. Jeanie was with them. They'd picked up Chinese takeout, and I shared it with them, eating on the couch in front of the TV. Jeanie wanted to hear how the trial had gone today, but neither Teddy nor I was in any mood to talk about it. When the food was gone, I drove home.

~ ~ ~

I called Dot's number, spoke briefly to my father, then asked him to put Dot on the line. We ran through her brief examination several times. Before today, Nina hadn't planned to call her to testify, but now we had no choice. Nina was dead set against returning my father to the stand and exposing him to another round of cross-examination. That left Dot to testify regarding his whereabouts the morning of the murder. We would also be using her as a character witness, asking her to testify to my father's gentle nature during the time they'd been engaged.

After I finished with Dot, I meant to go to bed early. But then Tanya called around eleven. "You're in luck," she said. "Sherrie was suspicious at first, but I talked her into it. I told her your regular girl was out of town and someone had recommended her. Only the price is going to be eight hundred."

The address Tanya gave me was a six-story apartment building in the Sunset, three blocks from Ocean Beach. When I got there, I went up the steps and punched in the apartment number to the intercom. The door buzzed and I went in.

I took the elevator up. The fourth floor was divided into three apartments, one in front and two in back. The door to the front one was ajar. Light spilled into the hallway.

"I told you not to look for me," a jaded voice said.

She was sitting on a low armchair. The light came from a lamp beside her. Her legs were crossed in fishnets and a short skirt, and she wore a push-up top beneath a denim jacket. Her hair was blond, brushed severely back. She was still beautiful, but I saw the lines of strain that had formed in her cheeks. She was expensively dressed and looked very different from the person I'd driven to Mendocino and back. Unmistakably, however, it was her.

"I'm sorry," I told her. "I know it was a cheap trick, getting you to come here, but I had to see you again."

She glanced around the room. "What you pulled tonight is just what Russell did. She hadn't even heard about him getting out of prison. No one bothered to tell her. So she walked into a trap."

Her stare was intense. At the back of my neck I felt a prickling sensation. Eric had never seen the body, according to what he'd told me. He didn't know which girl had fallen from the railing and which one had survived, which was the victim and which one had set him up. "You're Lucy," an instinct made me say. "You leaked that picture to the paper. Eric thought you were dead, but you're the one who's been blackmailing him."

She uncrossed her legs and leaned back, pressing her arms beneath her small breasts. "Lucy's dead, just like I told you. Russell Bell killed her. That's how it has to be. What did you want to see me for? Not for a fuck, I hope."

I came into the room and sat in the matching armchair next to hers. She put a hand on my leg and leaned over the arm of her chair onto mine. I felt a wave of heat go through me, triggered by the scent of her perfume. It was like she'd flipped a switch; sex was suddenly thick in the air. "Listen to me. I think Jackson Gainer had Russell killed to cover up Lucy's murder. Eric's protecting him." If she hadn't killed Russell, that is. The possibility suddenly presented itself to me, so obvious now that I knew who she was. Because who had a better motive than she did?

"That's because Eric Gainer knows he could never pick up a gun, pump bullets into a man." She sighted along an imaginary gun, pumped the arm four times as if with the effect of a weapon's recoil. "He's the kind that keeps his back turned while others are doing the dirty work."

Everything clicked into place, the possibility becoming more certain. I chose to test it. "I'd love to have seen the look in Russell's eyes when Lucy shot him." My eyes went to the small purse she clutched under her arm. Inside, I guessed, might be the gun that had killed Russell Bell. The key to my father's freedom, if I'd been a cop, and if this new suspicion was correct. My heart raced at the thought that the answer, at last, might be at hand.

She rose, her hand on the purse toying with the zipper, and began to pace the room. She could have the gun out in an instant, if it was in there. "Lucy didn't shoot Bell," she said. "I was going to do it for her, but someone got to him before I did. I guess Jackson decided he'd rather kill him than pay him. I was going to shoot him *after* he got paid, not before." She stopped and turned, her eyes sliding off every surface, flitting away from me. "What would be the point of that?"

She went on, pacing again. "Lucy was like Eric, in a way. She always counted on her friends to be strong for her. But unlike Eric Gainer, she always chose the wrong friends, ones that took advantage of her. This time was no different. I was never Lucy's friend, though I pretended to be. Actually, I hated her. I just hated Russell Bell more."

She stopped before me, looking down as if daring me to contradict her. I supposed the idea was that the repetition of the sexual torture and abuse she'd endured in her childhood had fractured her personality into at least two discordant pieces. Then she'd snapped and given Bell the justice he deserved, a justice that the legal system had been unable or unwilling to deliver. Maybe that's what had happened. The trouble was I couldn't read her. I was no psychologist, but I was under the impression that science had debunked the idea that any such thing as multiple personality disorder truly existed outside the sufferer's imagination.

I held up my hands. "You want Gainer. Right now you're biding your time, but the chance you're waiting for isn't going to come. He's surrounded by lawyers. They've got their stories matched. Eric thinks he's protecting Jackson and Jackson's protecting him. Right now, the element of surprise is on your side. According to Eric, Russell told him that he stashed the body in the freezer downstairs at Chen's house. Eric doesn't know the body isn't yours."

She turned midpace and stared at me with dawning comprehension. "You're trying to set me up. Your father's on trial for murder and you want me to confess to something I didn't do, so that you can blame me instead of him."

"No," I told her. "I haven't been able to put the right kind of pressure on Gainer. Moral pressure, I mean. That's the only kind a man like Eric is susceptible to. Russell killed you, he thinks, and he's convinced that Jackson killed Russell. If you surprised him, you could put the right kind of pressure on him, get him to tell the truth about what he thinks Jackson did. If he did that, then my father would be off the hook. And so would Lucy."

"Moral pressure? Eric Gainer? Are you kidding me? The man doesn't have a moral bone in his body. And your father's the son of a bitch who got Russell out of prison."

She was working herself up to something.

"I'm sorry to trouble you," I said, seeing the danger I was in. I needed to cut this short now and get out of there.

"I wish you *were* sorry." Her hand was still on the bag's zipper.

"I'm going," I said, moving toward the door, not turning my back to her. Then I was through it, and I let out my held breath.

I didn't wait for the elevator, but hurried down the stairs two at a time and out to the street. When I looked up, she was at the window, staring down.

I was home after two, and slightly closer to an answer than I'd been before tonight, now that I knew that Lucy Rivera was alive. What I didn't know was whether she'd killed Russell or merely been victimized by him again. Rather than go over and over in my mind what I'd just seen and heard, I spent the hours between 2:00 and 4:00 AM in front of my computer trying to focus on making an outline for Nina to rely on in her examination of Eric Gainer.

Chapter 22

"Are we ready to bring the jury in?" Judge Liu asked as Crowder pushed through the swinging gate, dropping her file box with a thud on the chair where Shanahan would normally be sitting. She was late, and we'd all been waiting in the silent courtroom for ten minutes. Where was her lead detective, I wondered. And what about Eric Gainer? He could be upstairs waiting in the DA's office—but if they planned to call him as their first rebuttal witness, he ought to be visible now.

"Your Honor, if I could just have a minute to confer with Ms. Schuyler. The state has a proposal for a plea bargain."

Liu blinked in surprise. It was a shocking development. The balance of the trial had appeared to have been tipped in the state's favor. Until this minute. "Use the jury room. Take the time you need, but no more than fifteen minutes," Liu admonished. "We've kept these jurors waiting long enough."

Nina shot me a glance. I touched Teddy's arm and we went through the swinging door into the well of the courtroom, followed closely by Dot. I put a hand on my father's shoulder. Through the fabric of his suit I could almost feel his anxiety. I let Crowder go first, then we filed into the windowless jury room with its conference table and dozen chairs. Nina sat in the chair at the head of the table and leaned back, apparently without expectations. The toll of the trial showed around her eyes. The rest of us and Crowder remained standing.

"Here's the offer," Crowder said. She too looked exhausted. "Second-degree murder, conditional plea for time served, you walk out of here today."

"What about Bell?" Nina asked, her posture betraying neither surprise nor appreciation, just the fatalism of a lawyer nearing the end of a hard-fought trial. "We'd need a nonprosecution agreement."

Crowder shook her head. "Not gonna happen. He has to take his chances." It crossed my mind that it might be a trick, that they were hoping to get Lawrence to plead guilty to killing my mother as a means of building up the case against him for murdering Russell, establishing motive beyond a doubt. If I'd been the DA on my father's case, I'd have gone for the jugular. I wouldn't have been offering any kind of deal today.

Whatever it was that had brought about this softening in the DA's position, Crowder wasn't telling. "I'll leave you to talk it over," she said to Nina. "I'm sure you know that I'm fully prepared to press forward. This is from over my head."

I speculated this could mean Jackson Gainer had leaned on someone in the DA's office, and Crowder had been told she needed to offer Maxwell a plea to protect Eric Gainer from being called as a witness, but speculation was all it was.

Or maybe my visit to Eric had achieved more of an effect than I'd realized.

"Five minutes," Nina told her, at which point Crowder left us there, wondering.

"She must have heard something that worries her from Eric Gainer," I said. Nina just shrugged. I recognized her indifference for what it was, a lawyer's recognition that only one consideration mattered now, whether to take the deal or reject it. The backstory was irrelevant.

"With a conviction on my record, I wouldn't be able to get my law license back," Lawrence said. "I wouldn't be employable."

Teddy reassured him, "You'll have a job."

"I'm ready to proceed," Nina told him. "But I wouldn't blame you for taking this offer. Other than that, I have no advice. I'm going to leave you three to talk it over. Whatever decision you make will be the right one." She rose, resting her hand briefly on my father's arm, and walked out.

There was a pause after she'd gone. Then Dot said, "It's the deal you wanted, Lawrence. All except the nonprosecution. We could walk out of here right now and be done with Caroline forever. I'm ready to say good-bye. Aren't you?"

He didn't respond, but gripped her hand.

Teddy said, "You can't think about the other case. Divide and conquer. This one, they've heard Shanahan testify about the confession. We have to cut our losses."

"Leo doesn't want me to take the deal," Lawrence said, reading it in my face. "Teddy does."

I hadn't intended to take a side, but Teddy didn't seem to see the danger of accepting this offer, only the immediate benefit of ending the trial. "You have to remember your plea in this case would be admissible in the next one. It would be evidence of your motive for killing Bell. All you'd have accomplished is punting to the next trial, while providing the DA with an admission of guilt to beat you over the head with. I feel good about this jury. I don't want you to admit to anything. You've been fighting for twenty-one years. Don't give in so close to the end."

My father's eyes were bright. "You don't want me to admit to something I didn't do."

"Pleading guilty doesn't mean admitting to anything," Teddy said, his voice tight. "You just stipulate to a factual basis."

"That's what it means to a lawyer," I told Teddy. "But I'm not a lawyer on this case. I'm sorry. I can't help it." Dot's eyes were hard, and she nodded to me. I turned to Lawrence again. "If you were my client I'd tell you to take the deal. But, speaking as your son, it makes me want to throw up, the thought of you giving them anything after all we've come through."

"You believe I'm innocent," Lawrence said. "You really believe it."

I couldn't answer, but I gave a nod. My encounter with Lucy last night had essentially confirmed all that my father had reported in his surprise testimony about his conversation with Bell. Bell had surprised Lucy and raped her, then faked her death and used that to blackmail Gainer, and either Jackson Gainer or Lucy had killed him for it.

"Teddy believes I'm innocent, and still he wants me to take the plea. So does Dot."

"Do what you have to do," she told him. "It's going to break my heart if they put you back in, that's all. And I don't care about you having a record, but Leo has a good point. They may just be setting you up, and I don't want to go through this again. I'm ready to walk back out there and testify for you. I've never been readier. Just promise me one thing. If you get off, we go straight down to city hall and get married."

He looked her in the face and nodded to her. She kissed him.

"I don't want you going back to prison for something you didn't do," Teddy said. "You'll have a conviction on your record, but who gives a shit? At least you'll be out here rather than in there. You lose this trial, then you'll have a conviction, and you'll be back inside for life, too."

"It's good advice he's giving you," I said. "It's the smart move. But remember, if they try you for Bell, the jurors will hear about this prosecution. Even if you win here, the DA can still argue that you only got off because you had Bell killed."

"But you all believe in me," my father said. Again I nodded. "Then I'll turn it down. Let's go back in there. Let's keep fighting."

"Leo," Teddy said. For an instant he resembled his old self. "Let me talk to Dad and Dot alone for a minute."

I could see that our father didn't want me to leave. His hand still gripped Dot's. I didn't get up. "You should probably listen to Teddy and take his advice," I told him, knowing he wouldn't. "He's been fighting for you longer than I have. I'm late to the party. I won't hold it against you if you take the deal. In your shoes, I'd probably take it."

"If you all believe in me, then let's go back in there," Lawrence said. "Let's go on fighting. You're right. Jesus. Twenty-one years. I'm not going to stop now. I'm not going to let those bastards beat me right before the end."

"This could turn out badly," Teddy said, looking at us with dismay. The one thing he no longer was was a gambler.

"He's told the truth," I told Teddy. "Every word of his testimony, it was the truth, and I know it now for a fact." I'd learned that much from my encounter with Lucy last night, that it was true Russell had *had her again*, as our father had testified. "I think we can make the jury see that you were trying to do what was right."

"I don't think you should listen to him," Teddy said. He looked both sad and grim.

"I hear everything you're saying, Teddy, and I know you're right, but I can't give in. Leo's right; they'll just use it against me in the next trial if I plead guilty here. I can do the time if that's what I have to do. It'll be different after this. You won't abandon me if the judge puts me back in?" Lawrence now asked me.

"No," I managed to say. "I'll visit you. Even if they convict you, this won't be the end. That confession should never have come into evidence."

"I'm going to turn down the deal," Lawrence said to Teddy. "You boys have carried me this far. But whatever happens now, it's on me."

With this decision, we went back out into the courtroom. Sitting at the defense table, Nina looked up questioningly. I caught her gaze and held my clenched fist before me. Nina gave a satisfied nod, her eyes half closing, then she looked down at her pad.

~ ~ ~

Shanahan came in the doors at the back and resumed his seat at the DA's table. Resigned and unyielding, he gazed across the courtroom at my father, seemingly trying to catch Lawrence's eye. When Lawrence looked up, Shanahan just nodded as if to say that it wasn't over between them, no matter what happened.

Judge Liu came onto the bench. "Anything we need to take up?" No doubt he'd already been informed that my father had rejected the DA's offer.

"Nothing from the defense, Your Honor," Nina said.

"Then let's bring the jury back in."

Once the jury was reseated, Nina said, "The defense calls Dorothy Cooper."

Dot took the stand and was sworn in. She sat very straight, her face all attention and nerves. Her hair was brushed back and she'd put on makeup during the break. She'd never testified in court before, and she'd told me in the hall that she wanted to puke, but when she returned Nina's greeting her voice was clear and strong.

Nina moved into the meat of the examination, asking Dot if she recalled the morning of Bell's death. In response, Dot described how she and Lawrence had decided on the spur of the moment to take a motorcycle ride down the coast. "Whose idea was it to make that ride?" Nina asked, establishing the important fact that the trip hadn't been preplanned, as it would've had to be under the prosecution's theory that the ride was a sham cooked up by Lawrence to provide himself with an alibi while a hired gun made the hit.

"It was mine," Dot answered firmly. "Lawrence didn't feel confident enough on the bike for such a long trip. But he was ready, and I told him so. We left at seven that morning. We wanted to get an early start so that we could be home in the early afternoon."

Nina had her retrace her route in detail, Dot narrating from the map in her head. She described the grocery store where they'd stopped to buy sandwiches, and told of eating them on the beach at Half Moon Bay. "It was nice," she said. "A moment of peace, away from our troubles."

They'd returned by two, and been surprised by a loud knock on the door shortly thereafter. She'd answered it and found a phalanx of police officers, dressed as if for combat. Bearing a warrant for Lawrence's arrest, they'd stormed in, made him lie on the carpet, and handcuffed him. She teared up, her voice swelling with righteous indignation as she described the scene.

"How long have you been engaged to be married to Lawrence Maxwell?" Nina asked.

"Nearly ten years. We'll be married the instant this is no longer hanging over his head," Dot told her. "One way or the other."

"Have you ever known him to be jealous?"

"Never. In the beginning, I was seeing other men, and I made sure Lawrence knew about it. He was patient, and he never pushed the issue."

At last Nina sat down, and Crowder rose. I felt myself beginning to sweat. I'd warned Nina that the alibi was shaky, but she'd had no choice but to proceed. Now we'd find out just how shaky it was. If Crowder had proof Dot was lying, the case could be lost in an instant.

"Tell me, what is your yearly salary?"

Nina objected, but Crowder was ready with her response: that she must be allowed to explore the witness's potential financial motive for giving testimony in this case. Liu ordered the lawyers to approach the bench, and the argument continued out of the jury's hearing, Nina no doubt emphasizing that of course Dot wasn't being paid anything. I knew the point Crowder was about to make, however, and I also knew she'd win.

For Liu, it was payback time for Nina's earlier transgressions.

The lawyers returned to their places, Nina with a smirk on her face as if Crowder had played a cheap trick that had no chance of working. Liu ordered the question read back to the witness, and Dot provided the answer: a relatively modest sixty-five thousand dollars.

"The morning you say you drove halfway across the state with no witnesses, what motorcycle was your fiancé riding?"

"A Harley," Dot said. "A current-model Softail. Chrome."

"And who paid for this spectacular and beautiful machine?"

"I did," Dot said, with an apologetic glance at Lawrence.

"Where did the money to pay for the bike come from? Savings?"

"I financed it. A five-year note. The rate was reasonable."

"Do you expect to come into some more money anytime soon, Ms. Cooper?"

"I don't know what you mean."

Crowder circled. "Didn't you just testify that Maxwell promised to marry you if he's acquitted here?"

"We've promised to marry each other after it's over. Whichever way the trial turns out."

"Wonderful. And if he's acquitted, and if he manages to extract a substantial settlement from the city, then maybe, just maybe, the two of you can buy a house with a garage to park those bikes in. And if you're really lucky, you can retire and tour the world. Is that the plan?"

Nina objected that this question was prejudicial, argumenta-
tive, and bullying, but it clearly had an effect on the jurors, who
seemed to be looking at Dot in a different light. Nina's protests
only seemed to underscore the damaging import of the things
Crowder was saying, but she had little choice but to object if she
wanted to preserve the issue for appeal.

Liu's only response was to instruct the jurors that comments
from the lawyers weren't evidence.

Crowder put her cards on the table. "Isn't it true, Ms. Cooper,
that Maxwell has made clear to you that if he's acquitted in this
trial, his lawyers will sue and are likely to obtain for him a substantial sum of money, in the form of a settlement for his alleged
wrongful conviction, and that if you help him, you can expect
to share in it?"

"We don't talk about financial matters."

"Does Mr. Maxwell earn any money?"

"Not much. He works in the law office a few hours a week."

"So you're willing to support him financially after your marriage?"

"Yes," Dot told Crowder. "If that's what it takes, I'm willing to
do just that."

"If that really is your plan, shouldn't you be saving money rather
than spending it?"

"I wasn't aware that my financial responsibility was on trial here,"
Dot said, at last fighting back. "Lawrence was in prison for twenty-
one years, and you're trying to put him back in. He deserves his
freedom, Ms. Crowder. My hope was that he would ride with me
and feel free, for however long we could make the feeling last. No,
I don't regret spending that money."

Seeming to realize that she'd pushed the issue as far as she could,
Crowder moved on and began probing the details of the alibi with
calculated skepticism. Dot gave her little material to work with,
other than the undeniable fact that there were no other witnesses
to their excursion.

Crowder closed with an unexpectedly gentle coup de grace, a series of questions that established Dot's deep belief in Lawrence's innocence, and also her freely admitted desire, apart from any financial motive, to see Lawrence freed so that they could spend their life together as a married couple, rather than separated by prison walls. A desire, Crowder suggested, that would in her mind justify lying for this man whom Dot believed in her heart to be innocent.

At last Crowder sat down, and I felt my shoulders drop in relief.

~ ~ ~

After lunch, Nina renewed her motion to exclude the confession and dismiss the case.

"Unless you've got something new, I'm not inclined to revisit my earlier rulings," Judge Liu told her. "But if you think you need to make a record, fire away."

"The state has produced no evidence that Mr. Maxwell was involved in the murder of Russell Bell. Mr. Maxwell's alibi stands unrebutted. The jury should therefore be instructed to disregard Bell's statement. Without the statement, there's no evidence that he murdered Caroline Maxwell. With Bell's statement excluded, the case should be dismissed."

Crowder stood. "The defense agreed that the confession could come in. Simple as that."

"Well, I've already granted relief from that agreement. The question is, without the confession, can the state still meet its burden of proving guilt beyond a reasonable doubt? For instance, do you plan to introduce any rebuttal evidence to the alibi?"

"No, Your Honor. As we've said, the state's position has never been that Maxwell pulled the trigger himself. The issue of Mr. Maxwell's possible involvement in Bell's death should be submitted to the jury."

"But I worry that puts us right back where we started, with little evidence other than Mr. Maxwell's obvious motive for wanting Bell dead."

Crowder shot a questioning glance over her shoulder at Shanahan, then turned to the judge again. "On rebuttal, the state plans to introduce additional evidence of Mr. Maxwell's involvement."

"Has this additional evidence been disclosed to the defense?"

"No, Your Honor. This information was just brought to our attention this morning."

Eric Gainer. It had to be. Nina was on the edge of her seat, but Judge Liu held out a hand. "We've already had more surprises than I care for in a murder trial."

"The witness in question was unwilling to cooperate with investigators until now. His lawyers contacted my office ten minutes before I was to be in court. I might as well say now that the witness is Supervisor Eric Gainer, and he intends to testify that Russell Bell told him that Mr. Maxwell threatened his life shortly after the preliminary hearing in this matter. If there's more, you'll hear it when I do."

Crowder was grim faced. I didn't envy her the position she'd been put in, forced to call a witness whom she hadn't interviewed, a witness Nina had already suggested had a motive to lie. Now I understood why she'd offered that plea: not because Jackson or anyone else had put pressure on her to keep Eric from testifying, but because Eric Gainer had showed up here at the hall this morning all but demanding to take the stand.

Liu went on more pointedly. "Assuming for the sake of argument that this witness's testimony is insufficient to make the confession admissible, can the state carry its burden without it?"

"We can. As we've been arguing all along, the evidence that was hidden from the defense in the first trial actually *reinforces* Mr. Maxwell's guilt. What the investigators didn't have the first time around was motive. Now the missing piece of the puzzle has been supplied in the form of the pictures that the defendant filed with his habeas petition, the one showing Caroline and her lover. The defendant's fingerprints are on the murder weapon. He has no alibi, and a strong motive of jealousy. It's a very straightforward case, and we intend to argue it as such."

"Ms. Schuyler?"

"We've heard no evidence that my client even knew of his wife's affair. Even if Your Honor isn't inclined to grant our motion to dismiss, he's entitled to a mistrial. You can instruct the jury to forget what they've heard, but they won't forget the accusation that Mr. Maxwell was involved in Russell Bell's death, and they won't forget the confession. Those genies won't go back in the bottle."

"But the defense is the side that uncorked them," Liu interrupted. "You're the one who first broke the agreement regarding the confession, and you're the one who introduced the fact of Russell Bell's murder. You can't complain about these things when you're the party responsible.

"I think Ms. Crowder is right," he went on. "I think we have to leave it up to the jury. I'll instruct the jurors to disregard the confession if they don't think there's sufficient evidence that Maxwell was involved in Russell Bell's death. But I'm not going to grant a mistrial, and I'm not going to dismiss the case. The court of appeals may feel differently, but you'll have to take that up with them. Ms. Crowder, let's get your witness in here."

Chapter 23

Eric Gainer had missed a patch of stubble under his jaw. His suit coat was wrinkled, his tie askew. At Nina's request, Liu had sent the jurors into the hall. Only if he concluded that Eric's testimony was sufficient to allow them to find that my father had murdered Russell Bell would they be allowed to hear it. The point of bringing Eric in was to shore up the idea my father had Bell murdered to keep him from testifying, which laid additional groundwork for the confession to come in. What Eric's point was in presenting himself here, I couldn't be sure.

Crowder's examination was brief. Without a jury to play to, she wasted little time. She asked Eric to state his name and occupation, then established he'd been Russell Bell's employer, after which she moved immediately to the conversation he claimed to have had with Bell shortly before Bell's death.

Eric's personality was on display to full effect, but for once his delivery was not calculated to charm. Rather, he wore a look of seriousness and concern, the haunted look of a man who was unable to forget the prophetic words he'd once heard. "I'd once told him that if he had any trouble about his past, he should come to me and I would help him," he said. "Well, a few days before he was murdered, he was driving me to a meeting, and he looked over at me and he said something like, 'I've been having a little trouble lately.'

"He went on to say he was going to be a witness in a case against a former cell mate, a man who'd confessed to him that he'd murdered his wife, and who'd later gotten out of prison. I knew he was talking about Lawrence Maxwell, of course. He told me Maxwell had called him, and had said he'd better keep his mouth shut if he knew what was good for him. Those were his words."

Watching Gainer testify, I felt like a man rearranging the last few pieces of a puzzle, but seemingly unable to find how they fit. I hadn't been able to figure out what he was doing here, why he'd suddenly thrust himself into the center of a trial that held such dangers for him, unless there was some greater danger he was trying to prevent. Hearing his testimony, though, I realized that he must understand that I was close to putting the puzzle together, and that if he didn't act to shore up the case against my father, the DA would have to cast around for other suspects. And, sooner or later, especially if more leaks emerged, their sights might settle on Jackson Gainer.

After just a few minutes, Crowder sat down, at which point Nina addressed Gainer without rising from the counsel table. She easily established that Russell Bell hadn't told Eric of any specific threat, only that Lawrence had told him he'd better keep his mouth shut.

Then she said, working from the notes I'd put together for her, "Supervisor Gainer, do you remember a woman named Lucy Rivera?"

"Of course I do," Gainer said. "How could I forget her?"

Nina rose to show Eric the picture from the newspaper, and asked, "This is Lucy in the picture with you, isn't it?"

"Objection," Crowder said. "Beyond the scope of the direct examination."

"Sustained," Judge Liu said, swiftly shutting Nina down without Eric needing to open his mouth.

"We have to be allowed to show that this witness has a motive to lie."

"Credibility isn't my concern. You can impeach him all you want if I allow Ms. Crowder to put this witness in front of the jury. But, right now, all you're doing is trying my patience, Ms. Schuyler."

I glanced behind me to where Jackson was sitting. He seemed not to hear the ensuing debate between the judge and the lawyers. His gaze was far away, almost sleepy.

Still Nina pushed against the judge's warning. "Someone has been blackmailing you anonymously with this picture, isn't that right?"

"No," Liu said, reaching his decision suddenly. "No, this examination is finished. I'm not going to allow the jury to hear this witness. I don't find that there's any relevance to this testimony. 'You'd better keep your mouth shut' isn't a threat. It's not evidence of anything, certainly not of murder. I see what you're doing, Ms. Schuyler. You're trying to turn this trial into a sideshow, and I won't allow it."

Never mind that Crowder was the one who'd called Gainer to the stand, and that this was a victory for Nina. Liu left the bench without allowing argument. His decision had been angry and rash, without a reasonable basis, but neither lawyer raised a protest.

I could only guess that Liu had little appetite for allowing one of the city's foremost politicians to be sullied on his watch.

Waiting for the judge to return, I glanced again at Jackson Gainer, who now wore a look of sullen, brutal disregard. In the judge's absence, Eric rose from the witness stand and walked out of the courtroom, followed closely by his brother and the lawyer who'd accompanied them. Crowder's face was somber.

Nina made her motion for a directed verdict of acquittal when Liu returned after the brief recess, but the judge denied it with obvious impatience. "We'll go straight to closing arguments. Unless the district attorney has another rebuttal witness."

Crowder didn't.

"Be ready in fifteen minutes."

I hurried out of the courtroom, to do or say what I didn't know, but Eric was already gone.

~ ~ ~

Standing beside my father as the jurors filed back in, Nina was unruffled. But I felt sick. I realized that part of me had believed that Liu would end the case right here. Now the case hadn't ended, and now my legs were weak and my breath was short. My father, glancing around, caught Dot's eye, then mine, but his face was rigid. Had he decided otherwise, the judge could be taking his plea. We would be walking out of here. Instead, we were launching the final battle.

The jurors, looking both bored and irritated, resumed their seats. Nina and Crowder stood ready. Liu gave a few brief instructions to the jury, explaining the purpose of the arguments they were about to hear. Then Crowder rose and carried her heavy binder awash in notes to the podium.

She began briskly. "The vicious beating of Caroline Maxwell was not the work of a stranger. It was the act of someone whose jealousy and anger had been building for years. If criminal defendants were to be believed, the world would be full of mysterious killers who slip away without a trace. But common sense tells us that's not how it is. Murderers don't usually get away, and they're not often strangers. Sadly, most murder victims are killed by the persons closest to them."

Crowder took up the photographs that had been put into evidence and went through them one by one, showing them to the jurors, walking back and forth in front of the jury box, holding each picture up, dwelling on the viciousness of the attack. I watched the jurors' faces as they studied the photos; most of them looked away. Whether that was a good or a bad sign I couldn't tell, but it meant that they weren't looking where Crowder wanted them to look, that she didn't have them fully in her power.

"I'm asking you to return a verdict of first-degree murder, meaning that the defendant made a cold, calculated decision to kill. Willfully, deliberately, and with premeditation is what the law says. Remember the admission he made to Russell Bell: 'it was a terrible thing but it had to be done.' This was no crime in the heat of passion. It was murder in cold blood."

Next Crowder walked them through the two compromise verdicts they might reach—second-degree murder or manslaughter. She went on in this technical vein, highlighting the jury instructions, trying to make the state's burden of proof seem less onerous. She, of course, glossed over the lack of evidence implicating Lawrence in Bell's death, instead treating the confession like an established fact. The jurors seemed to tune out as she droned on.

She ended on a note of attack. "You've heard Mr. Maxwell come into this courtroom and tell brazen lies. The only reason he can hope to get away with such lies is that most of those who would have contradicted him are dead, including Caroline Maxwell and Russell Bell. But his fingerprints are on the baseball bat. He has even tried to smear the character of one of this city's elected officials, San Francisco city supervisor Eric Gainer. But you've heard no evidence that Eric Gainer had anything to do with the events at issue in this case, certainly not with the murder of Caroline Maxwell. Or was Eric Gainer the mysterious stranger who framed Mr. Maxwell for murder, then slipped away into the night?

"You've also heard Maxwell put words into the mouth of a dead man, Russell Bell, words so transparently cynical and self-serving that I'm astonished he could expect anyone to believe them. But the truth is that Mr. Maxwell confessed to Bell. Dead men do tell tales.

"It's your job to see through the lies, to disregard the smear tactics, the distractions. This case isn't about what happened two weeks ago, and it's not about what happened two months ago. It's about what happened twenty-one years ago, when the defendant, Lawrence Maxwell, brutally murdered his wife. He confessed to that crime when he thought he had little chance of ever being released from prison, and he had Russell Bell murdered to keep that confession from reaching your ears.

"All the rest is an attempt to distract you from the task at hand, to sensationalize this trial and turn the serious purpose of this court into a paranoid farce. You heard from the defense that the blood type of the man who left the semen in Caroline Maxwell's body doesn't match the blood type of Mr. Maxwell or of the man with whom Caroline was having an affair. You've also heard a lot of talk from Ms. Schuyler that Mrs. Maxwell was raped. But the defense presented not a single piece of evidence that this alleged rape in fact occurred. The only medical witness you heard from testified that the evidence of forced sex was, at best, inconclusive.

"The reason is that no rape occurred. Let's put aside suppositions for which we have no evidence. The injuries noted in the medical examiner's report were almost certainly left by Mr. Maxwell when he beat her to death. The most reasonable interpretation actually supported by the physical evidence is that before her death, Caroline had consensual sex with one of her lovers, then was beaten to death by her husband when he came home and discovered her in a state of undress, obviously postcoital, shortly after the man she'd been with had gone. *'It was a terrible thing, but it had to be done.'* Unlike Mr. Maxwell, I don't pass judgment on her.

"Put the conspiracy theories aside. Look at the facts and reach a true verdict. Mr. Maxwell murdered his wife. He's guilty of first-degree murder. Caroline Maxwell has waited twenty-one years for justice, and you can give her that justice by swiftly returning a verdict of guilty on the first-degree murder charge against him."

~   ~   ~

"Brazen," Nina said thoughtfully a few minutes later, when she stood up. "That's a good word for what you've just heard. Listening to the district attorney, I was reminded of a memory from my childhood. My father was a military man. He was a man who, like Gary Coles, no doubt believed that he was on the right side in every conflict, and that whatever tactics he used were justified because they were done in the name of justice and cloaked with the power of the state."

I frowned, wondering where she was going. Normally I disapproved of lawyers telling personal anecdotes in closing statements. It never seemed to work, and always smacked to me of unpardonable vanity, drawing the jurors' attention away from the issues at stake at the most crucial moment of the trial. Still, I'd come this far with Nina; I was willing to give her the benefit of the doubt. Not that my father or I had any other choice. And I could see that the personal note resonated with one juror in particular, a young woman who'd told us during jury selection that she was a social worker. Nina's eyes returned to this woman again and again.

"One day, we were on a drive in the country when our car ran out of gas. My father pulled to the side of the highway. My mother beside him, my brother and I in the backseat, each of us knew that it was not permitted to state that we'd run out of gas. Eventually my brother hitched a ride and came back with a jerry can, enough to get us to the nearest service station."

Nina walked toward the prosecutor's table and stood beside it, her voice taking on power and conviction, chasing my doubts away. "I look at this man, Detective Shanahan, and I see my father sitting with crossed arms, refusing to acknowledge that the wheels will not turn. Evidence is the gas that a criminal prosecution runs on. In this case, the tank is empty and it has been from the start. Just because Detective Shanahan has the power to accuse my client, that doesn't make him a guilty man. We hold the state to its burden of proving criminal offenses beyond a reasonable doubt. When the car doesn't run, we're allowed to say so. We must.

"What evidence do they have? You heard the district attorney mention a baseball bat with my client's fingerprints on the barrel. Who cares? It was his son's bat, in his own house, an object that he'd probably touched a dozen times in the last month of his freedom, picking it up after the child had gone to bed, putting it back in its place in the closet. Who knows when those fingerprints were left? That's not evidence of guilt, of murder. There's no physical evidence other than what was hidden from the defense in the first trial, evidence showing that Caroline had been with another man before her death. Evidence that, if we had it today, could be subjected to DNA analysis, telling us the identity of the true killer. All we can know for certain today is that Caroline Maxwell's murderer wasn't her husband or her lover. The blood type of the person who left the semen doesn't match theirs.

"It matches the blood type of Keith Locke, though. You didn't hear from him, did you? The DA didn't want to bring him into court.

"The DA now theorizes that it *must* have been a crime of passion, that my client *must* have killed his wife because he *must* have known she was having an affair and he *must* have known she'd been with another man that day. The DA skips over the state's failure to produce evidence that my client knew of her affair, much less that he was there in the apartment that day. If he caught her with another man, where's that man? He's not dead on the floor, as you'd expect if my client were the vengeful, impassioned killer they've invented.

"And they have the temerity to accuse the *defense* of conjuring imaginary killers. Ms. Crowder went so far as to claim that the real killer didn't leave a trace behind. Her words—you just heard her say it. A killer who didn't leave a trace, none except for his semen in Caroline's body, which is the evidence that Gary Coles wrongfully hid from the defense, evidence that was subsequently destroyed. Angela Crowder wants you to forget that such physical evidence existed. She wants to conjure up a mystery lover for which there is no evidence whatsoever. But doesn't it make the most sense that the rapist who left his semen behind in Caroline Maxwell's body was the person who killed her, that someone with that blood type is the person we're looking for? It's the only logical explanation, yet the prosecution refuses to consider it.

"People, this case broke down twenty-one years ago, and they're still sitting behind the wheel with their arms crossed." She looked squarely at the jury, waiting for this to sink in. Then she went on to discuss the confession, showing the jury just how little evidence there was that my father had killed Russell Bell.

"You heard my client tell you that this so-called confession was a lie told by Mr. Bell, that Bell panicked after realizing that he'd made at least one incriminating statement to Mr. Maxwell, and that my client was going to turn him in to the police. Detective Shanahan swallowed Bell's lies, because they were exactly what he'd wanted to hear, coming exactly when he needed them. Those lies were what the detective knew he'd hear if he beat the bushes loudly enough.

"Mr. Maxwell's guilty, Detective Shanahan wants you to believe, because the state couldn't have made a mistake. Or perhaps because it would be too painful and embarrassing to admit that a mistake had been made. In his mind, it makes us weaker to admit that we were wrong. He's like my father refusing to admit that he'd forgotten to fill the tank. I happen to think it makes us stronger to admit mistakes, even terrible mistakes like this one, a mistake that resulted in my client serving twenty-one years for a crime he didn't commit.

"What a weak man my father was when he couldn't bring himself to admit that he'd forgotten to fill the tank with gas. What a weak man Detective Shanahan must be, for refusing to face the obvious fact that Lawrence Maxwell should never have been convicted, should never have been charged again, that there was never evidence of guilt. Mr. Maxwell and I are asking you today to be strong for the rest of us, to point out what should have been obvious from the start. The tank is out of gas. The car won't go. Return a verdict of not guilty and end this ordeal for my client, his fiancée, and his sons."

~ ~ ~

Crowder spent most of her rebuttal time on Lawrence's confession and the evidence, scant though it was, that he'd murdered Bell, dwelling on the phone calls between them, even on Lawrence's appearance at the funeral home. "His alibi, even if you believe it, is beside the point. We're not saying he pulled the trigger. Remember what Bell told Detective Shanahan, that Maxwell had orchestrated reprisals before, that he had a network of associates who would do his bidding. Men who'd kill for him. And remember, also, that the only evidence of this supposed alibi comes from Mr. Maxwell's fiancée, a woman with an obvious interest in the outcome."

Next she focused again on the technical aspects of the jury instructions, a tactic often effective for the prosecution in straight-forward cases, with the question of guilt already sewed up. Then, seeming to realize that she was losing the jurors' attention. Crowder flipped forward in her notes, then set them aside and went on without them, speaking directly to the jury.

"Listening to Ms. Schuyler's argument, you'd think that the state has maliciously set out to frame Lawrence Maxwell for the murder of his wife. But what motive does the state have to persecute an innocent man? He's *not* innocent. He confessed to murder, and then he murdered the man to whom he had made that confession. Ask yourself, who in this courtroom has the most at stake? It's not Detective Shanahan, and it's not me. No matter what happens here, we get to go home tonight to our families, to our beds.

"Who has the motive to lie? Obviously, the defendant does. After the last few days it should be clear to you that he'll say anything, anything at all to avoid being convicted of murder. Don't be deceived. Don't buy into his lawyer's conspiracy theories, into his desperate stories about what Russell Bell supposedly told him. The truth is that Russell Bell had put the past behind them, and he wanted nothing to do with Mr. Maxwell. But Mr. Maxwell wanted something from him.

"Mr. Maxwell has received due process of the law. No one in this courtroom disputes that he deserved this new trial after what happened twenty-one years ago. We've admitted our mistakes and we've made them right, and we've conducted this prosecution with dignity and fairness. The ultimate injustice would be if those mistakes were to result in the acquittal of a guilty man. Don't allow that. Return a verdict of first-degree murder and give Caroline Maxwell the justice she deserves."

Chapter 24

The jury instructions were complex and took more than an hour to read. In a droning, patient voice, Judge Liu instructed the jurors on the presumption of innocence, the burden of proof, and the charged offenses: first-degree murder, second-degree murder, manslaughter. Then, giving the state's version of the forfeiture instruction, he instructed the jurors regarding the circumstances under which they would be allowed to consider Lawrence's alleged confession.

My heart raced as Liu navigated this complicated instruction. I watched the jurors. Who knew what they were thinking, or if they even understood what they'd just heard? Liu had denied Nina's request to put blanks on the verdict form requiring the jurors to check *yes* or *no* in response to various questions, meaning that in the event of a conviction, we'd be unable to show that the jurors had failed to follow his instructions. We would know only the end result.

~ ~ ~

The courtroom was ours. The jurors were in the jury room. Judge Liu was in his chambers, and Shanahan and Crowder were presumably in the offices upstairs.

While Nina worked on her laptop at the counsel table, my brother, father, Dot, and I lounged in the gallery, our jackets folded over the back of the bench in front of us, our legs outstretched.

"The Grand Canyon," my father suggested. He and Dot had been throwing out ideas for the honeymoon they meant to take after their marriage.

"Europe," she countered, echoing Crowder's suggestion that they tour the world. "The Italian coast."

"Which one?"

"All of them."

"And then Spain," he told her. "Then ferry across to North Africa. Morocco. Casablanca. Tangiers."

He kept talking as if he'd have the chance to see all these places—the words rolling out of him with the lazy unflagging momentum of a person used to filling sleepless nights with harmless untruths.

In contrast with my father's apparent acceptance of whatever was to come, I was a wreck, unable to sit still with my second-guessing of Nina, thinking that Lawrence shouldn't have waived his right to a hearing before the confession came in. Since our conversation this morning, I'd begun to doubt that there'd be issues for appeal; more likely, our agreement meant that the appellate court wouldn't overturn a guilty verdict. There was no point in having that discussion with Lawrence now, after I'd just talked him into rejecting the DA's offer.

It was nearly six. In the world outside, commuters were boarding their trains, starting their cars, beginning their journeys home. Going back to their lives, their families. Teddy had phoned Tamara and told her he wouldn't be home for dinner. Jeanie had gone home, Teddy said, but Debra was there and able to stay.

The jurors could have left and resumed their deliberations in the morning, but the door to the jury room remained closed. We heard murmurs of raised voices behind it, intimations as heart-quickening as they were impenetrable. Often, juries would send written questions asking for clarification on a point of law, or for certain testimony to be read back to them. Such questions often provided clues as to which way the jury was tilting. This jury sent none.

No doubt Crowder and Nina each had their proxy in that room. Nina's would be the social worker in her twenties, with the tattoo and the vegan complexion. Crowder's proxy would be the stockbroker who worked in the Financial District and was always thumbing away at his BlackBerry during the breaks. The other jurors didn't appear to like him, but his voice would carry weight.

The social worker, by contrast, seemed on good terms with everyone, yet I guessed she'd have little experience imposing her views. I knew nothing about her, had nothing but my own ste-reotypes and prejudices to judge her by. But I was heartened by the sense I'd gotten from observing her over the past several days that she would care deeply that an innocent man not be convicted, while at bottom the stockbroker wouldn't mind at all. Of course I was just applying my preconceived notions. It could easily have been the other way around.

At seven fifteen, there was a firm knock on the jury room door. The deputy answered it and spoke a few words to the foreperson, a confident young manager at a software company whose sympathies I'd been unable to read. After that, things went quickly. The court-room deputy phoned upstairs, and a few minutes later Crowder appeared, with Shanahan not far behind. Judge Liu came out, but-toning his robe at the neck, and took the bench. My father, in his coat again, straightened his tie, kissed Dot on the lips, pressed his sweaty hand into mine, then Teddy's, and came out of the gallery to take his place at counsel table with Nina.

As he passed through the swinging door into the well of the courtroom I was painfully aware he was taking steps he might never retrace. If he were found guilty, Judge Liu would almost certainly order him taken into custody. If that happened, he'd be shackled and led out the secured entrance at the front of the room. That damp handshake might be the last contact I had with him as a free man.

I put my arm around Teddy's shoulders and squeezed briefly. Then we rose as the jurors came in. My eyes sought Nina's juror, the social worker. She looked exhausted. She didn't meet my gaze but didn't avoid it, either. The stockbroker, his tie loosened, looked like he just wanted to get out of there, impatient but not triumphant, as I thought he might be if he'd gotten his way.

"Ladies and gentlemen of the jury, have you reached a verdict?" Judge Liu asked.

"We have," the foreman answered. The stockbroker shot a look at Crowder.

The judge instructed him to hand the verdict form to the deputy, who brought the document to the bench. Liu studied it, and said, "I'll now read the jury's verdict into the record. 'As to count one, the charge of first-degree murder, we find the defendant *not guilty*.'"

Dot sagged beside me, catching herself on the back of the bench in front of her. I saw Lawrence's hand find Nina's. She looked down in surprise but didn't take her hand away.

"'As to count two, the charge of second-degree murder, we find the defendant *not guilty*.'"

At the DA's table, Crowder and Shanahan were stone-faced.

"'As to count three, voluntary manslaughter, we the jury find the defendant *not guilty*.'"

Lawrence lowered his face onto his hands, trembling with sighs, then sat up straight and let his head fall back. Then he was on his feet, turning to look for Dot.

Amid the chaos, they went to one another and kissed in a lingering embrace. A few of the jurors were smiling. One woman even wiped away tears. I wondered when their sympathies had turned to him, and realized it must have been during Dot's testimony. She'd humanized him, allowing the jurors to believe in him as she believed in him. That had been the difference.

For the first time in twenty-one years, Lawrence was truly free.

~ ~ ~

"I'd have thought you'd be with your family tonight."

We were at Tony Nik's in North Beach. "Teddy's with his family. Lawrence is with Dot. I seem to be the odd man out."

I'd already told Nina what a tremendous job she'd done, how wonderful she'd been. But I told her again, and added, "We ought to try a case together sometime."

"Sure, sure," she said. Eventually I paid the bill and we left.

"It isn't the end, you know," she told me after a bit, slipping her arm companionably through mine. "I didn't want to mention this to your father today. Let him catch his breath. But I'm pretty sure they're still going to try him for Russell Bell."

I nodded, her cool appraisal sobering me. In her company, with drinks in me, I'd begun to relax. Now I felt my shoulders tighten, though I'd already recognized the likelihood of what she was telling me.

"He won't be able to go through that experience a second time. Or third."

"With any luck, he won't have to. But we don't have to think about that tonight."

We walked up Columbus. At one point, as we paused for a light, I turned to her and tried to kiss her. She stopped me with a finger on my lips.

To cover the awkwardness of her rejection, I asked her if the story about her father running out of gas was true. "It might have happened," she said, looking at me with something like regret. "Maybe just not like that."

At the next corner we said good-night.

I was getting off the BART in Oakland half an hour later when my phone rang. It was Eric Gainer. I'd been half expecting his call, though maybe not so soon. It was clear to me that we had unfinished business between us. I pressed the Talk button. "Eric?"

He gave a cough, then spoke as if with effort. "I guess congratulations are in order. From the news reports, the consensus seems to be that after so long, the evidence just wasn't there."

"The evidence never was there. He's innocent."

"Well. Congratulations." His voice was tense.

"Are you calling just to tell me that?"

He breathed in sharply. "Look, can you come over to my place? Tonight? You see, something's happened, and you and I are the only ones who know the whole story. Lucy Rivera's alive, and she's here. She's told me some shocking news about my brother and Russell. The things she's telling me could be very significant to your father's case if the DA prosecutes him for Bell's murder. I think you ought to hear what I've heard."

"Okay," I heard myself say. "I'll be right over."

I ought to have suspected a trap, but the bait he'd laid out for me was too tantalizing to resist, especially after my conversation with Nina about the second case still hanging over my father's head. On the drive from the MacArthur BART back into the city, in a belated fit of caution, I called Car. I asked him to get to Eric's place as fast as he could, then park with a good view of the front, and be prepared to follow us if we left. And if things went bad, to call the police.

I didn't think things would go bad. With Lucy's help, I hoped to convince Eric that Jackson was behind Russell Bell's murder. Then, according to my half-formed plan, we would call the police and put the matter to rest. In ten minutes I pulled into Eric's garage. He came out to stand in the doorway, then turned to go inside. As I followed him inside, Lucy stepped from behind the kitchen wall and put the gun to my head. Too late, I realized my error.

Eric turned at the doors that led to the patio out back. "Thanks for coming over."

"I guess you didn't kill her," I said. "That must have been welcome news."

He gave me a warning in the form of a glance at Lucy. "You'll need to leave your car keys on the table there for me. Sorry, but Jackson may need to borrow them later. And your cell. Turn it off. Are we ready?" he said to her when I'd complied.

"Where are we going?" I asked, though I'd already guessed.

"Back to the house out there," Lucy said. "And then we're going to make a phone call." To Eric she said, "You're sure your brother can come up with the money tonight?"

"Normally, we wouldn't keep that kind of cash on hand. But this isn't exactly ordinary times. I knew we might end up having to pay someone, but I didn't know when. I thought it'd be Leo's father, but it doesn't really matter to me who gets paid, as long as this is the end of it. Jackson will have the money before morning."

I sat in the passenger seat of Eric's Cherokee, with Lucy behind me. He drove. "What's the plan?" I asked once we were out of the city.

Eric glanced over at me. "Don't you know? I thought you were the one who gave her the idea. The body in the freezer, I mean. This was supposed to be your show, not mine." After his experience in the courtroom, he wasn't above taking pleasure in asserting his power over me.

Car had been at his place in the Western Addition when I called. If he'd hurried, he might have made it to Eric's in time to follow us as we pulled away. But the Friday night traffic had probably prevented him from making it in time. In any case, if he was there as we left, I didn't see him.

"Russell could have been lying about the body, too," I said. "Maybe she went in the ocean and never came up." I didn't want to say, Lucy's lying. She was using Bell when he thought he was using her. She was in on the scam, and she shot him not for re-venge, but so she wouldn't have to share the payout you're making tonight. There's no body."

Lucy touched the gun barrel to my ear. "Then it's your lucky day."

Eric's hands gripped the steering wheel tightly. From time to time he glanced at my face. We crossed the Golden Gate Bridge. On the coastal highway, when we reached it a few hours later, we found long stretches where I saw no other headlights in either direction, just the dark curve of the headlands blotting out the sky, and the moonlit, seething Pacific.

"What'd she mean it's my lucky day?"

Eric glanced at me. "This is one of those times when it's good to be the one who picks up the tab. Nothing is settled until every-thing is settled. That's what Jackson always says. I'm no lawyer, but I think the principle applies."

"I'm a loose end, is what you're telling me."

"Jackson will be coming with your car. If there's no body in the freezer, you drive it home after we hand over the money."

"And if there is . . ."

"He doesn't need to know," Lucy interrupted.

"Sorry," he told her. "It's not really about you, Leo. It's just that she's got to have some insurance. We struck a deal. She'll help us take the body away, get rid of it. That's her end of the bargain. If her hands weren't dirty before, they will be now. And yours will be, too. You'll help her take the body away, and you'll dump it together somewhere where it'll never be found. Then your hands will be dirty, too. Either that, or we can do this the hard way. It'll look like self-defense. You'll be found with a gun. The window will be jimmied."

"You called *me*, remember? They'll get the phone records."

"Sure I did. To offer my congratulations. Then you started spout-ing a lot of nonsense about a body in the freezer at George's. I drove out here in the morning, meaning to check for myself, heard a noise, saw you running at me with a gun in your hand, and I shot you dead with the gun I bought when I started getting blackmail threats. Self-defense. That's as close to the truth as we can make it, Leo, and I think the story will hold up pretty well."

It was too risky to try anything while we were driving. I didn't doubt Lucy would shoot me if I made a move, and even if she didn't, there was no guardrail and a drop of hundreds of feet to the rocks below. If I was going to take action, it would have to be at Chen's.

Eric had calculated against this, likely betting that the glimmer of hope he'd offered me, of walking away if there was no body, or choosing to be an accomplice, would discourage me from rash acts. There was no question for me of going along with their plan, of helping her to dump the body. He must have known that. I could only hope he was playing along with Lucy with the goal of setting her up, and that when he phoned Jackson, the police would show up instead.

It was after 4:00 AM by the time we arrived. Eric parked at the end of the long driveway in the turnaround near the front door. He got out first. My heart dropped as he took a gun from the pocket of his hooded sweatshirt, a little snub-nosed revolver. He held it ready as I got out. As soon as Lucy was out of the car and had her automatic on me again, Eric put his gun away. He unlocked the door with a key he had, then quickly stepped inside and entered the alarm code.

We went into the living room. "Make that call," Lucy told him. She took out a cheap cell phone still in its package, the prepaid kind that was for sale at gas stations and liquor stores in every marginal neighborhood where drugs were dealt and cheap, untraceable communication was in demand.

Eric tore open the package, powered up the phone, and thumbed in a number. "It's me. Sorry to wake you, but we're live with that thing we've been expecting. A quarter million in cash is the price.

I'm at Chen's." He gave Jackson instructions about my truck, letting him know the keys were on the table at his house.

"Now what?" I asked.

"Now we wait," Lucy said.

"Unless you'd prefer we shoot you now," Eric told me. "But we're not opening the freezer until she has the money in hand. That's the deal. Think of it as the mystery box at the auction. You've got to buy to find out what you have."

"I don't even see why you'd pay her if it's empty."

"A deal's a deal. If we knew in advance she was in there, I'd pay more."

Motioning with the gun, Lucy directed me into a leatherette armchair set back from the massive central hearth. She and Eric sat on opposite ends of the matching couch facing it. I wondered how I'd misjudged him so thoroughly. The only light came from the hall. Lucy closed her eyes and after a few minutes was asleep, the gun in her hand, her chest rising and falling. Eric took his gun out of his pocket. I thought for a moment he was going to disarm her, and hope surged in me, but he just set the gun on his knee and held it there.

"So this is real," I said to him. "This is you."

"For about two months, I really believed I was a killer. At first, it tore me apart. I couldn't sleep. I couldn't look at myself in the mirror. But gradually, that feeling faded. Or I just got used to it. Probably the same way I got used to having lied when I identified Russell Bell. One day I was sitting in my office, thinking what if you put it in the balance—the world before and the world after? What difference does it make, one death? Once the idea came into my head, I realized I was right. It didn't matter. Not if I wasn't caught."

"You don't think there'll be any difference between that and what you're planning to do here now?"

"Sure. This will be a choice. That wasn't. The whole thing was a setup by Russell, a sadistic game, and now he's dead. I don't feel bad about that, either."

"Lucy shot him," I said. "It wasn't Jackson. You don't have to protect him."

"Anything's possible," he said with a yawn, as if it didn't matter one way or the other anymore, if it ever did.

We sat in silence for a while, me digesting that, trying to master my fear. I kept vacillating between disbelief and the impulse to make a move. That would mean testing him, however, and despite what he'd said, I couldn't convince myself that he meant to go through with it. Or maybe he knew that in the end I'd go along with his plan to make me an accessory to murder after the fact. I wondered who the other girl in the picture was, what she'd done to end up tangled in such a mess. Somewhere, someone must be waiting for her to come back, but she never would.

My greatest hope was that Car, having missed us at Gainer's house, had waited to see Jackson arrive and drive away in my truck, and that he would follow Jackson here.

And so we sat in silence. He kept the gun pointed in my direction, Lucy snoring at the other end of the couch, his own eyes remaining open. After another hour, the sky began to brighten. In the predawn light, the noise of the waves beneath the balcony seemed to draw nearer. I'd almost convinced myself that he wouldn't do it, that it was a bluff, and then Lucy started awake and he leaned down and kissed her on the lips. Her eyes widened in surprise and she reared away from him. "I've always wanted to do that," Eric said.

I recognized the rattle of my truck's engine as it pulled up outside. Jackson Gainer came in with a duffel bag in his gloved hand.

Lucy rose. Jackson stared at her for a moment, his eyelids heavy, the skin beneath them appearing bruised. "Here it is," he said, hefting the bag. "One hundred thousand."

For the first time Lucy seemed uncertain. She must have wondered if she'd miscalculated. Three of us, only one of her. "I thought you said a quarter million."

"This was all I could get together on such short notice."

With sudden decision, she crossed to the hall and took the bag from Jackson.

He pretended to offer my keys to me, then tossed them to Eric. "Why don't you move it while I have a look downstairs," he said to his brother. "There's a pullout up the road a bit. Make it look like he walked onto the property."

"Let's do this first," Lucy said.

"You got your money," Eric told her.

He walked out, handing his gun to Jackson as he went. I remembered Lucy's comment the other night about Eric turning his back while others did the dirty work for him.

"Eric," Lucy said sharply. But he was already out the door.

She had her gun in her hand and seemed to want to do something with it.

"Don't shoot Leo yet," Jackson warned her. "You're going to need the two of us to carry the body, if there is one. That's if Russell Bell wasn't a liar. I've been of the opinion all along that he was. I know Eric feels the same way. Leo, what's your bet?"

"Mine is that if she and I go down there, neither one of us comes back up."

Jackson seemed entertained by this. "What's the deal the three of you worked out before you called me? No body, you live? Body, you either help us dispose of it or you die? Only, if there's no body, how do we know that you'll keep your mouth shut about tonight?"

"That's your problem," Lucy said.

I didn't like him already knowing the terms of the deal they'd discussed.

"Leo's used to keeping nasty secrets. Think we can trust you with this one, Leo?"

"Sure. Here's a deal for you. We all go home and sleep in our beds, and we keep quiet about this. Eric refuses to testify when they charge my father with the murder of Russell Bell, and I don't say a word to anyone about tonight. I drop her off at the bus station in San Rafael."

"I like that. You respect my family's privacy going forward, and we respect yours. Otherwise it's your word against Eric's and mine. I don't know how far you'd get, but you could cause us some problems. I'll give you that."

"You two go on down ahead of me," Lucy told us.

"After you," Jackson said, nodding for me to go first.

The downstairs was a single open room, with a wall of windows facing the sea. The postdawn shadows of the headlands fell across the water. The room was divided between a TV and sitting area on one side, and exercise equipment on the other. Down here, the impact of the waves on the cliffs was felt rather than heard, and the salt smell was somehow stronger.

A small kitchen took up the end of the room opposite the window, the part that was below the grade of the surrounding property. Inside a walk-in pantry, a chest freezer hummed. Jackson threw open the lid and stepped back. "Leo, why don't you clear out all this crap so that we can see what we've got."

Frozen dinners, seafood, and meats filled the freezer nearly to the top. I began taking the items out and stacking them on the floor.

Halfway to the bottom, I lifted a box of steaks and saw a patch of blanket showing through the gap. The blanket, once a creamy white, was stained dark brown with old blood.

The body had been positioned with the knees bent to the chest, the head bowed so she would fit. Someone had wrapped the blanket around her in this position, then wound the blanket with thick nylon climbing rope, presumably the one that had been used to haul her off the rocks. The rope and the blanket together were encasing her in a tight cocoon. A towel bound her head. The only exposed flesh was at the feet, which were visible through the gaps where the ends of the blanket had been folded over. The skin of her heels was grayish, covered with ice crystals.

"Have a look," Jackson said to Lucy. "Then we'll get her out of here."

As Lucy stepped forward, Jackson stepped back, took the gun from the pocket of his coat, and extended it toward the back of her head.

She'd craned onto the balls of her feet to see into the freezer. Hearing my shout, she turned, diving to the floor as Jackson's revolver discharged into the wall. Plaster dusted them both. Lucy flipped onto her back as she landed, holding her automatic in both hands.

She squeezed off five shots at point-blank range, the bullets slicing into Jackson's groin, tearing bloody furrows up the front of his coat, blasting off a chunk of his jaw that created a look of openmouthed startlement as he fell.

"Arrogant prick!" she shouted, rolling away from the spreading dark pool. She got to her feet. "You thought you could take me?"

She now pointed the weapon at me. "Don't move or you'll be on the floor, too." She picked up her duffel bag and Jackson's revolver. Her scraped elbow was starting to bleed.

The gunsmoke stung my nostrils and eyes. "You've got the money. Just go."

"This can't be happening," she cried. "This wasn't how it was supposed to be."

"He was supposed to shoot me with your gun, not get shot with it, is that right?" I said. "That would have wrapped things up nicely. Jackson kills me, and the bullet in me matches the ones that killed Russell Bell from your gun. You'll have to go to plan B." I didn't know what plan B was, and I doubted she did, either.

"I *didn't* kill Russell. I told you that." She was jittery, agitated, and I wondered what kind of drugs she was used to taking. She looked like she needed a fix. "How strong are you?" she said. "Can you carry her?"

I had no choice but to agree.

I dragged the freezer away from the blood and tipped it over to get her out. Through the blanket, the frozen flesh was numbingly cold and hard as rock, but the climbing rope provided me with places to grip. Bracing the heavy mass against my thighs, I started for the stairs, one painful step at a time.

"Why're you taking all this trouble?" I said between grunts. "Who is she?"

She'd thought it through quickly. "Nobody special. Just somebody I met. No one would have missed her, but the photograph's in the press. If they find one of us dead, they'll expect to find us both. And if they don't, they're going to be looking for the one they can't find. And now evidently we're going to leave behind this god-awful mess."

"They'll be looking for you no matter what, after what's happened."

"Maybe, but there's a difference between looking and expecting to find."

I heaved the body step by step back up to the main floor, resting frequently, exaggerating how heavy she was. I wanted to give Car a chance to show up and save the day.

Halfway up the stairs, the towel came off the dead woman's head, exposing the glistening mess of her face, her dark hair matted in a dark encrustation of frozen blood. No one deserved to end like this, I thought. No one.

Outside, I got the body to the cargo area of the Cherokee, put my shoulder below it and with one heaving motion tipped it up. "Now what?" I asked.

"Now we wait for Eric to come back."

I sat on the bumper, head hanging. Four feet away, Lucy held the revolver in my face. I thought of where I was supposed to be in a few hours: with my father, helping him rent a tuxedo for the city hall wedding he and Dot had hastily begun planning in the giddy hours after the not-guilty verdict. I heard the crunch of footsteps coming nearer.

"I left the truck at the turnout," Eric's voice said. "Where's my brother?"

I didn't look up. There was only one way this could end for him. And only one way it could end for me.

Lucy shot him. As soon as she did, making the only move I could, I rushed her. I was nearly on top of her when the gun in her hand spoke in bright winking flashes. She stepped aside, and I stumbled and fell where she'd been standing.

After a while I rolled over, my legs pushing the gravel. My heels slipped in it, and my arms wouldn't obey me. There didn't seem to be much blood on my shirt, but I felt dizzy, and my hands and feet were cold.

I heard the Cherokee's rear hatchback slam, then the driver's door open and close. The engine coughed to life. Anger surged in me at this stupid end I seemed to have achieved, and with the strength of my rage I pushed myself up on one palm, my arm resisting every inch of the way. As I did this, the pain came alive in my chest like a clawing animal, and I crumpled as the Cherokee drove away.

The noise of the sea grew more distant. Great intervals of time passed between each crash and boom of the swell. A haze seemed to have descended. With my face on the gravel, I was barely aware of the daylight beyond the perimeter of the darkness that remained.

The wail of a siren roused me. I heard the sound of running feet, and someone calling my name.

Recognizing Car's voice, I told myself that everything was going to be okay.

In the hospital in Fort Bragg, Car slips through a curtain to crouch by my bedside. His voice is whispered, urgent. "Listen. Ricky Santorez is dead. He was killed yesterday in prison. Rumor is Bo Wilder ordered the hit."

My mouth's cottony, my head woozy from the drugs. I've been opened from belly button to sternum and stapled shut again. The bullet missed my major organs by millimeters, the doctors say. I'm going to be in for a long recuperation, but I'll live without any lasting effects. Just the scars, they promise. "Good."

"Leo, listen to me," Car says. "The corpse was mutilated. Whoever stabbed him to death cut off the ears, as trophies. They've got the whole prison on lockdown. They're going cell to cell, trying to find them. Only they're not going to."

I wonder if I'm hallucinating, if Car is really here, pestering me with this strange and disturbing news. I take another thumb press of morphine. "Good riddance."

"Stay with me. Not six hours after Santorez got cut up, someone dropped off a FedEx envelope at your office. The package was addressed to your dad, care of you. Inside was the ears."

Even through the morphine I realize this means the DA was right all along. I try to sit up but I can't.

"It's a message, Leo," Car says. "A message and clearly also a threat."

There's only one message Bo Wilder could be sending to us: that he killed Russell Bell, or rather, had him killed, in apparent continuation of the protection he'd given Lawrence in prison. And he wants us to know it. "What does he want?" This means that both Lucy and Jackson are innocent of Bell's murder, but my father may not be, depending on what contact he had with Wilder after his release. They haven't found Lucy yet. According to the police, she ditched Gainer's Jeep with the body in it and stole a car from a beach parking lot in Mendocino.

I wonder again about my father's whereabouts the morning of Bell's death.

"It may be months before we find out what he has in mind. But it doesn't take much imagination. A law office like yours could be a lot of use to a man like Bo, trying to run a criminal empire from behind bars. His people could use it as a home base, set up shop behind the attorney-client relationship to move money, hold drugs. He might want to use you as a go-between, carrying messages during client visits. It's the sort of thing Teddy always refused to do for Santorez, but Bo probably figures he can control you easier than Santorez controlled Teddy."

"So we nip it in the bud, go to the cops with our concerns right now."

"And tell them what? All we've got right now are the ears. No return address. It's only speculation piled on rumor that connects them to Wilder. And if we go that route, the police will never believe that your father didn't ask Bo to put out the hit."

I think about this for a long time, drifting on a haze of morphine. "Throw them in the garbage," I finally say.

I let my head fall back.